Celebrate Valentine's Day with three love-filled and laughter-warmed stories from Harlequin Superromance.

Elle Adams isn't sure Cupid is up to the task, which is why she's starting a Date-a-thon at her café, Cup O' Love. And Max Maxwell plans to use her pet project to prove that he's her one and only in "The Max Factor."

In "A Valentine for Rebecca," single father Will Blakely needs all the help he can get. Because his once-burned, twice-shy attitude just might cost him the very real love of Rebecca Potter.

Lucky Morgan from "Lucky in Love" gambled and lost when she proposed to her best friend, Joshua Watts. But she's not about to give up on him yet....

Who needs Cupid? Maybe we all do!

ABOUT THE AUTHOR

As a child, Debra Salonen wanted to be an artist. She saved her allowance to send away for a "Learn To Draw" kit, but when her mother mistook Deb's artful rendition of a horse for a cow, Deb turned to her second love—writing. She credits her success as an author to her parents for giving her the chance to realize those dreams. She and her high school sweetheart, who have been married for over thirty years, live in California surrounded by a great deal of family, quite a few dogs and views that appeal to the artist still trapped in her soul.

Molly O'Keefe grew up in a small town outside Chicago. How she ended up in Toronto, Canada, she's not quite sure. She sold her first romance to Harlequin at age twenty-five and hasn't looked back! She lives in Toronto with her husband, son, cat and the largest heap of dirty laundry in North America.

Susan Floyd started reading Harlequin romances when she was fourteen, and she hasn't stopped yet. No wonder that everything she ever wrote morphed into a romance complete with the happy ending. When she's not crafting "happily ever afters," she is teaching reading and writing classes at her local community college or bidding on "it" through eBay. She lives in Los Banos, California, with her husband, Michael, and their three dog children, Mr. Riley, Dexter and Tweetie-Pie.

WHO NEEDS CUPID?
Debra Salonen
Molly O'Keefe
Susan Floyd

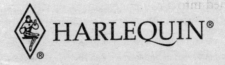

HARLEQUIN®

TORONTO • NEW YORK • LONDON
AMSTERDAM • PARIS • SYDNEY • HAMBURG
STOCKHOLM • ATHENS • TOKYO • MILAN • MADRID
PRAGUE • WARSAW • BUDAPEST • AUCKLAND

ISBN-13: 978-0-373-71392-9
ISBN-10:   0-373-71392-4

WHO NEEDS CUPID?

Copyright © 2007 by Harlequin Books S.A.

The publisher acknowledges the copyright holders of the individual works as follows:

THE MAX FACTOR
Copyright © 2007 by Debra K. Salonen.

A VALENTINE FOR REBECCA
Copyright © 2007 by Molly Fader.

LUCKY IN LOVE
Copyright © 2007 by Susan Kimoto.

This edition published by arrangement with Harlequin Books S.A.

® and TM are trademarks of the publisher. Trademarks indicated with ® are registered in the United States Patent and Trademark Office, the Canadian Trade Marks Office and in other countries.

www.eHarlequin.com

Printed in U.S.A.

CONTENTS

For the mastermind behind this concept—Mel

THE MAX FACTOR
Debra Salonen

Dear Reader,

Welcome to Cup O' Love. Come in. Sit in a comfy chair in the corner of the remodeled gas station and kick your feet up while you sip on a cup of the best coffee in Fenelon Falls, Illinois, and read about three friends, their love-hate relationship with Cupid and their attempt to turn the tables on the little imp. Be prepared to fall in love–with Elle, Becca and Lucky. We did!

Who Needs Cupid? was my first collaborative effort. I have to say it was a joyful experience thanks to my two fellow authors, Molly O'Keefe and Susan Floyd. Bouncing around ideas with these two bright, creative minds helped me remember why I love to write–it's fun! And working with Molly and Sus was the best!

I'd like to acknowledge two other Harlequin Superromance writers, as well. First Amy Knupp, whose husband, Justin, of Stonecreek Media helped demystify the WiFi setup mentioned in the story. Amy, thanks for being so supportive of your fellow writers and always ready to help. And then Melinda Curtis, who started this ball rolling in the first place. Mel, thanks for bringing me on board. I missed not having the chance to work with you, but you proved what a great team player you are when you named Susan as your designated replacement.

Warning: a lot of coffee beans were ground in the process of writing this book. I tested a number of varieties and will be giving away my favorite at my Web site, www.debrasalonen.com, in February. Drop by my blog and share a cup.

All the best,

Debra

PROLOGUE

"LET'S KILL CUPID."

"How?"

"Poison. I could leave a cup of strychnine-laced cocoa on the counter the night before Valentine's Day and—"

"That's Santa, Aunt Ellenore. Get your holidays straight," Becca said with a playful grin.

"Your niece is right. Cupid is a mythical being and commercial icon. You can't kill him," the ever-practical Lucky concurred. "Much as I might want to," she added in a low grumble.

"We can try," Elle insisted stubbornly. The three friends had spent their usual Friday night get-together bemoaning their status as single, eligible, underappreciated goddesses-in-the-making. Tonight, Elle was sick of self-pity. Lucky's recent unlucky experience at putting her heart on the line had pushed Elle firmly toward anger.

"What if we burn him in effigy? Right out front where the gas pumps used to be. Becca, you're an artist. You could create a papier-mâché piñata thingee with wings and a golden bow and arrows. All the people Cupid has burned in the past would come and cheer. It'd be a party. And good for business," she added, looking around her beloved but dying coffee bar. For nine months she'd poured her heart and soul—and savings—into Cup O' Love Café and Gifts, the sort of *Starbucks-with-heart* she'd established in her parents' remodeled Conoco station located at Main and Sixth in her hometown of Fenelon Falls, Illinois. Local residents hadn't exactly jumped at the chance to support her efforts.

"Elle, I love you. You're my friend. And I appreciate your outrage on my behalf, but…that's truly cracked." Lucky Morgan was in her early thirties. Smart about business. Truly clever when it came to eBay auctions. And adorable. Unfortunately she'd also just had her heart broken by a man who should have snapped her up in a heartbeat.

Where was Cupid when Lucky was making a fool of herself by asking Pastor Joshua Watts to marry her? Elle silently questioned.

"It's also against Fenelon Falls' fire codes," Rebecca added. Her niece was a few years younger than Lucky. A gifted artist, but far too modest and reserved for someone so beautiful. Sweet as the honey buns Elle served every morning, and chronically downtrodden, thanks to Elle's older sister, Jane.

Elle huffed impatiently. "You girls aren't helping. I thought we'd decided we were through being victims of the nearsighted little imp. Last year on Valentine's Day I was out with a guy who said he was divorced, but turned out to have left his wife the week before." She let out a long, defeated sigh. "Needless to say, our mutual attraction went nowhere."

"Were you his rebound fling?" Lucky asked, looking troubled.

"Just plain fling. He went back to his wife before the

month was out." Elle made a fist and pounded it on the coffee table where their bottle of wine was resting. "That's why I say we do something proactive this year."

Becca shuddered. "My mother's favorite word."

"Josh says the best revenge is a life well spent," Lucky stated, the quiver in her voice betraying her still raw anguish.

"He's a preacher. What do you expec— Hey, wait. That might work. We could use Cupid's pointy little arrows against him."

"I don't think that's what Josh meant."

Becca shuddered. "Will there be blood? I get queasy watching *House*."

Elle laughed. "No blood, dear heart. I promise. We'll use the Internet."

Lucky and Becca exchanged a look. "To do what? Set up a Web site that gives you ten ways to kill Cupid?"

"Maybe next year," Elle said patiently. "This year we'll try for something a little more upbeat."

"Will it help me sell more greeting cards?" Becca asked. Profits from the sale of her unique, handmade valentines helped to fund the after-school arts program Becca offered on the second floor of the Cup.

Elle nodded. "The more business I bring in, the more cards you'll sell. I guarantee it. That's why I've decided to look into the possibility of installing a WiFi connection at the Cup. I know that means sinking more money into what my sister calls a sinking ship, but if we could come up with some creative ploy that ties Valentine's Day and the Internet to Cup O' Love, I'd make back my investment in no time. And then I'd be able to say 'So, there' to Jane."

"You shouldn't worry so much about what my mother thinks," Becca said in a tone that captured her mother's scold perfectly. "Isn't that what you're always telling me?"

Elle nodded with chagrin. Since her arrival back in her hometown, the gulf between Elle and Jane had widened—partly because of Elle's perceived interference in Becca's life. Partly because Jane was…Jane. And Elle was Ellenore Adams, the girl most likely to screw up.

"People love to think they're getting something for nothing," Lucky said, appearing to give Elle's proposal serious thought. "What if you do some kind of online promotion that ends up with a big party here on the fourteenth?"

Elle refilled her wineglass. The three friends always began their Friday night get-togethers with tea or cocoa, depending on the season, but invariably they wound up opening a bottle of vino.

"It would have to be romance-related," Becca said. "People expect romance on Valentine's Day."

"Speaking of which," Lucky inserted, "when do I get my one-of-a-kind, handmade Rebecca Potter V-Day cards? People are going to start asking for them."

Becca rolled her eyes. "Mother gave me another account today, but I'm working on them. Really. Soon. I promise."

Elle's heart twisted. She wanted so much for Becca to honor her God-given talent and commit to her art, but her darling niece lacked the confidence in her abilities—and herself—to throw her mother's agenda aside and follow her heart.

Nobody spoke for a full minute. The only sound came from the hum of the cash register and the constant rattle of the wind against the windows. This was Elle's first full winter back in the heartland and her heart still wasn't into the cold.

"What if you sponsored an online dateathon?" Becca asked. "That might encourage people who didn't usually frequent the Internet to come into the Cup and use your WiFi."

Lucky looked intrigued. "Maybe you could have a MySpace.com format where people could post their bios, then all the potential Mr. and Ms. Rights would show up at the Cup on February fourteenth for a party."

Becca, who was in the overstuffed armchair she always claimed, sat forward like an eager student and gave a little clap. "Excellent. And you know who could set it up? Mr. Maxwell. Mom says Max is a genius about all things electronic."

Elle swallowed too big a gulp of wine.

Max. As in Arnold Maxwell. Her old classmate in high school. Class nerd. Boy she'd done wrong. Now, all grown up, Teacher of the Year two years running. A widower. *And* one of the few locals who came in to the café regularly.

She shook her head to refocus her wine-fuzzy thought patterns. "It's an interesting idea, but do we have time? It's already the fifth of January. I have no idea how long it takes to set up a WiFi system, but even if Max could do it right away, by the time I organized the publicity and built a new Web page…well, three to four weeks isn't enough time to fall in love."

"Elle," Lucky groaned. "You're the one who started this discussion. We're supposed to beat Cupid at his own game, right? Do-it-yourself matchmaking. How good do we have to be? It's not like we really expect anyone to fall in love, right?"

Becca nodded. "I'd settle for a date with a guy who didn't make fun of the sentiments in my cards."

Elle laughed. "You're right. We're talking dates, not marriage. And where do first dates usually take place?"

"At a coffee shop," Becca and Lucky returned in harmony. Their mingled laughter was a sound warm enough to melt the frost triangles in the corners of Cup O' Love's plate-glass windows.

The younger women filled their wineglasses, then all three friends prepared to toast their success. "So, what are you calling this online experiment, Elle? Do-it-yourself matchmaking dot com?" Lucky asked.

"How 'bout the Who Needs Cupid Alternative?" Becca suggested.

Elle shook her head. With appropriate solemnity, she held out her glass and said, "To the Cup O' Love Dateathon. Where, even if you don't find true love, you can still get a fine cup of coffee."

CHAPTER ONE

"ARE YOU SURE it's down here? All I see is a gaping black hole."

Elle Adams was squatting beside the concrete depression that had at one time housed the old Conoco station's car lift, trying her damnedest not to stare at the surprisingly fit and well-maintained rear end of the man doing a combat crawl on her behalf.

Selfless. That's what Max had become. But when had he acquired such a nice butt?

"Um, I think so. I seem to remember the contractor who remodeled this place telling me he'd installed a conduit to house all the wiring that went into the office. But that was shortly after we buried Mom. Jane and I were still settling our parents' estate and well...it was tough. Do you want me to call him?"

"Naw. I haven't given up yet."

Elle watched him roll to his side and shine his small, high-tech-looking flashlight around the crawlspace. She didn't even want to think about what was down there. Her father—renowned for cutting corners whenever possible—had helped build the two-story brick and wooden frame building in the early 1950s. Elle, Jane and their parents had lived in the apartment above the garage until Elle was ten.

The elder Adamses had kept the service station open until Boyd's heart bypass surgery, which had necessitated a partial retirement. They'd continued to rent the building to a succession of retail operations, but eventually a major chain opened a superstore twenty miles away, sounding the death knell for Mom-and-Pop-type stores across the county.

Only in the past few years had Fenelon Falls, a relatively untouched hamlet just an hour or so west of Chicago, seen a resurgence in commercial activity. Commuters were looking for big city convenience coupled with small town charm. The old downtown had undergone a rebirth, and Elle was determined to do her part—with or without her sister's support.

They were fast approaching the second anniversary of Elle's father's death. On Valentine's Day morning 2005, Boyd Adams had suffered a massive heart attack while shoveling the sidewalk so the florist could deliver the dozen roses he'd ordered for his wife. Giving Elle yet another reason to hate the holiday.

Not that she planned to share her feelings with anyone. She was a businessperson and V-Day meant *kaching* in the cash register, which is why she was now scrambling to get the WiFi installed. Cup O' Love Café and Gifts wouldn't be open this time next year if she didn't start showing some kind of profit.

She'd opened the specialty coffee bar nine months earlier. A ridiculous gamble, Jane had said, but one Elle's mother had supported before her death, which had come as a shock to everyone, except Elle.

Elle had returned home on the first anniversary of her father's death to help her mother recover from hip replacement surgery. Elle's two-week stay had turned into months as complication after complication took away her mother's will to go on. Until one lovely spring morning, Margery simply hadn't woken up.

A delayed victim of Valentine's Day, in Elle's opinion.

By then, Elle was too committed to her new business to back out. A month later, the Cup was up and running—right down the street from Jane's staid, respectable and flourishing accounting office.

"You are the most impetuous person I've ever known," Jane had complained when Elle'd first introduced her business plan. "Why would you assume that just because *you* find it annoying not to be able to buy a cup of fancy coffee in Fenelon Falls that everyone else in town does, too?"

Foolhardy. Another one of the words Jane used to describe Elle. But Elle wasn't done fighting. Even if she lost every penny of her investment, she would go down with a flourish.

After last Friday's brainstorming session with Lucky and Becca, Elle had called Max. "How much would it cost to set up a WiFi station—or whatever it's called—at the Cup?"

"I have no idea, but I'll find out."

And true to his word, he'd reported back to her with several options. The most affordable only required a DSL line and a wireless router, which he was in the process of hooking up...provided she had the right kind of telephone cable.

"Have you given any more thought to that dateathon idea I mentioned?" Elle asked.

Becca and Lucky had called every day since with ideas about how to make the concept work. They assured Elle the WiFi would bring in a younger, hipper clientele and the dateathon would generate good PR among older patrons. Age didn't matter. Cupid didn't matter. The only thing that counted was getting live bodies through the door to start spending money at her cash register.

Max scooted backward and sat up, brushing off the tattoo of lint left behind from the ancient army blanket she'd spread down to protect his charcoal-gray Dockers and a rust-colored corduroy shirt. It was early—not quite seven. He'd volunteered to come in before school to hunt for the line.

"I started playing around with the structure using MySpace.com as a prototype. People will pay a small sign-up fee and fill out a bio. The background design Becca came up with will look great. The trick will be in striking just the right balance between giving enough information to attract another person but protecting your privacy."

Elle nodded. "That's for sure. We don't want a swarm of kooks and creeps showing up at the party."

"I'm working on that."

"This won't interfere with your real job, will it?"

Max taught science at Fenelon Falls High, where they'd both graduated thirty-two years before. Back then, he'd been considered a geek. Math whiz, geometry tutor, chess master. The exact opposite to Elle's C-average, cheer-leader, chairperson of the cool clique. But they'd been friends. Of sorts. Until she'd blown it and callously trashed his heart. That, in hindsight, had been her first and most durable bad taste of Valentine's Day.

"Once I find the main line, the WiFi hookup will be a snap," he said, holding out a hand for help standing up. "You must have had plans to get a building permit. Show me the schematics. I should have thought of that first."

He brushed back a lock of his medium-brown hair, still ample and barely touched with gray. He still wore it in the same style he had when they were classmates.

Elle took his hand in hers and pulled. He popped right up, but didn't let go. In fact, he squeezed her hand ever so slightly. Just enough to make her heart do a funny sideways jump that reminded her how long it had been since she'd had sex.

The thought made her blush. Sex and Max did not belong in the same sentence. Max was a friend. One of the few townsfolk who patronized her place regularly. But he was also the boy she'd "done wrong," and her life was too unsettled at the moment to risk hurting him again—even if he was interested. Which, she was beginning to think, he might be.

He let go of her hand and bent over to retrieve the blanket, which he folded far more neatly than she would have. "Here," he said, passing it to her. "Keep it handy. This looks like the logical place to put a sweep, even if I couldn't find it on the first try."

Conscientious. Another of Max's defining traits. Not a word anyone in town would have associated with Elle.

"Maybe I should call an electrician. I don't want to waste your time." She'd heard through the Fenelon Falls grapevine that Max was once again a contender for Teacher of the Year—third year in a row—thanks to his Chess Team's success at state-level tournaments. Not that Max ever bragged about it.

Modesty. Something inherent in some people; others had to learn it the hard way.

"You know me, Ellenore. Can't pass up a challenge."

Ellenore. The old-lady name she'd always hated and had left behind the day she'd taken off for college.

"I do know you, *Arnold.* That's why I asked for your help."

The twinkle in his eye matched the impish smile on his lips. At fifty-one, Elle was no stranger to flirtation, both sending and receiving, but seeing what appeared to be a flirtatious glint in Max's eye made no sense.

Back in high school, Elle had been a tease. She'd used her beauty like currency. And Max hadn't wanted anything to do with her after she'd short-changed him over the Valentine's Day dance. By the time graduation had rolled around, the two hadn't been speaking.

"At least let me pay for your time. If this dateathon is a bust, you won't make a dime. What's the going rate for electricians? Do I need to make an appointment with my sister to dip into my retirement fund?"

His low masculine chuckle sent a shiver down her spine. He stood beside her, rolling down the sleeves of his fine corduroy shirt. She wondered if the shirt was one his wife bought before she passed away or if Max shopped for himself. Elle's mother had always dressed Elle's father.

"I'll treat you fair, Elle. Maybe we can work out a trade—free scones for life or something," he said cheerfully.

Fair. Max had always been honorable. But still. Her ex-husband had taught her not to put much stock in vague promises.

Before she could finalize the deal, a head popped into the back room where they were standing amid floor-to-ceiling boxes of graduated serving cups and lids. "Elle, there you are. Hi, Max. You haven't seen my gold necklace, have you?"

Max and Elle exchanged a look. The breathless declaration from Elle's friend and fellow Main Street business owner Lucille "Lucky" Morgan made her sound atypically frazzled. Lucky never lost her cool, even on subzero January mornings. That meant the necklace had more value than just the price of the gold.

"Um…nope. Sorry. Nothing turned up when I mopped."

"Was it valuable?" Max asked with typical guy obtuseness.

"No woman likes to lose jewelry—valuable or not," Elle said, giving him a slight push with her elbow.

He returned the nudge with a "What?" look.

"Well, um, sorta. Maybe not monetarily, but it has sentimental value," Lucky said. A blush made her already windchilled cheeks deepen in hue. Lucky didn't give away a lot—not when it was personal.

Before Elle could inquire about how to help, Lucky looked at her and said, "Did Jane call you about the Chamber of Commerce casino fund-raiser she wants to do in late spring? Of course, she didn't. I can tell by the blank look on your face. Maybe she will, though, right?" Lucky had a habit of asking then answering questions without giving the person she was talking to a chance to respond. Elle teased her about it all the time. This time she didn't bother.

Five years older than Elle, Jane was Elle's exact opposite. Jane's lack of support where the Cup was concerned hurt. Usually Elle could laugh it off, but deliberately excluding her own sister from an activity designed to benefit local businesses? That burned.

"Well, let me know what you hear," Elle said. "I'd be happy to put out the word on my weekly radio plug. I called them yesterday to let them know about the dateathon."

If Jane had ever made any effort to frequent the Cup, she'd know Elle served more than mochas, lattes, cappuccinos and espressos. Soups and sandwiches were her real moneymakers, thanks to the steady business she got from travelers on their way home from Chicago. *They* loved both the comfort food and the cozy, accommodating retreat Elle had created.

In their parents' will, Elle got the house and Jane the old Conoco building. At first, Jane had been adamant about selling the place but Elle had lobbied to keep it. Eventually they'd worked out a deal where Elle would pay Jane rent each month. An agreement Jane signed not out of love or familial loyalty, but because she didn't want to show a windfall profit that year. Jane was a CPA. Jane's husband was a CPA. And their only child—the most gifted artist Elle had ever met—was also a CPA.

Elle motioned for Lucky to lead the way to her office— a tiny room big enough for a phone and a desk, from which Elle snatched a marking pen. Once they reached the main room, she picked up a paper plate and neatly printed the words: Missing—Gold Necklace. Reward.

Without being asked, Max grabbed the tape dispenser she kept on the counter and attached the sign to the cash register.

"Thanks," Lucky said. "I'll give them a couple of Becca's cards, if she ever gets around to delivering them. Okay. I'd better get back down the street. I might have customers."

Her laugh told them that was a joke. Elle knew Lucky did far more business through online sales than she did with walk-ins. Sadly Lucky Duck Collectibles was on par with Cup O' Love when it came to scoring big with the citizenry of Fenelon Falls.

Jane had warned her. "This is the Midwest, not California, Ellenore. People take money seriously. They're not going to pay you two dollars for a cup of coffee when they can get it for ninety-five cents at the Bake-Rite or Hy-Vee." Elle had wanted her sister to be wrong. She'd wanted a lot of things. None of which had materialized.

"Oh, shoot, I have to run, too," Max said. "Catch you later. If you find those plans, set them aside. I won't be here for supper. I have a da…um…commitment. But I could pick them up on the way home."

Da…date? Was Max seeing someone?

To quell her curiosity—and the uncomfortable twinge in her chest—Elle focused on his choice of words. *Supper.* Elle was still trying to unlearn the West Coast way of dining where lunch was the middle meal and dinner involved putting on nice clothes and drinking wine.

Elle stifled a sigh. Moving home had been her decision, for many reasons that sounded smart, mature and selfless— at the time. Now, she was here. In Illinois. And despite what the locals thought, she made the best cup of coffee in town. Too bad she might go broke proving it.

She watched Max get into his dark blue Ford Explorer and turn across traffic onto Main. She hated the fact that she envied him. While she'd traipsed around the country, from job to job, always certain the next opportunity would make her wealthy, Max had managed to create a rich, fulfilling life without ever leaving…well, except for college. But he'd returned home, got married, bought a house, had two sons and worked at a job he apparently both loved and excelled at.

Elle, on the other hand, got pregnant before completing college, married and divorced within a year, became a single mom to daughter, Nora, who seemed intent on repeating her mother's mistakes. Although they spoke often on the phone, Elle hadn't seen her daughter in ten months because Nora was working on a cruise ship based out of San Diego. Nora claimed to love her carefree life, but Elle knew those love 'em and leave 'em romances would get old in a hurry.

But unlike her sister, who felt the need to run her daughter's life, Elle maintained a pretty much hands-off approach to parenting. Besides, she was certainly no authority on love, despite her vast experience when it came to dating Mr. Wrong. So, what business did she have instigating a dateathon? None. Was that going to stop her from doing everything in her power to try to save her business? Absolutely not.

WHEN MAX LEFT SCHOOL that afternoon, it was already dark. Short days and long nights—the only thing he really hated about winter. *Now.* He hadn't seemed to mind the season when his wife was alive.

He drove straight to his son's house in the new little subdivision on the west edge of town. Fenelon Falls was growing. There was even talk of building a new high school. He hoped it wouldn't happen before he retired. His wife had always said that change was good, but Max didn't agree. Except in a few specific cases.

Like where Ellenore Adams was concerned. She'd changed her name when she married, but had immediately changed it back when she got divorced. "I even changed my baby's name because the dumb jerk didn't want anything to do with either of us," she'd told him not long after she'd opened the coffee shop.

Elle was change personified. In high school, she'd wear

a wig on any given day or dye her long blond hair on a whim. She'd dated but never went steady—until their senior year when she fell for star quarterback, Lyle Patterson or something like that.

Over his years of teaching, Max had seen the same scenario played out time and again. Heartthrob girl falls for heartthrob boy. Occasionally, a third heart appeared in the picture. More often than not, this was the one that got broken. Max could personally attest to that, but he also knew that young hearts healed fast.

As he pulled up to the curb in front of the house, he realized he was whistling. Just from thinking about Elle. The irony of him whistling like a young swain from some silly musical wasn't lost on him. They were fast approaching the anniversary of his big emotional letdown. Not that either he or Elle ever mentioned that low point in their youthful friendship.

"Fool," he murmured under his breath as he got out of the SUV. "You're too old for this romance crap."

But he knew that wasn't true. He'd been a widower for nearly three years. Once the worst of his pain had abated, he'd started dating a few nice women from town, but they were all too much like Sarah, whom he'd loved with all his heart and wouldn't dream of trying to replace.

Elle was different. She'd been his first love, and whether she knew it or not, she'd changed his life. The attention she'd shown him in high school had altered how he'd thought of himself. In a good way. Instead of a freakoid nerd, as his students might say, he'd been halfway cool— for a nanosecond. Just long enough for Arnold to become Max. Not that Elle had any idea about the role she'd played in his improved self-esteem back then.

When she'd called to ask him about installing the WiFi connection, he'd decided to use the opportunity to change how she looked at him. Obviously the subtle approach he'd employed for the past nine months wasn't working. She treated him just as she did any other customer— friendly and grateful for the business.

He'd planned to ask her out on Valentine's Day, but this dateathon thing had thrown him for a loop. She was still the coolest girl in town—beautiful, adventurous and worldly. He was still the exact opposite—shy, serious and boring. If ten guys were interested in her, he was pretty sure he knew where he'd rank. Unless he screened the wannabe daters first.

He was her Web master. She'd directed him to keep out kooks and creeps. Had she offered any specific criterion on what constituted a kook or a creep? "No," he said aloud, his step lightening—until he hit a patch of ice on the walk.

Sobering, he paid attention to getting to the door safely. Wednesdays were his favorite day of the week. His standing date with the sweetest girl in town—his granddaughter.

He rapped twice then opened the door, calling out, "Hellooo. Grandpa's here. Where's my girl?"

The high-pitched squeal of his two-year-old grand-daughter was all the answer he needed.

CHAPTER TWO

THE EVENING RUSH, such as it was, had just ended when Elle looked up to see Becca walk through the door. Calf-length wool coat, hat down over her ears. At times, Becca acted much older than her years—especially after a day at the accounting office. It pained Elle to see her niece so bogged down in a rut of her mother's making, but she tried to keep her opinions to herself.

When Elle had offered Rebecca the space above the coffee shop to work on her art and her youth program, they'd kept the terms of their agreement to themselves. The last thing Elle needed was to listen to Jane accuse her of having some kind of Svengali influence over Becca.

"Hello, sweet niece, are you here for a cup of soup? Spicy chicken tortilla with all the toppings. People have been raving about it." *All six of them.* All from out of town.

"Sure. Sounds great, but could I get it to go? I need to hunker down if I'm going to get the rest of your Valentine's Day order done."

Rebecca was an amazing artist and she had an uncanny way of putting words to art to create unique greeting cards. Lucky had sold out of the cards last year.

"Sure. Not a problem. I'll put the toppings in a zip bag and you can add them to the soup when you're ready." As she scooped the thick, fragrant concoction into a foam bowl, Elle asked about Becca's day.

"Tax season is upon us. Need I say more?" Becca muttered. "But I got a new student for my art program. Penny Blakely. Her dad works for the probation department. No mom. Not sure what the story is there, exactly."

"Ooh, I've seen him around town," Elle said, pressing the plastic top over the container. "Quite the cutie—and the little girl is a doll, too."

Becca chuckled. She'd removed her coat and hat and hung them in the employee area behind the counter then returned for her tray of goodies.

"Cocoa?" Elle asked, studying her niece. Something was different. Cheeks a little too flushed, even for a winter day. And she seemed sorta edgy.

"No, thanks. I have bottles of water upstairs. This will be plenty."

Before Elle could ask what was bothering her, the door opened again and Max walked in. Although he'd said something about dropping by later, Elle hadn't really expected him this early. Not after a date. Must have been pretty short and uneventful, she thought. Not that it was any of her business.

She'd been called brash in the past but she'd learned there were some things you didn't want to know, so it was better not to ask.

"Hey, Max, how was your date?" Elle asked, unable to stop herself.

Becca gave her a surprised look. Had her tone given something away? Like the fact she'd been fretting about Max's date all day?

"Wonderful. Amber and I have a great relationship. I

give her anything she wants and let her get away with murder, and she loves me with all her heart."

Elle's heart plopped into the steaming cauldron of spicy soup until he added, "But when her pants need changing, I give her back to her mother."

"Her pants?" Elle croaked.

"She's two and not a bit interested in potty training, which is driving my son and daughter-in-law nuts."

His granddaughter.

Becca grinned as if reading Elle's relief.

"My son and his wife take a Pilates class or something on Wednesday evenings. I don't like to think of myself as a babysitter, so I call my time with Amber a date."

Elle's heart, which had returned to her chest cavity, was making a terrible racket. She didn't understand why. So he was unlike any man she'd ever dated—and there was a very long list of them. Still, he was off-limits, and she needed to remember that.

"I found those plans," she said. "Help yourself to some soup if you're hungry. I'll be right back."

Becca followed Elle to her office. "Is something going on between you and Max, Aunt Elle?"

"He's hooking up my WiFi. You know that."

Becca shook her head. "I mean that whole staring at each other like no one else is in the room. Are you two hooking up?"

Elle hunched over her desk so her niece wouldn't see her blush. "We're hooking up free Internet access."

Becca made an impatient sound. "I compose love sonnets on Valentine's Day cards, Ellenore. I know hot vibes when I see them."

"You can see vibrations?"

"You know what I mean. You're attracted to Mr. Maxwell."

"He's a great guy but not my type."

"That's a crock."

That was true. With a sigh, Elle picked up the rolled up set of plans and faced her niece. "The truth is Max and I have a history. Dumb high school stuff that still makes me cringe when I think about it. I broke his heart, and I'm not about to do something stupid that might wind up with history repeating itself."

Becca's lips formed a pretty but pensive moue. "I'm probably not the best person to be telling you this—look at the pathetic state of my love life, but I do believe that history only matters if there's a quiz." Her sincerity made Elle smile. "This is life, Aunt. He's a grown-up, and I'm pretty sure he knows the score."

But did he know how close Elle was to throwing in the towel and running away...again? Her bank balance was hovering around zero. She needed more business. She needed the support of local residents, but back in November, Lucky had mentioned hearing a rumor that some locals were staying away from the Cup out of loyalty to Jane. Some believed that Elle had managed to cut Jane out of their mother's will. Jane could have set people straight about their arrangement, but had she? Apparently not.

Elle's relationship with her sister was depressing, and whether Jane intended it or not, it undermined Elle's self-confidence. A part of her believed that if she couldn't get along with her own sister, how could she ever hope to succeed in a long-term romantic liaison?

But she didn't tell her niece that. She didn't say anything

at all. She let the subject drop as she hurried back to the counter to give Max the blueprints. If this WiFi thing brought in new business, she might just keep her head above water financially. If that happened, then she'd consider dating for real.

The Cup O' Love Dateathon was *not* real. It was a gimmick to attract customers. Besides, she'd tried online dating before and had been appalled by the superficiality. But Max was a different story. He *was* real.

MAX'S MOUTH was watering, partly from the amazing aromas emanating from the soup sitting before him and partly from the woman sitting across from him. She'd returned with the rolled-up plans under one arm then proceeded to show him exactly how to "fix" his meal.

"The key is in the toppings," she'd said, adding a layer of bite-size pieces of corn tortilla, right on top of the sour cream, cilantro, chopped green onions and black olives that were already floating there.

Max could read a certain vulnerability in her expression that he rarely remembered seeing in the past. Ellenore Adams had breezed through life, but no more. He knew that from bits and pieces of gossip he'd heard over the years. A mean-spirited divorce after her husband's rich parents dragged Elle over the coals. Jane once commented while she'd been working on Max's taxes that Elle's ex's family hadn't wanted anything to do with their son's baby. "Such a shame. Can you picture my sister as a single parent?"

Yes, Max had thought. Definitely. Her ability to embrace the best of life would serve any child well.

"Yum…" he murmured appreciatively as the spices enveloped his senses. Definitely a burn, but all the toppings tempered the heat of the chilies. "This is great. Where's your daughter these days?"

Elle explained about Nora's passion for travel.

"She sounds like a free spirit. Like her mother."

A sweet pink blush crept into Elle's cheeks. "I suppose you could say that. I moved around a lot more than my parents and my sister thought was wise, but every new job was a step up the ladder. I don't regret that, except that I think kids benefit from stability. Your sons seem to be doing really well."

Jason, father of Max's only grandchild, was a loan officer at the bank, following in his late mother's footsteps. Sarah had just been promoted to branch manager when she'd discovered that her breast cancer was back. Six months later she was gone.

Their elder son, Jared, lived in Chicago, where he was a lawyer for a firm that handled class action suits involving maritime companies.

"They both like their jobs. Their mom always told them to find something they felt passionate about, whether it paid well or not."

"Like teaching?"

He ate another spoonful of soup then nodded. "I hadn't planned on becoming a science teacher. Thought I'd go into research, but in college I discovered that no single thesis topic really grabbed me. My mind is a vast wasteland filled with unconnected bits of trivia. Perfect for education."

Elle laughed. The infectious sound made him feel good, youthful. He hadn't felt that way in a long time. The realization made him frown.

"Do you miss her? Your wife?" She shook her head. "Dumb question. Of course, you do. You were married a long time and very successfully according to Jane."

He wondered what that meant but his mouth was full so he couldn't ask. Elle seemed to read his mind because she explained, "Jane told me about your wife's death. Tragic, she called it because the two of you were the poster-models for the perfect marriage. Her words, not mine."

Max wiped his lips with the paper napkin he'd picked up from the dispenser. "Hardly perfect. Sarah was a sweetheart, but she had a stubborn streak unlike anyone I ever met. Even you."

"Me?"

He nodded, grinning so she'd know he was teasing. "Remember the time you refused to wear a dress to the Sadie Hawkins dance? I thought Principal Riley was going to have a coronary."

Elle made a dismissing motion with her hand. "Tell me what makes sense about letting—" she said the word with irony "—girls ask the boys out then insisting they dress like girls. I didn't go so far as putting dresses on guys, which I thought would have been appropriate, but I did choose to wear jeans to the dance. Very nice jeans with pink lace."

He remembered. He'd gone stag. As usual. He'd fallen a little bit in love with her that night, even though the principal had forcibly removed Elle from the gym. He'd decided she was his hero. His Rosa Parks, albeit for a less noble ideal. That was when he'd first decided to ask her to the Valentine's Day Ball. Since her jock boyfriend had broken up with her after his coach had threatened to sideline him if he hung out with a radical like Elle, the timing had been perfect.

She'd even agreed to go with him.

Until two days before the dance.

"So, show me the plans," he said, finishing off his soup.

Elle looked relieved to let the subject of the past disappear. "I heard Jane's calling the dateathon my last ditch effort to stave off the inevitable, but she thinks like an accountant. WiFi is hot right now. The dateathon might be silly, but if it gets people through the door, then my coffee and charming ambience will bring them back."

Max sure as heck hoped so, and he intended to do everything in his power to make sure that happened. He also intended to be Elle's date to the party.

CHAPTER THREE

SIX DAYS LATER, Elle was almost ready to call her plan a success. Max worked his magic almost overnight and suddenly anyone with a laptop or wireless-compatible handhelds could connect with the outside world at her little corner of it. Word had spread quickly—thanks to the power of the Internet, and she suspected Max the Teacher.

The majority of her new customers were high school and college students. Elle loved serving this vivacious crowd. It was almost like having Nora around. And the best part was they had money. And they liked to spend it.

On mochas and macchiatos.

And on the one-of-a-kind greeting cards Becca had just put on display.

The one thing these patrons weren't buying was the Cup O' Love Dateathon. The site had gone "live" yesterday, Martin Luther King Day. Since school had been out, there'd been a steady stream of young people in and out of the place. None had shown any interest in playing the dating game.

But now, school was back in session and the place was quiet again. Too quiet. Elle walked to the satellite radio receiver on the shelf and zeroed in on her favorite station. Songs she knew the words to.

"Um, hi. Um, could you help me? I'm thinking about

branching out a bit, dating-wise, and the girl who's helping me with my taxes said you're running some kind of romance contest or something?"

The woman was about Elle's age, although the heavy wool coat and knitted cap made it hard to tell exactly. "You bet," Elle said, barely catching herself from adding "cha" on the word. "I've got all the information you need set up at this table. Participants are going to create a questionnaire that other participants will fill out, then they can pick the most appropriate contender and meet here on Valentine's Day. We're having a party. Nice and safe, very public. Even those guys and gals who don't get chosen will be invited to meet other runners-up." Not losers, as Max had teased, when she'd outlined her idea to him.

"What if nobody replies to a person's questionnaire?"

Elle had tried several online dating services in the past and always had far more men interested in her than she ever could have dated. But she didn't tell Max that. "Then we've proven beyond a doubt that Cupid sucks," she'd joked.

"Either that or he has someone in mind for you who doesn't play games," he'd countered.

His reply had left her oddly breathless. That had been yesterday when she filled out the first dateathon application. So far, she hadn't had any hits. Which was a little unnerving, but until she had some competition to compare her list to, she wasn't going to worry about it.

Two hours later, the woman—Gloria, Elle learned—was still at the dateathon table, "Wow," she said, motioning Elle over. "Look at this. Three hits. My goodness, that was fast. Since I don't have a computer at home I'm going to have to come in every day to weed out the good ones, aren't I?"

That was the plan, Elle thought, forcing a smile.

Maybe I need a new photo on my home page.

MAX WAS PERCHED on his stool in the lab, half watching his honor students dissecting their frogs. The other half of his mind was focused on creating a man.

Just call me Max Frankenstein, he silently joked.

The man he was creating was going to submit his online résumé to Ellenore's home page. Max planned to add two or three men a day so Elle wouldn't get suspicious when no potential dates appeared under her name in the dateathon. This wasn't really cheating, he told himself, because Elle had already admitted she didn't plan on dating the winning name on her page. She was only participating to generate interest among her customers.

Since she wasn't really looking for a guy, then any of his imaginary alter egos would work, right?

"Mr. Maxwell, I can't find my frog's heart," a voice said.

"Maybe he doesn't have one. Like you," a deeper voice grumbled.

"Shut up, Peter."

Ah, young romance. A little bit like old romance, only more honest. He pressed Send, then slid off the stool and walked to the lab table where the heartless frog—and princess—awaited him. A really sharp scalpel was the answer. Missing heart—tiny and nonoperational—was right where it was supposed to be.

The princess in question stuck out her tongue at the less than gallant knight across from her then went back to work. Max smiled and returned to his computer to create another man. A heartless rogue, this time, he decided.

ACROSS TOWN, Elle let out a little gasp.

Lucky leaned over Elle's shoulder to read the page displayed on the laptop. "Oh, my, he's a naughty one."

"Naughty? I was thinking more like…deranged. I've got to talk to Max. He's supposed to be screening for sociopaths. Did you read what his hobby is?"

"Where? I missed that."

Elle pointed to the line that read: dissecting frogs for fun and profit.

Lucky made a face. "He must be joking. Nobody who really tortured amphibians would admit to it, right? That's just…sick."

Elle sent the possible suitor to her reject pile. So far, that was where all her interested beaus had wound up. She couldn't explain it. Not one bio had tickled her curiosity, much less made her want to type a reply. What was wrong with her? Had her standards changed? Was she losing her sexual drive?

"Do you think it's menopause?" she whispered softly.

Lucky frowned. "They can't all be going through the change. Some of them weren't that old. In fact, wasn't one of them seventeen?"

Elle laughed, as her friend had intended. "Yes, one was a kid. He reminded me of someone, but I can't think who. But that's not what I meant and you know it. There are things going on—bodywise—that tell me I'm past my childbearing years. Which, I'm happy to say, is a good thing, but maybe I should make an appointment with a doctor and check this out. Women going through the change still like sex, right?"

"You're asking the wrong woman. No older sisters. No

mom to ask about such things. I was counting on you leading the way when my time comes."

She sounded so sincere Elle had to bite down on the inside of her cheek to keep from laughing. "I could ask Jane, but I don't see that conversation ever taking place. The last time I asked her a personal question, she told me I shouldn't be thinking about such things and to go to church."

"Church? Really? What did you ask her?"

"Whether or not you could get pregnant when you'd just gotten over your period."

"Hmm…what did you do?"

"I got pregnant, of course."

Lucky didn't laugh. Instead she let out a deep sigh. "Going to church might have been an option back then, but it isn't going to be for much longer," she added cryptically, then stood up. "I have to go."

Elle didn't try to stop her. Lucky's disappointment in Pastor Joshua Watts seemed to be multiplying exponentially. The handsome young minister appeared to have a new agenda—both where the Fenelon Falls Community Church was concerned and in his personal life, where Lucky didn't appear to have a role.

Elle would have liked to help her friend, but as far as her attempt at beating Cupid at his own game went, she wasn't doing too well. She clicked on the next name on her "Persons of Interest" list.

A few seconds later, she groaned softly and closed her laptop. Her reject list was filling up with players who weren't in the same ballpark, let alone the same league.

CHAPTER FOUR

"So, Elle, how goes the quest for Mr. Right? Is Cupid smiling on you?"

It was Friday. Max's favorite day of the week. Well, Wednesdays were pretty great, too, because of his standing date with his granddaughter, but Fridays were special because chess club met at lunch. His A-team was made up of honor roll seniors who could drive and had permission to leave the school during lunch hour, so last week, when he'd mentioned the new WiFi at the Cup, he'd told them that this week's meeting would take place here.

Two birds, he'd figured: give Elle some business and spread the word among the faithful—people who lived and breathed the Internet. And, from what Elle said about her busy three-day weekend, he'd been successful.

As the members of his team swarmed behind him, Elle answered his question. "Cupid is a putz, Mr. Maxwell. If I see the little snot, I'm going to run over him with my car," she called over the sound of her cappuccino frother.

The eight students in line behind him started to laugh. He'd forgotten how much he liked her sense of humor. Edgy and smart.

"Who's the chicklet, Mr. M?" Abraham Jones, a stringbean who was continually asked to play on the basketball team but had no athletic abilities whatsoever, asked.

"I heard that, tall person," Elle said, returning to the counter. She secured a lid on a *grande* cup, slipped it into a corrugated band to protect against the heat then passed it to the woman standing just to Max's left. Luann Payne. Divorced. Two kids, grown. A member of the Fenelon Falls Community Church, which Max had attended regularly until his wife's death.

He nodded a greeting. She barely acknowledged him in her rush to grab a chair at the far table in the corner. A table adorned with red balloons and sparkly hearts.

Elle's lovely green eyes narrowed as she sized up his students. "My goodness, geeks have changed some since I was in school. Mr. Maxwell being the notable exception, of course," she added with a wink. "You aren't by any chance selling Hotties of Chess Club calendars, are you? You could make a fortune."

The twinkle in her eyes was only slightly touched with avarice. Max glanced over his shoulder. These were all great kids, and they handled their brilliance with a lot more style and grace than he'd ever possessed—prior to his almost date with Elle, that is. He wondered if she'd believe him if he told her what that near-miss date with her had done for his ego. Probably not. Max had a feeling she still felt guilty about chickening out.

"Ellenore Adams, meet the members of Chess On Fire. They smoked the competition last year and plan a repeat performance at State this year, too." He called out individual names. Waves, winks, leers and a "Yeah, baby" or two rounded out the greetings.

Elle and her helper quickly and efficiently filled their orders while the students hung out. All were technophiles, so they felt at home in a place that offered Internet connections and even a couple of laptops. Max was kicking himself for not bringing the club here before this. Some high school students frequented the Cup—he'd seen them here—but fewer than he'd expected. Probably because the magic hadn't happened. Yet.

He knew from experience that cool places appeared when the cool kids started hanging out there, creating a unique kind of drawing power. The Chess Club was a start. And the WiFi would help, once word got around.

"Hey, thanks, Max. I think I can make rent now," Elle said softly, sitting down at his table.

His students were making a lot of noise, but it was good noise. Happy noise. Elle didn't seem at all put off by it. "They're pretty neat kids. Smart and ambitious—just like you were in high school."

"Me? I wasn't the one who wanted to be the first female president of the United States," he reminded her.

Her blush made her look seventeen. "Oh, man, I forgot about that. I believe I used that slogan as part of my campaign for Student Body President. 'First step to the White House.'" They looked at each other and laughed.

The kid-noise eased slightly. Max could practically hear the little wheels and cogs in their brains turning. On the drive back to school there would be plenty of hissing and *pssts* as they discussed his love life.

Elle sobered and glanced over her shoulder. "Well, ambition only takes you so far when you're breast-feeding a baby because you're too poor to buy formula. After Nora,

I decided running the country wouldn't be enough of a challenge, anyway."

Her smile held a bittersweet edge. Max was certain she'd never looked lovelier. "Elle, would you like—"

"Hey, Coach, your bee-aach is lookin' to date other dudes in this Valentine thing," Morgan Myers yelled. "That just ain't right, man."

Morgan was forever trying to sound cool by using slang that he never quite managed to pull off.

Elle stood up, her chair making a screeching sound against the tile floor. "Hey, who are you calling a beast?"

Morgan, who was a foot shorter than Elle, slumped down to toddler size. "Um…sorry. But I heard that lady talking about a party, so I checked it out."

The rest of his students pressed closer to see what Morgan had found. Elle, who'd moved close enough to see where Morgan was pointing, said, "The dateathon is for singles over the age of twenty-one. I qualify but you don't."

"But you don't need some loser off the Net," Morgan said. "You could hook up with Mr. M. He's single," he added in a loud whisper.

"I know," Elle replied. Nothing in her tone implied that she might be interested in dating the man in question.

Max, whose face was burning, put his middle and index fingers on his bottom lip and whistled. Loud, piercing. "Time to go, Geek Squad. Do you want to get your off-site passes revoked?"

The mass exodus pretty much distracted Elle from the fact that his students were trying to play Cupid.

"Mr. Maxwell," she called out as he hustled the last team member—Kyla, who could never stop talking on her cell phone to her college-age boyfriend—out the door. "Weren't you about to ask me something?"

He'd been about to ask her out before his students reminded him that in the game of chess, like in love, it was usually better to stick to your plan. "My…um…team is doing timed matches at the mall tomorrow morning. I thought you might like to see them in action."

Her expression looked thoughtful. "I promised Becca I'd run interference with her mother tomorrow. Becca needs the time to work on her cards. Her mother thinks she's going to the office. I volunteered to take Jane to do something sisterish." She rolled her eyes. "What that is, I have no idea. But if it involves shopping, and I can drag Jane along, we'll be there."

Max nodded, but he didn't have a chance to say anything more because several horns started honking. He threw up his hands and dashed away. Coming here was probably a mistake. Young people, although often ridiculously ego-centric, were also amazingly astute. He might have blown his grieving widower façade all to heck.

Not that he wouldn't miss his wife for as long as he lived, but she would have been the first to berate him for not making more of an effort to find someone new, someone he could love again—or someone he'd never stopped loving.

THE BEST THING about Saturdays, Elle thought as she cleaned the snow off her windshield, was having help. Three college students who attended school in Chicago during the week but came home every weekend because their significant others lived here had jumped at the chance to make money peddling coffee. Elle used the opportunity to do all those things she couldn't do during the week, like sleep in, run, work out, play.

Shopping for a Valentine's Day outfit with her sister didn't fall under any of those headers—well, except maybe the exercise one, she thought an hour later as she carelessly thumbed through the spring collection of underwear at the lingerie shop. Jane had most immodestly held up three or four peignoirs that had made Elle blush.

If Jane is still having sex and she's five years older than me, then I need to rethink this menopause thing, Elle told herself. Too bad none of the men who had visited her site had shown the least bit of potential. Too old, too young, too needy, too strange.

"Ellenore, can you come here a minute?" a voice called from the dressing room area.

Elle's throat closed up and her mouth went dry. She coughed delicately. "Sure." Holding her breath, she peeked around the corner. "Which room are you in?"

"First on your right, but you don't have to come in. I just need you to see if you can find this style in a large. The medium just doesn't work for me."

There was something very un-Jane in her sister's tone. Defeated. Almost tearful. Rather than question the reason behind the tears, Elle snatched the royal-blue scrap of material that appeared through the gap in the dressing room curtain and ran to the racks.

"Large, large, large," she murmured under her breath. "She sits at a desk all day, what does she expect? I run my little tush off from dawn to dusk and my butt isn't getting any smaller, for heaven's sake."

After way too much scrutinizing, she found the size in question and dashed back to the changing area. "Here it is, Jane. I bet it'll look great on you. Blue always has been your color." Liar. Jane needed subtle, not garish.

A faintly mumbled, "Thanks," filtered past the thick pink curtain.

Elle hesitated, rocking back and forth on her thick-soled walking shoes. With a stifled groan, she took a step closer and wiggled one finger between the curtain and the wall of the booth. She put her eye to the opening.

Jane was sitting on the pink patent leather stool, fully dressed, crying. Elle clawed her way into the room and squatted in front of her sister. "Jane, what's wrong? Is it Phil? Is he having an affair?"

Her sister stiffened as if shot. "Of course not. Why would you say such a thing?"

"I don't know. Statistics. Men in their mid-fifties go a bit crazy, right? I'm sorry. I've never seen you cry. Even at Mom's and Dad's funerals you were such a stoic. I was a blubbering idiot, but you held it together."

Jane reached into her purse and took out a small package of tissues. She withdrew one, carefully refolding the package and returning it to its designated spot. After a deep inhale, she blew her nose. "Well, it's not Phil. He and I are fine. A little distracted by work, which is to be expected in the weeks leading up to April 15, but this will help in that department," she said, lifting the crumpled silk teddy in her lap. "No, it's Rebecca. She's been like a stranger lately. Head in the clouds. Mumbling under her breath. I swear if I didn't know better I'd think she was using drugs."

"Drugs," Elle exclaimed, moving back so quickly she lost her balance and wound up on her bottom. "That's ridiculous. How could you think that? She's a freaking CPA, for heaven's sake. You double-check all the tax returns she does. Wouldn't there be glaring mistakes if she was strung out on something?"

Jane dabbed the corner of her eyes. "I…I guess so. I didn't think about that. But she's always been a high achiever. She might be able to do both."

Elle wanted to slap her sister. The woman was obtuse. If something didn't fit into Jane's world, it wasn't of value. Like Rebecca's art.

"You're right, Jane," Elle said standing up. "Rebecca is an overachiever. She's got the most amazing brain. It lets her do things with both hemispheres."

Jane's brows scrunched together in a most unflattering way. She wasn't dumb. She knew about right brain, left brain. "Are you talking about her cards? That's a hobby. Gives her a little money on the side. Nothing more."

"She's an artist, Jane. Your daughter may work numbers during the day, but at night she's an art slut." Elle knew exactly what she was doing by using that term. She was tripping a few of the mommy-issued landmines Becca so carefully tip-toed around. Jane could overlook "dabbling," but Becca's cards had become a business, and Elle's support, however benign, would be viewed as a betrayal.

"Jane, before you go off all half-cocked and indignant, could you, just once, look at this from your daughter's point of view? Denying her art is like closing off one part of who she is."

"Don't tell me about my daughter. I *know* my daughter.

I know where she is. I know that she's safe. I might not approve of her hobby, but at least she's not sleeping around on some floating brothel."

"'Floating brothel'? Where the hell do you get off calling an internationally chartered cruise ship a red-light district on water? You don't know—"

Jane stood up, letting her elegant underwear choices fall to the floor. "I read, Elle. There was an article in one of our church magazines recently about the sins that get committed on pleasure cruises. Phil and I thought about taking a cruise for our thirty-fifth anniversary, but once I read up on the subject…"

Elle had no words. Her sister had always been rigid and narrow in her views of the world, but when had Jane become so sanctimonious?

"But what your daughter does or doesn't do with her life is not my concern. Rebecca, however, *is* my concern and I want you out of her life."

"She's my niece."

Jane crossed her arms like a tin soldier ready to draw a weapon and fire if Elle said another word. That had never stopped Elle before. "She's an adult, Jane. She can pick her friends, even if she can't account for her family. Plus, she pays me rent."

"What?" Jane said, nearly choking on her gasp.

"For the upstairs. Her paints smell, and this way she has room to spread out. I get a percentage of the sales from her cards, plus Becca works for me when she's not lashed to your counting-house desk. It's fun work. She can interact with people—men—her own age. Who knows? She might even meet someone and fall in love."

Jane's eyes narrowed and she said something Elle hadn't heard in years, but with every bit of antipathy she'd used in the past. "I hate you."

CHAPTER FIVE

ELLE MEANDERED through the small mall that had been built a few years after she'd left Fenelon Falls. As in other towns across the country, there had been a big push to move shopping away from the old, established downtown core to a centralized, indoor enterprise under one roof. Also like other towns, the plan hadn't been a complete success. New warehouse stores came in and further divvied up the spending dollar. More people drove into Chicago for their "big" purchases. Hence, both the mall and the downtown suffered.

But Fenelon Falls' downtown had experienced a recent rebirth. Outside grant money, which Jane's Downtown Association had been responsible for getting, had been used to refurbish the infrastructure. The facelift had attracted shop owners like Lucky.

The mall, in contrast, looked dim and frumpy, like an aging aunt who never dressed well. The few randomly placed skylights merely added to the grayness, given the high clouds and icy wind that had blown in overnight. Elle was thankful for the protection the roof afforded but little else.

She was downright miserable. Fighting with her sister always made her blue. And not being able to reach Nora was compounding the problem.

She spotted an empty bench across from Betty's Hallmark shop and sat down. She punched in Nora's number again. Still no answer. Not surprising, she told herself. Nora usually called when she was in port, but they might go weeks without talking.

She left a message, then tried the other number she'd been calling. Her niece. Poor Rebecca deserved a heads-up. Her sister was on a rampage. Not that Jane would storm into Cup O' Love and create a scene. That was not Jane's style. But she would track down Becca eventually with a long list of reasons why Rebecca should give up her art and focus completely on the life her mother had in mind for her.

Rational. That was Jane.

Irrationally Elle wanted to scream, rant and kick something or somebody. But that was her.

Too bad the weather is so crappy, she thought, getting to her feet. *I need a run.*

Three women a few years older than Elle walked past, arms pumping, Nikes squeaking on the tile. Mall-walkers. She'd heard about them. Dodging shoppers seemed like a silly way to exercise, but maybe she should give it a try.

She looped her purse strap so it lay across her chest and started marching. She felt silly, particularly when she reached the middle rotunda where five card tables were set up with chess sets between two players.

She'd forgotten about Max's team's exhibition. She made a wide detour, hoping to avoid their coach. She was too upset to talk to anyone.

"Hey, what's your rush?" a deep voice said from just behind her.

"I'm walking the mall. Which Jane would probably compare to street walking," she muttered. *Grow up, Ellenore. You are not blubbering about your fight with your sister to Max.*

"Elle." He put a hand on her shoulder.

She stopped dead. Touch. She'd been craving touch. Max's touch, actually. In her night dreams. In her daydreams. Whenever she read one of the silly bios that showed up on her dateathon page. She was pretty sure this need was hormone related, but since she hadn't gotten around to making an appointment with a doctor, she didn't know whether or not to blame menopause.

"What?"

"That's a good question. Something is wrong, but what? Since you've got that stubborn look on your face, which I can recognize because my wife was the queen of stubborn, I can only assume that your outing with your sister was a bust, which means you need an outlet for your frustration but mall-walking isn't the answer."

She'd never heard him talk that fast in her life. "So what is the answer?"

"Come with me."

Forty-five minutes later, she was standing at the locked door of the high school, shivering so bad her teeth chattered. "Am I going to detention?" she asked, trying to be a good sport.

He'd apologized repeatedly for taking so long to wrap up the Chess Exposition, but the members of the team turned out to be very talkative. And they'd introduced her to their parents and friends, with sweet little comments, like, "Wait till you try her mochas."

Although this cut into Elle's pouting time, she found that her bad mood was so altered she didn't really need whatever cure Max had in mind. "Maybe we should go to the Cup for some hot cocoa," she said. *And warn Becca.*

"Patience. This will be good for you. I promise."

Good for me? She knew he hadn't meant that as a double entendre, but her heart heard it as such. With just the tiniest of prompting, she could imagine them sweaty and breathless after sex, asking the question that nobody actually asked after sex.

"Are you coming?"

Elle startled. A hot blush clashed with the icy cold of her cheeks. The door was open and Max was waiting. "Sorry," she said hurrying inside. "I think I left my mind at home this morning."

"No problem. What I have planned doesn't require brain power."

She followed him a few steps then stopped and inhaled deeply. "My gosh, this place smells just like it did when I was a student here."

He grinned. "I know. It's weird, isn't it? A mix of gym clothes left in lockers, bubblegum, wet tennis shoes, raging hormones…it never changes."

The sounds their rubber-soled shoes made against the pristine floor seemed to echo and made Elle feel guilty about being there. "Should we be here? Will you get in trouble?"

Max grinned and motioned for her to follow as he headed toward the gym. The school had expanded some since she was a student here. New classrooms had been added, but the extralarge gym appeared to be the same.

Max opened the double doors. To her surprise, they

weren't alone. A dozen or so joggers, two or three groups of walkers and even a guy in a wheelchair were making the round on the second-floor gallery. "There's a street entrance on the other side of the building," Max said. "On weekends and every evening, except for game nights, the public can use the facility. Much better feng shui than the mall, wouldn't you agree?"

"Feng shui?" she repeated, laughing. "Don't let my sister hear you say that. She'll accuse you of letting my Californianess rub off on you."

He snatched her wool cap from her hands and started up the steps. "I knew Jane was behind your bleak look. Want to tell me about it as we run?"

They found an empty spot on a bench to drop their coats and gloves. Elle was glad she hadn't dressed up for her shopping excursion. If she'd been in Santa Rosa with her friends, she'd have been wearing girlie shoes and hose. And she wouldn't have been so glum. Only Jane could make Elle feel small and stupid and…bad.

"We had a little tiff. Sisters. Can't live with them, can't kill them for a bigger piece of the inheritance," she said, trying for flippant. She took off jogging before Max could comment, but he caught up with her without a problem.

He didn't say anything right away. They seemed to silently agree to find their own personal space among the runners before talking. Around the middle of the second lap, Max said, "Jane is a good person, but I don't think there's much joy in her life. Not sure why. Your parents always seemed happy."

That made Elle think. Her father, for sure, had been an easygoing person. Everyone in town loved him. He'd pump gas for old ladies, long after full-service went out of fashion. He was notorious for extending credit to people who were equally notorious for not being able to pay. The only time she could ever recall her parents arguing was over money. Their mother had handled the books for the service station, a chore Jane later took over.

"Obviously they loved each other," she said, slowing down enough to talk. She wasn't in nearly as good shape as she had been when she'd moved home. She'd worked in sales for a software company that believed strongly in keeping its employees fit. An on-site gym had been just one of the perks. But since opening the Cup, those darn mochas were catching up with her. "What with Mom dying of a broken heart and all."

Max missed a step. "I hate to disagree, but dying after losing a mate, doesn't necessarily define the quality or quantity of feelings you had for that person."

Elle felt her cheeks turn even warmer than they already were. "Damn, if I had a spare foot it would be in my mouth. Sorry about that."

His smile let her off the hook. "If I'd have died a few weeks after Sarah, she'd have smacked me upside the head and made me get back in my body. She didn't suffer fools lightly. When her cancer came back, she told me right there in the doctor's office, 'This is it. I fought a good fight, but I'm not going to make beating cancer my new job. It's going to win, Max, and you are going to have to go on without me.'"

Tears filled Elle's eyes. She'd never met Max's wife. The few times she'd returned home to visit her parents and sister, she'd never seemed to find time to call up her old friends. "Jane said she was a really good person. A saint, I believe, were her exact words."

Max hooted so loud people turned to look at them. "Sarah would be the first to laugh at that. She was a wonderful mother, an honest banker and big Bulls fan, but she wasn't perfect. Nobody is, Elle."

His words were still echoing in her mind an hour later when she watched him bend over to take a drink from the water fountain. She wanted to reach out and touch his hair. A stray lock, damp from sweat, had fallen over one ear. But she stuffed her hands in the pockets of her heavy coat and looked around instead.

Her loud intake of air must have sounded like a gasp of fear or shock because Max looked up so fast water trickled down his lips. "What?"

Heart pounding in the silliest way, she pointed. "Am I having a déjà vu moment?"

A six-foot long banner, crudely written in red and pink block print surrounded by extravagant arrow-pierced hearts, proclaimed: The Winter Ball. Saturday. February 17. Bring Your Valentine.

Max wiped the water from his mouth and took a deep breath. He'd grown more or less inured to the many social events taking place around him. He volunteered to chaperone—or rather was required to chaperone—two or three per year. This had never been one he'd chosen.

"Some things never change," he said, striving for casual. "The administration tried to combine this dance with the Sadie Hawkins a few years ago, but it didn't work. No matter how sophisticated the kids get, there's a core group that still likes their social functions."

She was staring at the banner as if it had some power over her. Max decided now was the time to put their old demons to rest. "Elle, let it go."

"Huh?" She looked at him. "What do you mean?"

"This was the dance that didn't happen between us. We both know that, but I think you're reading way too much into it."

Her eyes narrowed. "I was a stupid, shallow twit, Max. I thought I'd blown it with the love of my life. He broke up with me a month later when I refused to put out. How could I have been so stupid?"

He'd always hated it when she belittled herself. "Would it make you feel better if I told you I only asked you to the dance because I was hoping to get laid, and rumor had it you were easy?"

Her mouth dropped open and a second later she gave him a shove that made him stumble backward. "That is not true."

He grinned. "I know. I just wondered if it would make you feel better if I told you that."

She started laughing. "You're crazy."

"I know."

"I really have felt guilty about dropping you when Kyle came groveling."

Kyle. Right. Kyle Peterson. Super jock. Super jerk. "I know. But, just for the record, you didn't break my heart beyond repair. Slightly bruised, I'll admit, but nothing that time and a few sexual encounters in college couldn't cure. So, can we finally put this to rest? We all make mistakes in high school. We wouldn't be human if we didn't."

She took a deep breath and let it out. Then she held out her hand. "You're a good person."

"At the risk of sounding redundant…again, I know. Hey, I almost forgot. I told my daughter-in-law I'd swing by and spend a couple of hours with Amber so she could run to the store. Wanna come?"

"Won't Amber be jealous?"

"Not if you bring her black olives. Her parents don't like her to have candy, but she's a sucker for black olives."

"If we could swing by the Cup, I just happen to have a can left over from my tortilla soup. I'm in."

CHAPTER SIX

"NICE PLACE," Elle said an hour later.

She was sitting on the floor of his son's family room, cross-legged, in stocking feet, with his granddaughter settled snugly in her lap. Amber hadn't warmed to Elle immediately, but about half a dozen black olives had done the trick. Now, Max was feeling a little left out.

He glanced around. "Yeah. Sarah helped them buy it before she died. I mean, she helped them fill out all the first-time buyer applications, cross all the t's, etcetera. She was really good with that stuff. Maybe that's why she and Jane were friends. They both liked numbers."

"Huh? Your wife and Jane were friends? Jane never mentioned that. Come to think about it, Jane has never mentioned having friends, other than Phil. I know she's active in the community and at church, but I guess I've never really seen that side of her."

He shrugged. "They weren't close, but they probably had lunch together once or twice a month."

"Hmmm," she murmured, bending down to whisper something in Amber's ear. The baby girl chortled and flopped sideways, holding out her arms toward Max.

"Rumpa," she called. Her language skills were pretty

advanced, but her name for grandpa hadn't changed since the word first came out of her darling little mouth.

He moved off the couch and walked on his knees to where the two were sitting. Amber more or less launched herself into his arms. "Hey, presh, let's show off for Elle." He helped the child stand, and then they swung their arms back and forth to the tune of "Ring Around the Rosie." Amber knew about half the words.

"Wow," Elle cried, clapping gaily. "That's amazing. My little girl loved that song. We'd dress up like princesses and dance till we were dizzy."

"I bet you were a cool mom. Fun and adventurous."

Her smile faded. "I don't know about that, but Nora is a pretty fabulous person. Graduated from college with honors. Had a bunch of job offers in the Bay area, but decided she wasn't ready to settle down. Right now, she's entertainment director for a cruise line. She books performers and handles the shows. When she has time off, she goes into the villages—not where the tourists are, but the ones that are really poor and don't have running water and schools, and passes out books and money and toys. I donate to her cause every month. Not a lot, but a little goes a long way when there's no bureaucracy involved."

Max had no idea, but he wasn't surprised. Elle always had had more depth than anyone in town gave her credit for. "What time do you have to be back at the Cup?" he asked.

"Four. I considered closing early on weekends, but we get enough theatergoers to make it worthwhile."

Max shook his head. "I can't believe you're open seven days a week."

She shrugged. "I have good help on the weekends, thank

heavens. I almost never have to go in on Sunday. And if business keeps picking up I'll be able to hire another person during the week. Did I tell you we've seen a twenty percent hike in sales since the WiFi went in?"

"That's good. Do you have plans tomorrow?"

She nodded. "Absolutely. Laundry, grocery shopping. I have to make up the menus for the rest of the week. And I thought about going to church to support Lucky. Did you hear about Josh's plan?"

He could tell his question made her uneasy—hence her change of topic. "I did." And even though he knew and liked Josh, he didn't want to talk about the church or its pastor. "So, would you go out on a date with me?"

"Huh?"

Not the answer he was hoping for. "Brunch. Next Sunday. My son in Chicago wants me to meet his new friend. Um, did I mention that he's gay? Meeting your child's lover for the first time is awkward regardless of their sex, so I thought maybe having you along would make things easier."

Her mouth dropped open. "Why? Because I'm from the San Francisco area?"

He laughed. "No. Because you're nice."

"Oh." She didn't speak for a moment. "How do you feel about him being gay?"

He shrugged. "Jared is who he is, and he's a really fine person. His mother had a rough time accepting the truth when he was in high school, which can be brutal when someone is different."

"Tell me about it," Elle murmured.

"But they reconciled completely before she died."

Elle got to her feet, then bent over and picked up Amber. "I'm glad. I know what it's like to feel disapproval from someone you love over something you have very little control over. That probably didn't make sense, but you know what I mean, right?"

He did. "Your sister doesn't know about Jared." At her look of shock, he qualified, "At least, I don't think she does. The last time we talked about some question on my taxes, she asked me when we were going to match my unmarried son to her very eligible daughter. I gathered she'd been trying to pair the two up since high school. Apparently she and Sarah never spoke of the subject of Jared's sexuality. Or, maybe like me, she just didn't want to burst Jane's bubble of denial."

"Odd. I wonder what Jane's going to say when she finds out her daughter has a crush on a divorced man with a child?"

A door closed and the sound of voices, Amber's parents returning from shopping, ended the conversation. Max and Elle said their goodbyes and left.

As he opened the passenger door for her, he remembered that they'd gotten off track and she hadn't answered him about the brunch date. When he brought it up again, she said, "I'm afraid I have to pass. I have a lot to do to get things set up for the Valentine's Day party at the Cup."

"I understand. Then how about a movie next Saturday night? They're doing a Movies of the Seventies revival at the old Grand Theater."

She looked skeptical. "Haven't they heard of Netflix?"

"Theater popcorn can't be replicated in a microwave. I don't care what Orville Redenbacher says."

Her laugh was sweet and tantalizing and almost enough of a push to make him confess that he'd been manipulating her Web page so only total losers—and his bogus mystery men—were showing up in her In box. But not quite. Call him superstitious, but this time he wasn't taking any chances. He'd show up on Valentine's Day at Cup O' Love and declare himself. The rest would be in Cupid's hands.

ON THE FOLLOWING Monday morning, Elle was at her desk, putting the finishing touch on her food order. Business had been steadily picking up. Nearly a dozen people—mostly women—had signed up for the dateathon. And everyone, except Elle, it seemed, was getting hits from interesting, eligible men.

Becca and Lucky tried to reassure Elle that she was still "dating material," but Elle had to wonder. Fortunately the upturn in business was keeping her too busy to fret about her apparently polluted dating pool. A steadily increasing number of people were showing up to make use of the WiFi—and buy coffee and other goodies. She was about to e-mail her wholesaler, when the phone rang.

"Hello?"

"Mom?"

"Nora?"

"Who else? Unless you've recently given birth or adopted without telling me."

Elle felt a serene warmness wash over her. She loved her daughter, her voice, her humor. "Nope. You're my one and only." She tried to keep her tone light, but Nora wasn't fooled.

"What's wrong? You sound blue."

"You're right. It's probably that light deprivation sickness I've heard about. Either that or I'm sick of not getting along with your aunt."

Nora groaned. "I told Bjarne things probably hadn't improved on that front."

Elle sat up straight. "Bjarne? Who's Bjarne?"

Nora let out an uncharacteristic giggle. "A coworker. Well, he works in corporate, but he's great, Mom. He plays five instruments and speaks four languages. Or is it the other way around? He's from Denmark. Blond hair, blue eyes and smart, Mom. Oh my God, he's so smart. You're going to love him when you meet him."

"You're bringing him home to meet your mother? Wow, that's a first."

Elle didn't mean for the observation to sound critical. This really would be a first. Although Nora had mentioned other boyfriends from time to time, she'd never gushed about one and never suggested that he might be a part of her life long enough to visit the Midwest.

"We have two weeks at the end of the month, and we decided to fly to Chicago and rent a car. We'll stay with you a few days then drive to New York. His parents are going to be in the States on business and they'll meet us there. Maybe you could fly out for a couple of days, too."

"Wow, this really is serious, isn't it?" Elle said softly. "Oh, honey, I'm so happy for you. Can you e-mail a photo when you're in port next? I'd love to see him."

They talked about all the vitals: how they met, why they're perfect for each other, what they think might happen down the road. Elle was thrilled for her daughter, and just a little bit bluer when she hung up.

Her baby had probably been the most independent child on the planet, which had been a boon considering how much growing up Elle had had to do as a young mother, but that self-reliance was a mixed blessing, now. If Nora and this young Dane married, they would probably spend their time split between two countries with a very wide ocean separating them.

For a time, Elle had been able to pretend that by coming home to the Falls, she'd set the stage for the last part of her life quite nicely. She would have family nearby—a sister and niece whom she could call on if something happened. She'd even fantasized that Nora would be so charmed by the quaint little town that she'd relocate here, too, once she got over her wanderlust.

But the chances of that bucolic scene happening seemed like pure fiction. Jane didn't want anything to do with Elle, and she'd ordered Elle to stay away from Rebecca. Her business was at a make or break stage. She only had so many productive years left to add to her retirement fund, and presently the Cup O' Love was more a drain on her energy, her health and her resources.

"Give me one good reason to stay," she muttered under her breath as she rocked back in her father's cranky old chair.

A loud screech made her wince. If that was an answer, it was pretty lame. But with a tiny stretch of the imagination, she could almost hear the word "Max" in its echo.

CHAPTER SEVEN

"DID WE LIKE THOSE movies back when we were young?"
Elle asked, discreetly trying to dislodge a kernel of popcorn
from between her back molars.

Max laughed. "In my own defense, I don't think I saw
any spaghetti Westerns back then. My friends and I liked
to pretend that we were too smart for such plebian pulp.
We'd get somebody's parent to drive us to the city to watch
something with subtitles."

They paused in the foyer of the old theater to zip up their
jackets. Temperatures had dropped steadily throughout the
week. Word of a storm—a big one—was on everybody's
lips. They'd had flurries off and on all winter, but the really
bad stuff had missed them.

Until now, Elle thought, when Max opened the heavy
door for her step outside. The bite in the air chilled her
lungs when she inhaled. "I had to give up on foreign films.
I become engrossed in the action and forget to read until
it's too late."

"Ah…the beauty of DVDs. I have a couple I bet you'd
like. You'll have to come over some time for a marathon
culture immersion. Instead of popcorn, we can eat treats
endemic to the country. Edemame for *Rashomon*, arguably
Kurosawa's best, I'm sure you'll agree," he said teasingly.

DEBRA SALONEN   67

"Croissants and brie for *Amelie*. I promise you'll love it. And…what would be appropriate for a Russian film? We could watch either *Andrei Rublev* or *War and Peace*."

"Umm…vodka?"

"Vodka! Perfect. Sarah was a connoisseur. Some people claim that potato vodka is the best, but Sarah was a grain enthusiast. I'll buy her favorite."

They turned right to get to where Max's car was parked. As they strolled down Main Street, Elle decided Fenelon Falls had never looked better. The deco-shaped reproduction streetlights glowed like orange candle flames, giving the scene a Norman Rockwell painting quality.

She tried to mute her curiosity but was only a few steps beyond a circle of light cast by the theater's marquee when she said, "Somehow I can't picture your churchgoing banker wife as a vodka drinker."

He took her arm—in the way people do when they're walking on icy ground—and pulled her close so their shoulders touched. "Sarah came from a big, boisterous Polish family. They all smoke and drink and eat raw hamburger and onions." He shuddered. "They tell me it's an acquired taste, but I think it's genetic. Both my sons like the stuff."

Elle glanced sideways and saw a puff of frosty air leave his lips. He had gorgeous lips. *Did I know that in high school?*

"Anyway, she wasn't the kind of person to shortchange herself—banker joke—when it came to life. She organized a major family vacation every summer, either we rented a cabin at the lake for a month or did some traveling. One year, we went to the rain forest in Belize. Another time we took a canoe trip in Northern Ontario."

"Wow. Sounds like you had a great life together. Must be pretty hard, now. To be alone, I mean. Since I never had that kind of togetherness—well, not for long, anyway, I'm used to being alone."

They'd stopped walking, and he turned so they were facing each other. "Alone and lonely aren't the same thing," he said. "I keep busy, like you do, but don't tell me you don't have nights when the walls close in and you think you'll go mad if you don't have someone to talk to."

Her mouth went dry. How had he guessed? "That's what friends are for," she said, striving for flippancy.

"Friends can only do so much. Your kids have their own lives and can't be expected to fill in all the gaps. And an electric blanket may warm the bed, but it's hell to snuggle up with."

He was inviting her home, she realized. To his bed. To snuggle…and more. But she couldn't do that. She couldn't take the place of his dead wife.

"I…um…I'm not Sarah."

He closed the distance between them and put his lips just inches from hers. "No. You're Elle." Then he kissed her. A real kiss. The kind she hadn't experienced in months, or longer. Maybe ever.

Her arms knew what to do even if her mind wasn't working. She looped them around his neck and kissed him back. Forgetting the fact that they were dressed in six layers of clothing and standing on Main Street.

How long they kissed, she had no idea. Why they stopped, she wasn't sure, either. But his low chuckle prompted her to open her eyes.

"Wow. I've waited nearly forty years to do that."

His tone was so serious, Elle panicked. She didn't do serious, right? She was footloose and fancy-free and immune to commitment. At least, that was what she'd always been told. Nobody took her seriously, and this was definitely the wrong time in her life to try to make a personality change.

"Max," she said, dropping her chin to her chest. "I don't think this is a good idea."

"Why?"

"You know why."

"Because your boyfriend might want you back?"

She looked up. A low hit, but deserved. "Because I'm flaky Ellenore Adams. Airhead blonde. All body, no substance. It's just a matter of time before I screw up, cut my losses and leave. That's what I do."

He ran the edge of his leather glove along her jaw, which jutted out defiantly, as if she had a right to be proud of that history. "That was never you, Elle. You let people believe that. Just like your dad let people think he was a bumbling, goofy old Joe, who only knew how to pump gas and change tires. But I got to know your dad before he passed away. He came to all the local chess matches, and he and I would play a couple of times a month. There were times he showed glimpses of brilliance. Daring, gutsy moves that reminded me so much of you."

Elle couldn't quite take in what he was saying. "My dad played chess? But I used to beat him at checkers."

Max's shoulders lifted and fell. "Did it never occur to you that he let you win? Dads do that for little girls they love unconditionally."

Tears pooled in her eyes and her nose started to run. She

dug in her pocket for a tissue, but Max produced a cotton handkerchief. She'd never met a man other than her father who carried one.

"Speaking of chess," he said, turning her to one side so he could use the streetlight to see to dry her tears, "wanna play? I have a stack of boards in the back of my truck. Never leave home without 'em."

She took the hankie from him and blew her nose. "The last time I played was in high school when you tried to teach me."

He put his arm across her shoulders in a companionable way and started toward his SUV. "And I seem to remember you showed great promise."

She snorted. "You were probably so busy looking down my shirt you just didn't see my mistakes."

"Could be. Feel free to use that gambit tonight, if you're serious about winning."

Because she knew he was teasing—the view down her shirt wasn't that great anymore—she laughed. It struck her that she laughed more in his company than with any other man she'd ever dated. Did that mean she was in love?

The possibility suddenly seemed all too real.

MAX HADN'T BEEN BACK to Elle's parents' home since her mother's funeral. He knew that the house had gone to Elle and the gas station to Jane because Jane's husband, Phil, had mentioned the arrangement one night at the Elk's club. He wasn't surprised to see that Elle had already put her own stamp on the simple, one-story bungalow.

"I like these colors," he said, admiring the deep, taupe walls of the living room.

"Thank you. Jane said it was ridiculous to paint when

my business was so iffy, but I told her I thought fresh paint would attract younger buyers if I do have to sell." She shrugged off her coat and hung it up in the coat closet.

His was next. Irrational as it seemed, that gesture gave him hope. Would she bother hanging it up if she was going to send him home after their game of chess?

"Cup of tea?" she asked, heading to the kitchen.

"Sure. But nothing with caffeine, please. I'm saving up for my java jolt for the morning."

The kitchen, he noticed, was relatively untouched. White walls and old-fashioned four-inch square tile that was a mottled blend of tan and brown with dark grout. His kitchen had looked almost identical before Sarah had it gutted just a few months before she died. He'd tried to talk her out of starting such a big project when she was so weak, but she'd claimed it was her mission to leave him a house he could be happy in.

Happy. How a ten-thousand-dollar remodel job was supposed to make up for losing his mate, he had no idea, but he'd given her free rein.

"You've been my only honest-to-goodness Falls regular, you know," she said from where she stood at the stove, her back to him.

"I kinda guessed that. Can't figure out why. Your prices aren't that much higher than other places and your coffee is a thousand times better tasting than that light brown swill they sell at the bakery."

She glanced over her shoulder. "Thank you. I think so, too. Jane says locals are slow to warm to outsiders. I was so dumb I didn't know she meant me."

Max heard the hurt in her tone. He walked over to her

and put his arms around her. "I'll never understand your sister, but I do agree that there are quite a few people in small towns with a certain mentality toward change. Give them time, Elle. They'll come around."

Her deep sigh pushed her backward slightly in his arms. He liked the feeling. A lot. He loved her scent, a blend of cinnamon and coffee—even when she wasn't working. "I don't know how much time I've got, Max."

Her words jolted him. Hard. Like someone had jabbed him in the chest with a cane. "What do you mean?" he asked, stepping back. His voice must have cracked because she pivoted on one heel, her eyes wide with alarm.

"Oh, dear. What a stupid thing to say! I didn't mean it like that. I'm well. More or less. I think I might be going through the change, but I'm healthy as a horse. What I meant is I can't afford to keep dipping into my retirement fund to shore up a losing business. I put every penny I could into my 401K when I was working in sales. It's not a fortune, and it has to last. I didn't mean to sound like such a drama queen."

His heart returned to its normal pace. He held out his hand to her. "I should have known that's what you meant. And if it makes any difference, I know women are all different, but Sarah said menopause was the best thing that ever happened to her."

"Huh? Surely she was too young to have—"

"It might have been connected to her treatments, but she was all done with symptoms when she was forty-two. She called her hot flashes 'power surges,' and said they served as a reminder to have sex more often."

Elle chuckled and shook her head. "I think I would have liked her."

"I think so, too."

They looked into each other's eyes for a long while. Max read something that told him she was thinking about sleeping with him. When the kettle started whistling, she turned off the stove and said, "Let's skip the tea. And chess. I have something better in mind."

Then she led the way to the master bedroom. A room that might have once belonged to her parents, but now was home to a glamorous, sexy woman who wasn't afraid to display her treasures.

CHAPTER EIGHT

"CLASSY."

"You like the color? Jane called it olive-green. I almost kicked her in the shin." Elle quickly snapped on the bedside lamp, an updated version of a Tiffany design with a heavy sculpted base.

"Sage," he said, walking from the doorway to the dresser where her eclectic collection of vintage jewelry was displayed. "My favorite color. Sarah redid the kitchen in a Craftsman design and the walls are about this shade. Maybe a little darker."

He picked up a glittery, slightly vulgar necklace of square garnets, diamonds and finely wrought silver. She'd unearthed the piece at an estate sale in Oakland and loved it on sight. "This is fabulous. Will you wear it for me?"

She swallowed loudly. "Are you kidding?"

"No."

"It's early-American harlot. Are you sure that's the right tone to strike for our first time?" She couldn't believe she managed to sound so cavalier when inside her heart was barely pumping enough oxygen to keep her from feeling light-headed.

His grin turned wicked. "You're right. I'll wear it."

Elle laughed and some of her nervousness disappeared.

She kicked off her shoes and hopped up on the bed to watch him as he replaced the necklace on its clear acrylic stand and moved on to her collection of enamel butterflies. He'd given her her first one. A cheap trinket he said he'd found at a rummage sale. She hadn't believed him.

She'd framed the dozen or so pins, clips and charms on a black velvet background. He pointed to one with azure wings and a brilliant yellow body. "You kept this."

"Of course."

"It's the first thing I ever bought for a girl. I remember how badly my hands were sweating when I gave it to you. My voice cracked and I thought I was going to be sick."

She leaned forward. "Really?" She could picture the moment, vaguely. Boys had been giving her things since she'd first developed breasts. She'd accepted it as if she were entitled, not because someone went to a lot of effort to pick out something she would like. "I was a shallow twit. I didn't deserve it."

He turned to face her. "That's not true. Obviously. You kept it. You valued it." He walked to the bed. "In a way, that says you valued me."

She couldn't deny that. Whenever she thought back to her high school days, Max came to mind. He'd been so different from the boys she'd usually dated. He'd made her feel smarter, better somehow. "I've always valued you, my friend."

He put one knee on the bed and leaned close enough to kiss her, but he didn't. Not right away. Instead he asked, "Do you believe that friendship can grow into something stronger?"

"I don't know," she answered honestly.

"I do."

"Show me."

And he did. Gently, gracefully, intelligently. He kept things simple, making sure she was comfortable with each step. Getting naked. He teased her about the line left by her hipster panties. "No grandma undies for you, I see," he said, tracing the imprint across the middle of her quivering belly.

Underwear talk made it easy to segue into health talk, which made it very simple to admit that she had a supply of condoms in her bedside drawer…just in case.

"I would have expected nothing less, Ellenore. You always were far more responsible than anyone gave you credit for being."

His praise felt good. So did his hands on her breasts, and his heat against her skin. A shiver of desire shot through her and a silent voice chortled, "Power surge." Loving and being loved was a powerful sensation. Life-affirming. She'd missed sex, she realized. But more than that, she'd missed this feeling of rapture, though if she was honest, she could honestly say she'd never before felt quite like this.

My hand is touching Ellenore Adams's breast. The thought was so mind-boggling, Max almost laughed. But explaining his giddy reaction would definitely ruin the mood.

And the mood was amazing. Comfortable but far, far from complacent. He wanted to do everything, taste every inch of her, find out what made her breathless, hot, wild. But he also wanted to savor every salty drop of sweat and sweetly smothered cry.

"You're beautiful," he said, looking into her eyes.

Her grin said she didn't believe him. "You're in pretty

amazing shape yourself. Chess did this to these shoulders? Who knew?"

He laughed. "I started working out at a gym when Sarah's cancer came back. A friend who lost his wife a couple of years earlier said exercise would keep me sane, plus she'd need my help as things got bad."

She ran her hand, lovingly, over his shoulder and down his chest. The muted light hid a few imperfections, but it couldn't hide the fact that their bodies were much older than when they first were attracted to each other. "It seems surreal that we're here in bed together, given our history."

He didn't want to get into that again. There wasn't room for any ghosts in this bed—hers or his. He tossed back the covers, exposing them both to the chilly air.

"Max," she exclaimed.

He rolled them both over so he was on top. With arms braced so only their bellies were touching, he said, "Elle, once we do this, things change. There's no going back. You mix certain chemicals and they not only stay mixed forever, they become something new. You understand that, right?"

She wiggled her hips and ran her hands down his back to his chilly butt. "Max, this is sex, not a science lesson. Get on with it."

And he did. Teacher became student. Friend became lover. The chemistry worked...for both of them.

CHAPTER NINE

ELLE COULDN'T BELIEVE how fast the weeks had flown by. Today was Monday, February 12. Only two days left before her big party.

She and Max had been together half a dozen times since that first night at her house. "We need to take things slow," she'd told him. Both because of the uncertainty of her business and to avoid the inevitable gossip that came from living and owning a business in a small town.

Elle didn't know if Jane had heard about them or not. She and her sister hadn't talked since their big blowup. Jane hadn't called or stopped by the Cup, even though Elle saw her drive past on her way to the office every morning.

The snub hurt more than her sister could possibly know, but Elle tried to rationalize that Jane had been busy lately. Becca had mentioned that in addition to the crush of tax preparation, her mother had been volunteering to help the Conner family. Not only was Rachel Conner undergoing treatment for cancer, but the poor little girl and her mother had been involved in a terrible car wreck during the blizzard that hit the area.

Elle and her friends hadn't gotten together for one of their wine and whine sessions in way too long. Becca, it seemed, was constantly on the run. She'd suffered a creative crisis not because of Jane's bullying but because of Will Blakely. The man had publicly denounced the sentiments in Becca's Valentines, without realizing she was the artist who'd made them.

Elle and Will's daughter, Penny, had tried to collaborate on a scheme to bring the two together, but, so far, their efforts had been a bust. Elle wanted her niece to be happy—as happy as she was, but she knew love followed its own path, with or without help from meddling aunts, well-intentioned friends or, it seemed, the Internet.

She looked around Cup O' Love and smiled. A dozen patrons, at least. All occupied with their morning brew, a newspaper or their online connections. She could now name eight or ten regulars who were eagerly awaiting February 14. They were most vocal about their online suitors and readily discussed the state of their courtships.

Elle, however, had nothing to report. She had yet to receive an e-mail from anyone remotely interesting enough to consider asking to the party. She couldn't decide if this was because the few who'd responded to her page were just all wrong for her or because she'd already found Mr. Right—Max—and none compared to him.

She smiled, picturing him asleep in her bed as he'd been when she'd left for work that morning. Humming under her breath, she stirred the tomato bisque soup once more then moved the Crock-Pot to the self-serve stand. She replenished the crackers and made sure there were plenty of spoons. The wind had picked up again during the night, resculpting the snow drifts in a way that made the landscape look harsh and cold. People needed hot soup on days like this.

She wondered if Max would be in for lunch. He usually

took a lunch, but on the nights he stayed over, he had to return home, shower and dress for school *and* make a lunch. She glanced at her watch. Eleven-thirty. She had time to check her Cupid's Picks page.

"Wow. Twelve entries. Now this is more like it."

As she read the first one, her smile changed to a puzzled frown. Ron B. He was single. No kids. He liked older women. Dislikes: "People who think it's funny to call other people names."

"Huh?" she murmured, hoping the man included a photo. So far, only a few of her rejects had attached an image, and those had been so blurry, she would have been hard-pressed to pick them out in a lineup.

"Yes," she exclaimed. "A picture."

Of a beautiful black Lab. Nice pink tongue. Cheerful red and white kerchief. "My best friend, Jeremiah," the caption read. "He's better looking than me. Sorry."

Elle shook her head, made her gut reaction in the box provided and watched as Ron B. disappeared into Cupid's red heart icon. So far, he'd probably gotten the best ranking from her, but she sincerely hoped he wouldn't show up on Wednesday for a date—dog or no dog.

"This was a really bad idea, wasn't it?" she muttered after two more dismal entries failed to interest her. Each of them sounded impossibly young and immature. Their responses reminded her of…of…she couldn't quite pin it down, but the niggling idea disappeared when Rebecca walked in the door.

"Hi, Aunt Elle. Smells good in here. And look at all these people. Cool."

Elle closed down her page and got up. She walked to

where her niece was standing and gave her a hug. "How are you? Still getting flack from your mother?"

Rebecca didn't answer. Instead she opened her coat and took out a plastic grocery bag, from which she withdrew a two-inch stack of folded cards and envelopes. "I was going to drop them off last night, but when I drove by your house, I saw Mr. Maxwell's truck out front. Did you go out on a date?"

"Um…sorta."

"Oh. Well, I would have run them over this morning but Mom gave me four new tax clients."

"Honey, I'm sorry. How will you have time for your art classes?" Rebecca looked so bleak, Elle wanted to kick her sister in the back of her high-tech ergonomic chair. "Come on, kiddo. You need a cappuccino. I can tell."

"Why does Mom hate art, Aunt Elle?"

Elle held the stainless steel mug to the frother. It made too much noise for her to answer, so she used the time to think about the question. Did Jane hate all art or just her daughter's?

As she poured the fragrant caramel-colored liquid into a paper cup, she said, "Jane is a lot like your grandmother. They both craved order and routine. Numbers give you that. They're clean and neat and you can usually tell at a glance when you've made a mistake. Art definitely isn't that clear-cut."

"She has a few paintings on the walls. And some photographs that someone told her were going to go up in value someday."

Elle shrugged. "We've never had the same taste in anything, especially art. I'm really sorry if my big mouth made things tougher for you."

Rebecca shrugged. "I'm a grown-up. I can handle it."

Elle agreed. She just hoped her sister wouldn't burn any bridges she'd later regret.

A few minutes later, the noon rush hit. Several new faces. A few older folks who looked kind of familiar, like maybe they'd been customers of her parents or something. And four of Max's chess club members. The latter ate two bowls of soup each and bought drinks, cookies and coffees. Her cash register had never looked so healthy.

As she was standing at it, sorting bills, she happened to glance at the Valentine's Day table. One of Max's students whom she couldn't remember by name pointed to the screen of the open laptop and laughed.

That's when it hit her. *They* were responsible for the new entries on her page that morning. She wondered if Max had put them up to it. *No, of course not.* They were just lusty young boys and this was a game to them.

On a hunch, she picked up a box of candy hearts and walked to the table. "Hey," she said, "which one of you has a Lab named Jeremiah?"

The shortest one, with curly brown hair and glasses, looked up. "I do. How'd you know…oh, damn."

His blush was endearing, and she knew his friends would tease him relentlessly for blowing their joke. So, she presented him with the little candies and gave him a kiss on the cheek, then sent them back to school. Let their teacher worry about discipline. That wasn't her thing.

MAX COULD TELL something was up with the kids in his first class after lunch. His conscience made him worry that his ever-perceptive students had somehow guessed that he'd gotten lucky—better than lucky—last night. But as he covertly listened, he picked up bits and pieces of some embarrassing fiasco involving four of his chess kids.

After a quick quiz, the class broke into small groups to work on their science fair projects. He moved stealthily and ambushed them when they were huddled together, deep in conversation.

"Do you think she'll tell Mr. M?"

"Naw, she's cool. She gave you candy hearts. I think she likes you."

"Really? Like maybe she'd let me see her naked?"

"You are one sick little pup, Pete. If Mr. M finds out—"

"Finds out what?" Max asked.

The three seniors suddenly looked as mature as his granddaughter. They stammered and hemmed and hawed until the story finally came out.

"You hacked into Ms. Adams's Valentine's Day Dateathon page?" *How did I miss that? Oh, right, I was in bed with Ms. Adams.* "Why?"

"Because we like her and whenever we checked the Cup O' Love's home page, we'd only see one or two hits listed under her name. We couldn't figure out why," the acknowledged leader of the group said.

"So, we bypassed the gatekeeper and sent in our names. Well, not our real names," Peter Ellison added.

"I see. Well, you do know you're supposed to be twenty-one to participate in this dateathon, right? And there's a charge."

Peter looked down. "Yeah, we know, but we spent all our money on lunch at the Cup."

Max fought back a smile. "You know Elle…Ms. Adams

didn't set this up so a bunch of high school boys could flirt with her. I take it she found out somehow?"

"Pete can't keep a secret," Ham said.

Peter blushed a brilliant shade of red that nearly matched the little square box sticking out of his breast pocket.

Candy hearts. Max had seen them for sale at the Cup.

"Did you apologize?"

They nodded in unison.

"But did you grovel?"

They looked at each other. "Huh?" their tenors hummed.

"Here's a hint. She likes butterflies."

And she's quite fond of having her belly button licked. But he'd keep that little tidbit to himself.

CHAPTER TEN

ELLE LOVED the four o'clock lull. It gave her time to make whatever roll-up she had in mind for the day. Today's selection would be chopped black olives, salami, three kinds of cheese and strips of roasted red pepper.

If her sandwiches went over as well as her soup did at lunch today, she'd be able to say with pride that Cup O' Love had its best day of business ever. She crossed her fingers and knocked on the wooden chopping block just in case.

She heard the exterior door jingle, but she kept rolling the cracker bread.

"A delivery, Elle," Noreen, her part-time assistant, said. "You have to sign for it."

That was surprising. Usually if Tony, the FedEx guy, had something for her, he just left it on her desk. "I'll be right there."

She secured the roll-up with toothpicks, then wrapped it in plastic wrap and carried it to the display case. She sold roll-ups by the inch and wouldn't cut it until someone ordered a specific size.

She looked around as she wiped her hands on a towel. No Tony.

"Over there," Noreen said, motioning with her head.

The man in question wasn't wearing a uniform. He looked more like an attorney than a messenger boy.

"I'm Ellenore Adams. You have something for me?"

He turned on the heel of his shiny black shoes and produced a sealed manila envelope that bore her name and the Cup O' Love address. "I need to sign something?"

He had a small receipt book. The kind offices used to keep track of petty cash. She signed her name, then looked at him. "Who are you? Who do you work for? I don't think I've seen you around before. Do you want a cup of coffee? On the house."

He was young, mid-twenties, she'd guess given the number of blemishes. Her suggestion appeared to come as a surprise to him, but he stammered a "No, thank you" and left in a hurry.

"Odd," Elle said, carrying the envelope to her office. It was lightweight, only a page or two. A few weeks earlier she'd gotten a registered letter inviting her to a time-share hotel in Hawaii. Maybe this was something similar, she thought, ripping open the seal. There was no return address. What kind of company would pass up the chance to plaster its logo on…

The thought disappeared as she scanned the piece of paper. Her hand began shaking and she placed it flat on the desk to finish reading the six paragraphs of typed print, which she saw carried a notary seal on the bottom.

"She's kicking me out?" Elle murmured, squinting at the words that made no sense. "For letting her daughter use my empty second-floor space?"

"A clear violation of rule 7, subparagraph 3 of a signed lease," the letter said.

"Rule seven?" Elle repeated. "What rules? What lease? What the hell is she talking about?"

Her voice rose as her hysteria grew and must have carried beyond her open door because a second later two people joined her in the tiny cubicle. Lucky, who snatched the paper off the desk and started reading it aloud, and Max, who was looking at Elle with such concern, Elle almost burst into tears.

"Your sister sent you this?" Lucky asked, her voice taut and angry. "What a chicken-poop thing to do. Noreen said she had some snot-nosed messenger boy deliver it, too. She wasn't even woman enough to tell you face-to-face that she was revoking your lease."

"Revoking?" Max grabbed the page and scanned it. "Did you sign a lease, Elle?"

Had she? Jane had wanted to keep everything clean and neat, and Elle had agreed. She'd always heard that was the best way to do business with family. "I don't know for sure. I might have. I signed something, but I thought it had to do with power of attorney if anything happened to me. That made sense, I thought, with Nora so far away and hard to reach."

"You must have signed a lease, too, since she acts so confident. I don't picture Jane as the type to bluff."

Elle's stomach turned over. Had she blown it again? Trusted the wrong person and wound up in trouble? But not Jane, a small voice cried. Her sister wouldn't publicly humiliate her and kick her out. Not when Elle's business was finally taking off.

"Today was a good day," she said in a small voice. "Best sales, yet."

"Listen," Lucky said. "I don't know much about the law, but I do know you're entitled to due process. She can't just kick you out in three days. That's silly. Ridiculous."

"Three days?" Max asked, his brows drawing together.

"Cease and desist by February 15, it says. Wednesday is Valentine's Day, right? Elle's dateathon party. What's Jane going to do—show up the next day with the sheriff in tow?"

"Her husband goes duck hunting with the sheriff," Elle said, starting to feel that same numbness she had when the doctor had said her mother was dead. The sense of finality was so profound and suffocating, she could hardly draw a breath.

"Elle." Max took her shoulders between his hands and made her look at him. "I'll call Jared. He's a lawyer. He'll give us some idea where you stand, but it would probably help if I could fax him a copy of the lease."

She looked into his eyes. Max. In her corner. She suddenly knew she wasn't going into this battle alone. The realization made her start to cry.

"Oh, Elle," he said obviously misinterpreting her tears. He pulled her into his arms and wrapped her in a tight hug.

"Oh," Lucky peeped.

The look on her friend's face made Elle ease free of Max's hold. Lucky had put her faith in one man's hands and wound up losing all hope. Elle wasn't going to lose her head over this. She'd been in tight spots before and she'd gotten out of them without some man coming to the rescue.

"The lease should be in my file cabinet, if I have a copy. Jane was insistent that important papers stay with her…in case I burned down the place my first week of business."

Max was tempted to use a word he heard too often from

the lips of his students. It described Jane perfectly. Watching the woman he loved stoically thumb through the files in her desk drawer made him want to storm the accounting office and face down Elle's sister in person.

He checked his watch. Jared would still be at the office, he was sure. When he'd dined with his son and Jared's new friend, Ricco, a few weeks earlier, a great deal of the conversation had been devoted to Jared's workaholic tendencies.

Personally Max thought his son could do better, but he'd managed to keep his opinion to himself. Maybe all parents thought that way, although after hearing Elle's enthusiastic gushing about a young man she'd never met—based solely on her daughter's assessment of the guy—Max had decided to take a lesson in tolerance and let his son come to his own decisions in matters of the heart.

"Can I use this line?" he asked, picking up the phone.

"Of course." she answered without looking up. A second later, she said, "I think this is it." She produced a single piece of paper.

Five big letters across the top of the page read: Lease. Max's stomach released a dose of acid usually reserved for watching a tight chess match in which one of his players was losing.

He punched in his son's phone number then looked up when he felt Elle's hand on his shoulder. As the call went through, he gave what he hoped was an encouraging smile.

"Thank you," she mouthed silently.

Or was it, "I love you"?

WHEN ELLE RETURNED to the front part of the store, she was shocked to see every chair taken and a line at the counter.

Rebecca had apparently jumped in to help when her aunt had failed to emerge from her office as promised.

Elle was touched, but she wasn't sure having Rebecca's help would aid her cause. Rebecca's mother was determined to make Elle pay for helping nurture Rebecca's artistic side. Peddling soup and sandwiches was probably even higher up on Jane's list of no-nos.

"Thanks, sweetie. I appreciate your pitching in, but you should probably take off. Aiding and abetting the enemy might not sit well with your boss."

"Aunt Elle, this is ridiculous. Mother is being a complete putz. I can't believe it…okay, I can believe it. But I'll fix things. Honest. This doesn't have to get out of hand."

It already had.

Rebecca was removing her apron when she said, "Guess what? We sold a bunch of my cards. Can you believe it?"

Elle gave her niece a one-armed hug, then motioned for the next person in line. "Of course, I can, doll. They're the best cards in town. I'm only sorry your mother can't see that." To her customer, a rather handsome young man who had one of Rebecca's cards on his pile of goodies, she said, "You have good taste."

He leaned partway across the counter to reply, "And everything here tastes good, so we're even."

"Have you been here before?"

He shook his head. "No, but my younger brother comes here all the time. He said his chess coach brought him here for lunch one day. Raved about the place."

The power of word-of-mouth. If her sister had helped spread the word when Elle first opened up, maybe it wouldn't have taken so long for Cup O' Love to catch on.

"Thanks," she said, handing him his change. She was about to say, "Come again," but changed her mind. No use encouraging him to return if she was going to be closing in three days.

The rest of the day flew by. She sold out of soup and sandwiches. A dozen new people signed up for a last-minute attempt to find a match on the dateathon. Two women announced to the entire room that they'd found their soul mates while drinking their decaf lattes.

"How is that possible?" Elle muttered. "They're my age, for heaven's sake."

"What are you mumbling about?" Lucky asked. She'd decided to stick around to show her support, although she flat-out refused to enter the dateathon because she only wanted one man and Josh Watts would never in a million years sign up for that kind of thing.

"I'm shallow and vain, aren't I, Lucky? I haven't grown and matured in the least in thirty years. I'm facing eviction from my own sister and my mind keeps harping on the fact that not a single soul in cyberland finds me attractive."

"Maybe there's something wrong with your Web page," Lucky said, wiping down the inside of the glass display case.

"I thought of that, but a couple of Max's students sent me profiles. They were totally wrong for me, of course, but kinda sweet."

Lucky shook her head. "What are you going to do if your sister finds a way to enforce this? I know Max's son said you were being denied due process, but Jane has a certain following in town. She's like the town matron. When I first opened my store, I remember somebody saying I'd never make a go of it if Jane didn't give me her endorsement."

"Oh, pah, I don't believe that. She's my sister, not God. Free enterprise will prevail." Although it was becoming increasingly obvious just how little Jane had done to help Cup O' Love succeed. And that hurt. A lot.

"Did you tell Jane that Nora is coming for a visit?"

Elle shook her head. "Never got the chance. But, now, I'm not sure she should bother. Nora has always liked Jane, and with my folks gone, Jane and her family are all we have. This would really fracture future relations. Nora loves me. She'd never understand why Jane is doing this."

"Why *is* Jane doing this?"

"Maybe she thinks I'm trying to come between her and Rebecca. That by letting Becca use the upstairs without Jane's okay, I undermined their relationship. All I know for sure is I did sign the stupid lease. And I did blab about renting the upstairs to Rebecca, although for the most part there's never any money exchanged. She fills in at the counter when she can and I take that off her rent."

"You should have bought the the building, too. Why does Jane have so much say?"

"At the time I was thinking about starting Cup O' Love, I still hadn't sold my condo. Jane wanted to sell, but I talked her into letting me rent this place. It was better for her taxwise, and I used the profits from my condo to remodel the house." She looked around with regret. She really loved it here, and she was sure her parents would have been proud to see the way she'd saved the old gas station and turned it into a vital new business.

"If my sister wants to be queen of the town and feels threatened by my being here, then maybe I should just leave. I'm not a fighter, Lucky. That isn't my style."

"Everybody has to fight sometime, Elle."

"She's right, Ellenore," Max said, coming up behind them. Elle had almost forgotten that he was in the office making calls. She'd delivered him the last bit of roll-up before someone else bought it, but she'd been so busy she hadn't checked on him again. She'd more or less assumed he'd gone home. "Jared called me back after he did a little research and said the time constraints of this demand are absolutely ridiculous. He'll fax you some information that you can use to argue a stay if she takes this to the sheriff. I don't think it will come to that, but we'll have some legal recourse, just in case."

We? "Thank you, Max. I appreciate your help. Really I do, but—"

He gave her a flinty look and said in a stern teacher voice, "Now, stop talking so fatalistically and tell me you'll go to the Winter Ball with me on Saturday."

She looked at him as if he'd lost his mind. "I beg your pardon? Did we walk through a time warp or something? The same Winter Ball I screwed up for you a hundred years ago?"

"No. That was the Valentine's Day dance. This one takes place the Saturday *after* Valentine's Day because there was a regional basketball meet scheduled in the gym last weekend. Coach Erickson broke his ankle when he tripped over a photographer from the paper. He and his wife usually chaperone this dance. He asked if I'd trade the Winter Ball for graduation night. I said yes, on one condition. That you'd be my date."

"Well, that was rude. The man was probably in pain. And I can't go. I have a lot to do."

"Like what?"

"P…pack."

He glanced at Lucky who was watching their conversation as if she were at a tennis match. He grabbed Elle's hand and led her toward the easy chairs in the corner. "Let's sit down and talk about this. You and Jane obviously have issues that have nothing to do with Cup O' Love. I'm guessing she's still processing the loss of your parents, but I could be wrong. People handle grief differently. My sons are a perfect example, but I digress. If you agree to ask Rebecca to move her art studio, I'm certain Jared will be able to convince Jane to back down."

"Kick Becca out? That's not right. She's so happy there, and her cards are a huge success. With a little support, she could…" Elle sighed. She'd known all along it would probably come to this.

"You sublet a portion of the building, which is in violation of your lease."

"And if Jane succeeds in kicking me out, then Rebecca will have to leave, too. Score two for Jane."

He nodded.

Elle muttered a low epithet but she knew she had little choice, legally. And knowing Jane, hell truly would freeze over before she backed down.

"What a mess! I swear, I'm not sure I *want* to live in the same town as my sister."

Max's heart rate shot up. He couldn't let her give up and run away. Not again. "I'll talk to Jane. She and Sarah were friends. I'm sure I can talk some sense into her."

"This isn't your battle, Max."

"I know, but I really need a date for Saturday. The chess

team will never let me live it down if I show up stag. In case you hadn't noticed, we geeks are changing our image. Will you go with me?"

She made a moue with her lips that told him she was thinking—about how to say no. She'd done the same thing when she'd broken the news that her loser hunk of an ex-boyfriend had come groveling back and insisted on taking her to the dance. "I don't know if that's a good idea, Max. Wednesday is Valentine's Day. What if Mr. Right shows up on my dateathon page between now and then?"

His heart started beating a little easier. Her tone made it clear she didn't think that would happen. "I'll take my chances."

"Okay, for Coach Erickson's sake. Besides, it's not like men are flooding my dateathon page. Except for a few underage geeks. Do you think there's something wrong with my e-mail address? Maybe it's corrupted."

Or your Web master is. "I'll take a look," he said, inwardly wincing at his deceit. He needed to tell her the truth, but in his head, he'd built up an image of what would happen on Valentine's Day. Elle would open her dateathon page at the party and read his profile, which he couldn't post sooner because it would include a marriage proposal. She'd look up, with tears in her eyes, and he'd be there, on one knee with a ring.

Too fast? Probably. *Insane?* Possibly. But *wildly romantic?* Absolutely. His wife used to call him a die-hard romantic, and given the fact that he was still in love with the girl-that-got-away and was prepared to make a fool of himself in public no doubt meant she was right.

CHAPTER ELEVEN

JUST ONE MORE DAY till Valentine's Day, or V-Day, as Elle chose to call it. The day most likely to disappoint you, she'd always figured. In high school, this was the day she'd turned left when she should have turned right. Instead of listening to her conscience—and her heart—she'd chosen the "popular" route. After all, everyone said cheerleaders didn't date nerds.

She'd been a coward back then, and she was still a coward. She'd let other people "handle" her sister. Max's son, Jared, who had to be one of the most caring and intuitive people she'd ever spoken with, had acted as an intermediary, faxing and e-mailing Jane until she backed off—once Elle agreed to have Rebecca move her art studio out of the old Conoco station.

Rebecca had claimed to understand. "I know this is what Mom wants, Aunt Elle. She's never approved of my art and this is her way of eliminating something she thinks is bad for me."

"How can art be bad for you?"

"It takes my focus away from my career. You know how busy accountants are this time of year. She was sure I'd overwork myself trying to do too much. I guess this is her version of *tough love*."

She'd shown up after closing last night to pack her things. Elle had brought up a couple of empty plastic crates and volunteered to help, but Becca had wanted to be alone.

Elle had gone home alone, too. She'd thanked Max for his help then asked for the same kind of space she was giving Becca. Time to think.

And what she decided was her sister was a control freak who made Cupid, nasty little imp that he was, look like a saint.

All morning long, her thoughts had bounced around from their most recent argument to disputes from childhood to that bleak time after their mother had died. Elle was tired of letting Jane set the rules.

She hadn't had a chance to talk to Becca this morning. She hoped she wasn't about to make things worse between mother and daughter, but she needed to clear the air with her sister. About a lot of things, including Elle's role in her niece's life.

"Noreen, can you handle things for an hour or so? I need to go see my sister."

Noreen looked slightly terrified at the prospect of working the coffee bar alone, but she nodded gamely. "You'll be back before lunch?"

"Absolutely." She grabbed her jacket from the back of her chair in her office. She took one last look at the fax Max's son had sent. He'd added a personal note on the cover sheet. "Don't give up. Dad seems happy. Looking forward to meeting you."

Damn right she wouldn't give up, she thought, hurrying outside. The temperature had warmed to ten degrees above zero, and the snow underfoot crackled as she marched down Main to her sister's office.

She opened the door and walked into instant warmth.

Rebecca was at her desk in the foyer. Stacks of folders occupied every square inch. "Aunt Elle, what are you doing here? Did I forget something in the studio?"

"No, dear heart," Elle said, sloughing off her jacket. "You left the place spotless, and looking at that empty space this morning broke my heart. Is your mother here?"

Becca stood up. "Um, yeah, she is. Um…you know last night—"

Elle didn't want to hear her niece apologize for not accepting Elle's help. "I understand," she said, cutting Becca off. "This isn't about you. This is between me and Jane. And, believe me, it's long overdue."

"But…"

Elle marched to Jane's office and walked in without knocking. Jane was facing her computer, her back to the door, but she swiveled in her seat when Elle said, "Jane, we need to talk."

Jane didn't ask Elle to sit down, but Elle was too wired to stay still.

"I know we've never been close. Even as a little kid, I knew you didn't like me. I never understood why. I didn't steal your toys or take clothes from your closet or borrow your car without asking. I didn't do anything to deserve your wrath, but I've always been on the receiving end of it. Why?"

Jane didn't reply at first, then she said, "Because everything was so damn easy for you. You didn't have to get perfect grades—all you had to do was blink your baby blues and smile and your teachers passed you. You didn't have to work. I started helping out in the gas station office when I was ten. If not for me and Mom, Dad would have given away more gas than he sold."

"I was five, Jane. What did you expect me to do?"

"I maintained a four-point average and got three scholarships so I could go to college. Mom and Dad gave you a free ride, and what did you do with it? Partied. I was the one who convinced them that they should cut you off until you brought up your grades."

"You what?"

She shrugged. "I told them you'd never appreciate your education unless you earned it." She made a scoffing sound. "Of course, you immediately got pregnant, married and divorced without any kind of child support, which meant you needed Mom and Dad's help anyway. So I guess the last laugh was on me, right?"

"Wow. You really do think you're God." Elle stepped to the desk and leaned over, placing her hands on the blotter. "For your information, I paid Dad back every cent I borrowed after my divorce. We're talking thirty years ago, Jane. Thirty lousy years, but I still have a copy of the canceled checks. Do you know why? Because Dad wrote a little note on the back of each one telling me how proud he was that I was getting my life together and what a good mother I was." Tears filled her eyes. "Do you want to see them, Jane? They included interest."

Jane blushed. "Mom didn't know."

"Why does that surprise you? She was so tight-fisted, this was probably the only spending money Dad had to call his own. I bet he used it to buy her flowers on Valentine's Day," Elle said, her voice cracking with emotion.

"She always said if she didn't keep a tight rein on Dad's spending he'd move them straight into the poorhouse."

Elle got her emotions under control and nodded. "I

know. And she was probably right. Dad was generous to a fault, but he knew he had a safety net. There was never any doubt that they loved each other and complemented each other. And you're a lot like Mom. Everybody's safety net. But I'm living proof, Jane. Sometimes the fall doesn't kill you."

"What does that mean? That you're better than me because you take risks? You bounce around the country, changing jobs on a whim. Raising your daughter without any boundaries, any rules?"

Elle straightened up and let out a deep sigh. "My daughter turned out great. Happy. Confident. You'll see that for yourself when she comes for a visit later this month. As for my work history, I call it the school of hard knocks. I graduated summa cum laude. But for your information, I was with the same company for nine years until Mom fell and needed help. I came back because I thought I owed us both that time together. Family was more important to me than money."

Jane's lips tightened.

"And my early years were a good proving ground for sales. I learned how to run a business. Cup O' Love is succeeding—despite your lack of support. I don't care that you've never walked through the door to buy a cup of coffee. I don't need your help, Jane. Next week, I'm going to see about securing a loan to buy the building. If you don't want to sell, then you're going to be stuck with me as a tenant because I'm not moving, Jane. Ever."

She turned and took a step away. "That's all I have to say, except…Happy Valentine's Day. I'd have brought you a Rebecca Potter card, but we just sold out."

FIRST THING WEDNESDAY morning, Max arranged for a substitute to handle his afternoon classes. He left the high school at noon and headed straight to the Cup. He'd gotten very little sleep the night before since he'd spent so much time rectifying his deceit.

First, he forwarded all the e-mail from men who had responded to Elle's dateathon page. He'd tried to stack the odds in his favor by redirecting her applicants to his trash bin, and he wasn't proud of that "nerd" maneuver.

Second, he'd filled out his own personal sheet, answering her questions as honestly as possible. This wasn't the elaborate proposal he'd originally planned. In fact, compared to a few of the guys who'd e-mailed her, his bio wasn't outstanding in any way. Except that he knew her and loved her. The real her, not the Elle she'd described on her dateathon profile.

Last, he'd called Potter Accounting Services and left a message on Jane's answering machine telling her that he planned to find a new accountant. "You talk about building up local businesses, but you've never shown the least bit of support for Cup O' Love. That tells me I need to find a company that walks the walk, not just talks the talk."

The Cup was bustling when he walked in, after driving around the block twice to find a parking place. Seeing the upsurge in business did his heart good, but he didn't see Elle behind the counter. Noreen, Elle's regular helper, and two other employees were dashing madly while a line of customers waited. Everyone seemed in high spirits. He wasn't sure why…until he noticed a sign above the cash register that read: Half off any purchase for all dateathon participants.

He knew the party wasn't scheduled until seven, but the party atmosphere was unmistakable. He glanced at the far table—the one adorned with red and white hearts.

Elle. Seated at a laptop with five or six women crowded around her. All were smiling. Including Elle, who looked so amazingly beautiful—joyous, even—that he couldn't move. Until she looked up and their gazes met.

Her smile changed to a look he wasn't sure he dared interpret. Triumph? Satisfaction? What did that mean?

He walked to the table. "Hi. Can we talk?"

She glanced sideways as if seeking permission from her peers. Max checked out the women. Locals. All single, in the thirty to sixty age range. Two gazed at him curiously. Two snickered. *Good grief, are we back in high school?*

"Actually I'm kinda busy…catching up on my e-mail. From the past couple of weeks," she said pointedly.

Max felt himself blush.

"Max, how could you? You're my Web master. I trusted you."

He looked at the toes of his boots and wished he could crawl under the table.

"All this time I thought men must find me repulsive, undesirable. You're a teacher, Max. You know what that might mean to my self-esteem."

Three giggles and a snort made him look up. The mischievous twinkle in her eyes made his heart stop for a second. Two of the women started to laugh openly with comments like, "Make him grovel, Elle" and "Don't let him off too easy, honey."

Max wasn't sure who that one came from. He didn't care. All that mattered was Elle. "I cheated. I admit it.

Partly because I could...once a nerd, always a nerd. Partly because I didn't want some guy slipping in the back door while I was being noble and waiting for you to notice me."

She pointed to the computer screen. "Did you mean everything you said in your profile? Even the part about getting married again?"

Max took an unplanned step back. When he'd filled out his profile, he'd left out the M-word, deciding it was too soon to bring up the subject. They'd only started dating again. He hadn't even met her daughter.

A sudden hush fell over the room.

"Marriage?" he asked.

Elle nodded. "This is *you,* isn't it?" she asked, pointing to the screen. "I certainly hope so because I've just e-mailed all the other potential dates who signed up on my list to let them know that I picked Arnold 'The Maximum' Maxwell to be my valentine."

He scrambled to see what she was looking at. In the upper right hand corner was his photo—the one on his school ID, which he hated because it made him look like a science teacher. That definitely hadn't been there last night. Further scrutiny proved that someone had been tinkering with his remarks.

"We especially liked the way you answered question number four, didn't we, ladies?"

Her friends laughed.

He quickly read the line in question. "Oh." He couldn't stop the blush that heated his face. "Um, that would be a slight exaggeration. In fact, I'm not even sure that's anatomically possible."

He looked around. Someone mumbled something about "Maybe that's how he got the nickname Maximus."

Max's cheeks burned. "Um…there's a simple explanation, and when I get my hands on the meddling, overachieving juvenile delinquents who doctored my answers, I'll…"

"Hug them?" Elle asked. "It seems appropriate. Since they did build a formidable case for why I should date you and nobody else."

He looked at her, and he saw something he hadn't noticed before. She wasn't smiling because she was amused. She was happy. "They did?"

She nodded. "Absolutely."

Max, who knew that in chess there was always one move that decided a victory, made it. He went down on one knee and proposed. Partly because he was swept up in the moment and partly because he'd learned the hard way that life came with no guarantees and, while this was a new day and sometimes the nerd did get the girl, he wasn't taking any chances on letting Elle get away again.

To his profound surprise—and relief, she said, "Yes, Max, I think I will."

Their kiss was accompanied by a group hug that Max could have lived without and an ear-deafening applause that seemed to make the plate-glass windows rock. Slowly they made their way though the throng of well-wishers toward Elle's office. Elle had just paused to share a tearful embrace with Noreen when the bell over the door jingled. Their mutual gasp made him look.

Jane.

Elle tightened her grip on Max's hand as her sister stepped across the threshold. She had no idea what to expect from Jane. Today had been that kind of day. From telling her dearest friend goodbye to seeing Max's name on her dateathon page—along with fifty or so other profiles. She hadn't given the other men a single glance, but she'd read his intently, and she'd known immediately which answers were his and which had been tweaked. By the members of his chess club, she'd guessed.

That demonstration of devotion provided the little extra push Elle needed to admit the truth. She loved Max. They were meant for each other. But Jane still had the power to make living in Fenelon Falls unpleasant.

Jane's chin lifted proudly as she looked around. Customers not privy to the family drama being played out detoured around her to get in line and order.

Elle squeezed Max's hand and whispered, "I should probably handle this order myself. Wait for me?"

"Not a chance," he said with a smile. "I've always wanted to learn how to make a latte."

They were standing side by side at the cash register when Jane stepped forward. She didn't say anything for a minute, then she cleared her throat and announced, "A grande cappuccino decaf, hold the whipped cream…please."

Elle reached across the counter. Their hands met. "My pleasure. Welcome to Cup O' Love. I named it after something Dad always said. Remember?"

Jane, with tears in her eyes, nodded. "Coffee is just coffee unless the person closest to your heart makes it, then it's a cup of love."

Elle sniffled. "Are we going to be okay now?"

Jane nodded. "I took roses to Mom's grave today. And

put some on Dad's, too. I… They both loved us very much. And, if the upstairs is still available, I think Mom and Dad would be tickled to know their granddaughter was using the space to create her art."

"Her very successful card business," Elle corrected. "Would you like to see her Valentine to me?" Elle had left it displayed on the counter.

The outside featured a woman pulling a bright red heart from a laden tree. Below were the words: I pick you. Opening it, she read the inscription aloud. "Dear Aunt, If given a choice I could not have picked a better aunt…or friend. I love you. Becca."

Elle blinked back tears.

"It's wonderful," Jane said.

"I know."

"Where is she? She left a message on my cell about helping Lucky and Josh…"

Elle honestly had no idea. Well, maybe one idea. She didn't get a chance to explain, though, because Max reached past her to hand Jane her coffee, which Noreen had helped him make. "Here you go, Jane. Happy Valentine's Day. Oh, and by the way, you can disregard the message I left on your machine this morning."

Jane looked confused. "I haven't checked my messages. I needed to do a little soul searching, so I ran by the church before I went to the cemetery." Her eyes filled with tears. "I still can't believe Pastor Josh is selling out and leaving Fenelon Falls."

Elle didn't know what message Max was referring to, but she did know that Jane didn't handle change well. And whether Elle was the catalyst or just an innocent bystander, ever since her return home, things had been evolving in Jane's life. With Becca. With the impending loss of the Fenelon Falls Community Church. With their relationship.

She looked at Max, hoping to signal him not to mention his proposal or the dateathon. *Later. When Jane's had time…* Max's eyes narrowed and he shook his head. To Jane, he said, "Change happens, Jane. Nothing stays the same, and I, for one, am indisputably grateful because I just asked your sister to marry me and she said yes. I have witnesses." He motioned toward the women still gathered around the WiFi station. They backed him up, with hoots and whistles.

Jane's mouth dropped open and the cup in her hand started to wobble. In the past, Elle might have apologized for causing a scene, but not this time. She waited, her breath caught in her throat, to see how Jane would react.

"C-congratulations?" Jane stuttered.

That appeared to be good enough for Max, who beamed. "Thanks. Elle will fill you in on the details later. Right now, we have to call the kids. I want to be the one to tell my boys, and you know how fast gossip flies in Fenelon Falls. Plus, it might take us *hours* to reach Nora. Right?" he asked Elle. His mischievous wink told her phoning wasn't the only thing they'd be doing.

"Come to the party, Jane. Please," Elle called to her sister as Max tugged her toward her office.

She wished Jane would come. Possibly, Becca would put in an appearance. With Will. Lucky wouldn't be there. She was already on another road.

So much had happened in such a short time. At the rate their lives were changing, one almost wondered if Cupid—or some outside hand—was directing things.

But all thoughts, divine or otherwise, disappeared from her head the moment Max closed the door of her office behind them and pulled her into his arms. Unfortunately his kiss didn't last long enough. "I love you, Elle," he said, his tone serious. "But I feel like a heel for messing with your dateathon page. I should have let you make up your own mind without any tricks."

"Why did you do it?"

"I guess I was afraid some slick dude might slip in and sweep you off your feet. You're still the coolest girl in school to me, and always will be."

"Some slick dude," she repeated with a giggle. "Max, that terminology has been passé for twenty years, at least. But I can understand why you might not trust me."

He tightened his hold slightly. "No. That's not it. Ellenore Adams, you changed my life when you agreed to go to the Valentine's dance with me our senior year. Just knowing that I was worthy of your friendship was a validation that only a kid—a nerd—in high school can truly appreciate."

"But we didn't go together. I backed out two days before the dance."

"I know. Which means…you still owe me."

She smiled. "We're going to the dance on Saturday. Will that make us even?"

He nuzzled her neck. "It's a start. Ask me again in thirty-whatever years from now."

Elle looped her arms around his neck and hugged him tight. She'd started this dateathon as a way to best Cupid at his own game. And whether Cupid had a hand in this gambit or it was all Max, she really didn't know…or care. She'd found her match, and that was all that mattered.

A special valentine to Joe, Dana, Evan, Teagan
and especially—the champ—
Anlun Meyers

A VALENTINE
FOR REBECCA

Molly O'Keefe

Dear Reader,

No other holiday carries the burden of expectation quite like Valentine's Day. New Year's Eve doesn't even hold a candle to my anticipation of the Lover's Holiday. For years I was one of those women who liked to pretend I didn't need or want the cards or flowers, that I would not fall victim to the commercial shlock of the holiday. Foolishly my husband believed me. I suffered in passive aggressive silence for about two years and then explained to him that I did want the emotional shlock and a ten-dollar bouquet of flowers. He's caught on and I stopped pretending, and now Valentine's Day is one of our favorite holidays. Last year our valentine was our son—which will be difficult to top this year.

It was in this anticipation and expectation that the idea of *Who Needs Cupid?* was born. This anthology has had lots of great input, beginning with the fantastic Melinda Curtis who started this project on an early-morning walk in Seattle. Debra Salonen and Susan Floyd have been perfect partners in crime and I have enjoyed this process immensely! I hope you have a great time at Cup O' Love!

Molly O'Keefe

P.S. Please stop by www.molly-okeefe.com or visit www.drunkwritertalk.blogspot.com and join in the fun!

CHAPTER ONE

January 18—Thursday

"HEY, MS. POTTER, what do you think?" Tony DeLona slid a thick piece of white sketch paper under Rebecca's nose.

She glanced up quickly at the grinning twelve-year-old and then down at his paper.

The assignment today had been perspective and Tony's project was a pencil sketch looking down at a skateboarder in motion. She sucked in an astonished breath and glanced at Tony. He grinned back, his dark eyes twinkling.

"I think it's awesome," she said and the boy's smile could have lit up her studio for hours.

She wished the rest of the kids in her after-school program had a tenth of his talent. But she also wished Tony had about a tenth of his new crappy attitude. Tony had changed in the past year, and it was more than just the awkward changes every boy his age went through.

His parents were in the middle of a terrible divorce. And Tony was getting lost in the shuffle.

"I really like the holes in the jeans and the untied shoe-laces. Very real and kind of funny." She pointed to those details in the sketch and Tony nodded, taking in her praise like new grass takes in water. "You might think about adding a little more to the area outside the sidewalk."

"I wanted to, I just sort of ran out of time." She handed him the sketch, and he took it, blushing so hard he nearly ignited.

"Hmm, I wonder why you ran out of time?" She laid it on thick and Tony's ears turned red.

"Ms. Potter, I told you—"

"I know, I know, it wasn't your fault. But guess what?" She stood and circled the old Formica kitchen table that served as her desk, so she was right beside him. "It is. You were a half hour late, Tony, and you've got to take responsibility for that. There's no note from your teachers, so I have to tell your mom." She shrugged. "You're not a little kid anymore."

Tony scowled and she held her breath, wondering if maybe she'd pushed too hard. These days she could feel Tony's usual good spirits becoming gloomy. She braced herself for the "whatever" teenagers so loved to say and she so hated to hear, but instead he shrugged.

"Sorry, Ms. Potter."

She smiled and patted his thin shoulder. "Tony, I just want you to be able to spend every minute you can on your drawing. You're really talented." She said it earnestly, willing the boy, who was just growing that tough outer shell of indifference, to believe her.

Encouragement at the right time could do wonders. Or so she assumed, mostly because she'd never had it.

"Cool?" she asked.

"Cool," he said and headed for the door, his book bag hanging off one shoulder.

Rebecca heaved a big sigh as the silence of her empty

studio enveloped her. Ten kids ranging in age from six to thirteen for two and a half hours was enough to challenge anyone. Some days, when the kids behaved and picked up eagerly on the lesson of the day, the time flew by, but other days... Other days she wondered why she didn't just take that full-time accounting job her parents kept offering her.

She made a face at the thought. She was proof that having a degree in accounting did not actually make one an accountant.

But no matter how terrible the day, how much finger paint was splattered on the walls, how late Tony was, or how much glitter Dora ate—thinking it was ˙cookie sparkles or fairy dust—she liked kids. She liked their creativity. Their guilelessness. Their innocence. She like the way their brains worked, free from cynicism and the darker thoughts of maturity. They were honest and fair and didn't judge.

Completely unlike adults.

More importantly, she *got* them, and they *got* her. It was adults who seemed mysterious and unreadable. A roomful of adults always made her feel as if she'd walked into church naked.

She turned and found Penny Blakely, her newest student, still in her spot in the far corner. Her pale blond hair covered her face as she bent over her work. Her fingers held a red crayon in what could only be called an eight-year-old's death grip.

"Penny?" she asked, making sure her voice was low and careful. The girl's head snapped up, her blue eyes huge in the twilight.

"Hey, sweetheart." Rebecca smiled and approached the

quiet child. She climbed up on the table in front of the one Penny sat at and put her feet up on a chair. She'd kill the kids for sitting like this, but breaking her own rules was one of the perks of being the teacher. Since she'd paid for the secondhand tables and chairs, she figured she could do what she wanted.

"Whatcha working on?" Rebecca had asked the same question every day for two weeks. And every day Penny answered the same way.

"Nothing," she muttered and covered her drawing with her hands so Rebecca couldn't see it.

"Who's picking you up tonight?"

"My dad. Aunt Elaine has choir."

"Okay." Rebecca checked her watch. Five minutes. *Five minutes before Will Blakely walks through those doors and you say something stupid. Or do something stupid.*

Her hands were suddenly dripping and her stomach wanted to reject the meager lunch she'd managed to eat a few hours ago. Just the thought of Will Blakely drove her blood pressure someplace unhealthy.

"You've got about five more minutes if you want to finish that or…" *tell me what's making you so sad?*

The little girl had a sustained unhappiness surrounding her that could break the most jaded heart and Rebecca's was far from jaded. But whatever it was in Penny's young life that had caused her to be so cautious was a secret the girl wasn't telling.

"I'll finish." She bent back over her red masterpiece. Rebecca, who'd tried for two weeks to reach out to the little girl, still had one more surefire weapon in her arsenal.

"Well, then I think I'll join you." Rebecca stood and

grabbed her own card stock and India ink from her desk at the front of the room.

She sat down next to Penny and spread out her work, making it impossible for the girl not to see her sketches and materials. She made a big show of pushing up the sleeves of the old red cardigan she'd knitted during one of her knitting phases. Penny cast curious glances as Rebecca dipped the end of her pen into the black pot of ink. She took a piece of the thick white paper and drew a cartoon version of Penny with big eyes and pencil-straight hair. She made sure the girl was watching and added a tall fairy princess hat, a lion tamer's whip in one hand and a crayon in the other.

From the corner of her eye she saw Penny smile, and Rebecca added a ballerina tutu and big galoshes. She put some birds and butterflies and little bits of fairy dust in the air around her.

Penny giggled and Rebecca finally looked right at her.

"I thought you were working?" Rebecca asked with all the false indignation she could muster.

"That's me!" she said in her little girl voice.

Rebecca managed to look surprised. "You know, I think you're right. Let's just make it official." She dipped her pen back in the ink before adding a big P to the ballerina tutu and then in small print she wrote under the drawing Super Penny.

"For you." She pushed the drawing over to Penny, who beamed with all the sunshine of a June day.

"This is for you," Penny said, pushing her own work over to Rebecca. This time, Rebecca's surprise was real. She opened the folded paper. The red masterpiece was actually a giant heart that took up most of the page. In the corner, written in Penny's precise print, were the words: For Ms. Potter.

Rebecca had gotten plenty of hand-drawn cards and gifts in the year she'd been teaching this class, but this one, either because of its sheer unexpectedness, or because of Penny's big sad blue eyes, made her blink back tears.

"You're nice, Ms. Potter."

"Thank you, Penny," she managed to say past the lump in her throat. "So are you."

"It's for Valentine's Day," Penny said.

Rebecca's heart seemed to stutter. "Is that coming up already?" she muttered. She knew it was, of course. Lucky Morgan and Aunt Elle had been harassing her for weeks about supplying Lucky Duck Collectibles and the Cup O' Love Café with cards, but it didn't make the encroaching holiday easier to accept.

Dumb, stupid holiday. Dumb, stupid holiday that allowed her to keep her art program running, dumb stupid holiday that every year made her feel like the kid picked last for kick ball.

Dumb, stupid holiday.

"It's in four weeks." Penny nodded. "I know because Dad put a big black mark on our calendar."

Rebecca swallowed and tried to think about ice and cold but she still felt the blush creep up her face, until she thought the tips of her ears would ignite.

Valentine's Day was coming up, and she had a crush on Will Blakely.

Was there anything in the world more pathetic than a twenty-seven-year-old woman with an unrequited crush on Valentine's Day? And considering how every crush she'd had since Eric Northfield in fifth grade had crashed and burned, she could only hope that she'd catch Will picking his nose or kicking a stray dog or yelling at his daughter, before Rebecca's foolish heart led her to dangerous places.

There was nothing like being lovelorn and alone on Valentine's Day to bring her future into crystal clear focus. Tea cozies. Coffee cake. Pants with elastic waists. Hairy legs.

"Do you like cats, Penny?"

"I love cats. Why?"

Rebecca sighed. "I'm thinking of getting like six."

"We have a dog," Penny told her with a solemn nod. "Pirate. He's got a black spot over his eye."

"Then let's just…" Rebecca reached over and added a dog with a pirate patch over his eye to the sketch.

"Hello?"

Rebecca's head snapped up at the sound of the deep voice. She put her hand to her heart and felt it beat in time to the words *He's here. He's here. He's here.*

Will Blakely walked into the room and grinned his crooked grin. His blond hair, tousled by errant breezes or his own long, strong hands, glinted under the lights. Rebecca barely swallowed a whimper.

Who could be immune to such beauty?

All he needed was a heavenly chorus and the image would be complete.

The way he walked into the room made Rebecca feel smaller, girlier. She wanted to bat her eyelashes (which were far too short to be effective) and giggle (which she, as a rule, did not do). She felt like Scarlet O'Hara without the beauty or plantation. And it wasn't just because Will was tall and broad, and she'd spent hours imagining the body beneath his down jacket and black dress pants.

It was his confidence.

Will had grown up in Fenelon Falls, five years ahead of her in school so their paths had never really crossed. He'd moved back six months ago and was a juvenile parole officer for the county, which probably helped him foster that confidence, but Rebecca knew he'd always been that way. Will Blakely had always been picked first for kick ball.

And that epitomized the insurmountable gulf between them. Those picked first never even glanced at those picked last. Even when they grew up.

But it didn't stop her from looking. And dreaming.

"What are you guys working on?" he asked with a smile. His deep voice echoed around her studio and she wished it would get caught in the corners, behind the big jugs of finger paints and the cans of brushes so she could hear it later.

His blue eyes seemed to lightly touch Rebecca, just stroke her ever so softly.

"Nothing," Rebecca and Penny said at the same time and put their hands over their sketches.

Will's thick eyebrows shot up, and Penny and Rebecca smiled at each other.

They'd gone from untouchable student and concerned teacher to coconspirators in five minutes.

I guess I've reached her, Rebecca thought with a mix of pride and relief.

"Well." Will smiled again, though this time it seemed more sad, like the secrets she and Penny kept excluded him. Rebecca felt sudden sympathy. Whatever sadness surrounded Penny surrounded Will, too.

A beautiful, sad man, with a beautiful, sad daughter...just my type.

She knew he was divorced, but that was it. She could certainly find out more just by hanging around the café downstairs. The town, particularly the female portion, had gone berserk when Will and his daughter had moved back to Fenelon Falls to be closer to his family. Speculation about everything from his divorce to the size of…well, certain private things had been rampant. As well, Will and Pastor Josh had rekindled their old friendship, so Becca could get the details from her own friend Lucky, but listening to gossip about Will seemed a terrible invasion of privacy and if there was one thing Rebecca valued, it was a man's privacy.

Which was probably why she hadn't actually been witness to a man's privacy in eons.

"Grab your stuff, sweetheart, and let's go get some dinner." Will rubbed his hands together and when his daughter walked by he pulled her to him in a quick, hard hug.

So much for catching him being mean to her. The guy was a devoted father. On Penny's first day at the after-school program, he'd come by early to drop off a card and a box of crayons, asking Rebecca to make sure the gift sat at Penny's spot when she came in.

It was the most considerate gesture Rebecca had ever seen.

Her own mother had at one time thrown out every crayon, colored pencil and marker she'd owned in an attempt to get her to pay better attention in school.

"How's she doing?" Will asked when Penny was on the other side of the room, digging her stuff from her cubby.

"She's good." Rebecca nodded and started stacking things so she didn't have to look into those blue eyes of his. "She's still very quiet in class…"

"That's what her teachers have said since preschool." He cast a worried glance over his shoulder. "I keep hoping she'll grow out of it, or feel comfortable enough to be herself in class at some point."

"I do think she's opening up with me." Rebecca could feel the heat emanating from Will. She could smell the winter air on him and something minty on his breath, and she awkwardly stepped back, hit the chair behind her and dropped her pen.

Nice, excellent. You're like all three stooges rolled into one woman.

She bent for the pen, but Will beat her to it, and she looked up at the ceiling, praying for a quick death.

"Really?" he asked, handing her the pen, which she took, making a special effort not to touch him. "You think so? She's always liked art, but since we moved here she's been so intensely private, I'm beginning to wonder if she's ever going to open up again."

She unfolded the heart picture and showed him. "She gave me this today. It's my first of the season," she said, like that had anything to do with their conversation.

He touched the red heart. "Valentine's Day," he muttered and she detected a wealth of disapproval in his tone. He smiled, but the humor was glacial. "I wish I could forget all about it."

The pain she heard took the air from her lungs. All she could do was stare at the curve of his eyelashes against his cheek and long to say something that would diminish his pain.

He stared down at the red heart like it was a death threat.

"I'm ready, Dad," Penny said from underneath a hat, scarf and pale pink winter coat.

He turned to her and laughed. "You sure are. Ellenore's got some chicken noodle soup warming up for us downstairs at the café. How about we take that home?"

She nodded, the purple yarn pompom on the top of her hat bobbing.

Me, too, Rebecca thought, dying a little. *Warm me up and take me home, too.*

She sat at her desk and busied herself with the stacking of papers so as not to look at that handsome man who seemed to hold her heart.

"Bye, Ms. Potter," Penny cried, though it was muffled by her scarf.

Rebecca smiled and waved at the little Michelin girl.

"Bye, Ms. Potter," Will echoed.

She waved at their retreating backs and when the door shut behind them she sat back in her chair.

She shook her head and smiled at her own folly.

"What a seriously good-looking man," she said aloud.

But then, because she knew she'd already spent far too much time thinking about the gold of his hair and what she imagined would be the thick, rough texture of his hands against the soft parts of her body, she swiveled in her chair and flipped up the January page on her Far Side calendar.

There it was. February. Accompanied by Gary Larson's deer exchanging paper hearts. She pulled her red marker from her pocket, bit off the cap and circled Wednesday the fourteenth.

V-Day.

She could avoid it no longer. Aunt Elle and Lucky needed cards and she needed the money those cards brought in.

The Fenelon Falls Young Artists Program was kept financially alive thanks to several sources. Of course, the student fees, but she had to raise the fees every year just to cover materials, so things like electricity and rent weren't covered.

Luckily the rent Elle charged for the spacious, sunny, second-floor studio situated above the Cup was next to nothing. The building used to be Rebecca's grandparents' Conoco Station a million years ago. Now it was owned by her mother, and Elle had converted it to the cool, retro Cup O' Love Café filled with old filling station memorabilia and sadly, very few customers. Rebecca helped out on the weekends and the money she made paid for rent.

The third major source of income for the after-school art program were the cards, journals and paper gifts Rebecca had created over the past two years for Valentine's Day. Last year, both Elle and Lucky had sold out of them.

She found it hilarious, if not a little sad at times, that she managed to so easily create the messages and sentiments the lovers in Fenelon Falls found perfect to exchange. Easy. All she had to do was open a vein and bleed.

She'd poured every romantic and sexy thing she'd yearned for onto pink and red card stock. Just thinking about the paper made her fingers tingle and the ideas she spent the whole year imagining crowd inside her begging for release. Any kind of release.

Because even though she knew it was unlikely that she would ever find the kind of love she wrote about and drew, she believed in it. She hoped for it with every breath, every scratch of pen on paper.

And she knew that most of the people exchanging her

cards would never guess that it was her, the quiet studious art teacher/accountant who created them. Accountant by day—tortured Cupid by night.

She never signed a single card. A few people knew she made them. Elle, Lucky, Pastor Josh. Her parents.

Though it had just about killed Jane and Phil Potter that their daughter was the one sketching hearts and writing sweet little poems on cards the whole town exchanged. And it was the fact the holiday was so close to tax season that added insult to injury. People were asking year-round for more cards, and she'd been thinking that after tax season was done, she might branch out into birthday cards. That would probably send her parents right over the edge.

She put a little black x on today's date, Thursday, January 18, counted the three and a half weeks until V-Day and then dropped the January page back down. She bent and pulled from the bottom of her filing cabinet her red card stock, which was the color of rubies.

She took the top piece and dipped her pen into her pot of ink.

She drew a little sketch—not of Will exactly, but of the idea of Will. A man who held lightning bolts and hearts in the palms of his hands. A shirtless man in boxer shorts and winter boots. She added long hair, blowing in an unseen wind and a look of unshakable confidence.

Love God, she printed beneath it.

She smiled grimly and pulled out another piece of red card stock.

One down. Dozens to go.

CHAPTER TWO

January 19—Friday

IT WAS FRIDAY. Penny *loooved* Fridays. Not as much as she *loooved* Saturdays—because of the hot chocolate and cartoons—but Fridays were definitely second best.

Wednesdays were last. Dad always called Mom after dinner on Wednesdays and that ruined everything, but that was over for this week.

Today, she and Dad were going to Grandma and Grandpa's for dinner and she would get to see all her cousins. Even Joe. Which wasn't great, but she could live with it.

And it was free draw day with Ms. Potter. She could draw whatever she wanted—for two whole hours.

She put down her red crayon and picked up the yellow and colored her mother's hair in big curlicues. That's how she remembered it. Bright yellow and curly and blowing in the open window of the car.

"We're going places, kiddo," Mom used to say and Penny would unroll her window and wish she had curls that bounced around in the wind, rather than straight hair that got in her mouth and eyes.

At least she had the color right.

"Hey, Penny, whatcha working on?"

Penny looked up from her picture. Ms. Potter was wearing Penny's favorite shirt today—she wore it every Friday (another reason to like the day). The light blue T-shirt with the pretty painting on it.

Monet, she'd told Penny the last time she'd worn it.

Ms. Potter sat down on the table in front of Penny and smiled. Ms. Potter was pretty. Not like Mom was—not many people were pretty like *that*. But Ms. Potter's hair was straight and soft and was a pretty brownish-red that changed color when she wore something green or when she stood under different lights.

Hair that changed color was much better than curls.

"More valentines?" Ms. Potter asked. She tilted her head and smiled.

Penny put her hands over the picture, flat, so she could feel the thick wax on the red car and the blue sky and the yellow of her mother's hair.

She was going to tell Ms. Potter about her mom. She'd decided Wednesday after Dad had hung up on Mom and then sat in the dark kitchen staring out the window.

Penny had watched him from the hallway, where he couldn't see her and tell her to go back to bed. She stood there and decided that her cousin Alyssa might be right.

He was lonely.

Watching him, Penny had decided Dad needed a girlfriend.

Dad needed Ms. Potter.

Ms. Potter was the nicest woman Penny had ever met. She smelled like perfume and paint. She was perfect.

"You don't have to show me, Pen—"

"What's your real name?" Penny asked. She needed to

know that kind of thing if Ms. Potter was going to be Dad's girlfriend.

Ms. Potter's eyes got wide, and she smiled her big smile that made the little dents come out in her cheeks. "Rebecca is my first name and everyone calls me Becca. But I've always thought that my real name is Anastasia."

Ms. Potter…Becca…was joking. She did that a lot. Penny liked that, and so would Dad. He always said the best thing in the whole world was laughing. He'd laugh all the time with Ms. Potter.

Slowly Penny peeled her fingers from her picture, and then she pushed it toward Ms. Potter. *Becca.* Ms. Potter climbed down from the table and slowly turned the drawing so she could look at it the right way.

The picture was of her mom leaving, driving away in that red car with no roof, with that guy—Mom told her to call him Uncle Jim—but he wasn't an uncle. In the picture, Penny and Dad were standing in front of their old house in South Carolina crying tears so big they made a river at their feet.

"That's my mom," Penny said, pointing to the woman with blond curls in the driver's seat.

"Did she leave?" Becca asked in a quiet voice.

Penny nodded.

"Do you still feel like that?" Becca pointed to the big blue tears.

Penny thought about it and decided she didn't. Not anymore. She hardly ever cried about Mom.

"No," she told Becca.

"Can you draw me a picture of how you feel now?"

Penny pulled another piece of the scratch paper that

Ms. Potter had all over the room and she picked out crayons from the big box that her dad had given her. Becca walked away, not far, just over to one of the other tables, but Penny was glad she wasn't watching her.

Privacy. That's what her dad called it when she let him go to the bathroom with the door shut.

Becca was giving her a little privacy.

One more thing to like about Becca.

REBECCA STARED DOWN at the second picture Penny had drawn. Will was helping Penny into her coat on the other side of the room and Rebecca wondered if there was some kind of student/teacher confidentiality that meant she shouldn't show Will these pictures. But Penny was only eight, and Will needed to know what was going on in his daughter's head.

The second picture touched Rebecca even more than the first. In it, Penny walked beside her dad. They were both wearing thick jackets and hats with yarn balls on top. Big snowflakes were falling down around them and Penny was looking up at her dad, watching him cry huge tears that turned into icicles before they hit the ground.

It was so private. So honest.

"I'd like to have Penny come in three days a week instead of just Thursday and Friday," Will said, approaching her with his checkbook out. "She loves this class so much, it's blowing my mind."

Her heart beat erratically from the knowledge of the sadness that lay just underneath all of his grins.

Rebecca stood up.

"Hey, Penny, would you go down and see if Elle has any more muffins? I'm just about dying for a muffin," she said.

"Sure," Penny agreed readily.

Rebecca waited until the door shut behind the little girl before handing Will the pictures.

"Your daughter drew these today." He tucked the checkbook into his parka and took the two pieces of paper. "She willingly showed them to me, probably assuming I wouldn't share them with anyone else, but I know you're worried about your daughter and these drawings are the best insight into Penny that I've had since she's been in my class. Please don't tell her that I showed them to you, otherwise she may never let me see another one."

Will blinked rapidly. "All right," he finally stammered and looked down at the drawings. His grin faded and the bright color in his cheeks followed. Rebecca stared at her hands, wanting to flee from the tension that had filled the room. He flipped to the second picture, of Penny watching Will crying icicle tears.

"She said that's how she feels, now. About her mother leaving," she murmured. "She said she's sad for you."

"Oh…wow," he breathed. He rubbed his mouth with the back of his hand, and Rebecca longed to wrap her arms around him. She'd never seen someone more in need of a hug in her life.

She touched the sleeve of his jacket, a weak, silly thing considering what she wanted to do. "I think it's a good sign."

He nodded and handed the pictures back. His blue eyes were flat and sad, without their usual sparkle.

Rebecca folded her arms across her chest, to keep herself from touching him again.

"I guess my daughter and I have some things to talk about," he whispered.

"Will, I—" She had no clue what to say.

I'm an art teacher, she thought. *An accountant-slash-art teacher, I don't know what I'm doing!*

Luckily she was saved by Penny's smash and bang arrival back into the studio.

"No muffins, but I brought you a scone. Elle says you shouldn't send kids to do your dirty work. If you want free stuff get it yourself." Penny's smile was bright and unfettered and both Rebecca and Will smiled back at her. It was impossible not to.

"Thanks, Penny. I appreciate it."

Penny dropped the scone on the corner of Rebecca's desk and turned bright eyes to her father. "Dad, I'm ready!"

"Gotcha, sweetie!" he said but his voice cracked and he took a deep breath. "Thank you, Ms. Potter. Thank you very much."

Finally his eyes met hers and Rebecca felt scorched by all the emotion there—the gratitude and grief.

For a moment, just one second in time, she got lost in his eyes and suddenly the opportunity was right there—tangible and welcome—for her to touch him. Really touch him. She imagined her fingers in his hair, her head tucked under his chin. She could almost feel his arms around her, his hands on her back, her lips at his throat.

His eyes were warm and wide, surprised maybe. She didn't know, but she could sense that he felt the same.

"Dad! I'm hot!" Penny cried, and both Becca and Will jerked as if they'd been in a trance. The moment ended, and Penny and Will walked out of her room, leaving Rebecca to sit down hard in her chair.

A pile of red card stock was at her elbow and she

pulled the top sheet close, fumbled for her pen and dipped the end in ink.

She drew a heart on the outside. A heart with a bandage across it and limping on crutches. On the inside she drew another heart kissing the wounded one, the crutches flying off into the air and the bandage falling unneeded to the ground.

Your kiss heals me, she printed underneath the image.

She sat back. No way was that card going to be a big seller but she so badly wanted to kiss away Will's pain. And perhaps have him take away a little of hers.

And it made her nervous. Feeling that way put her beyond a crush, put her in that warm but dangerous area closer to love.

As WILL AND PENNY left the Cup, he scratched at his neck, where he was still hot. He burned with a strange awareness that Ms. Potter knew too much about him. His wife had left him and he was still a wreck and Rebecca Potter *knew*. It wasn't like he went around advertising that. He'd actually begun to believe he was doing all right. That he was over the divorce.

His daughter clearly saw something he didn't.

Two years had gone by, and he had the sinking suspicion that while he'd gotten over Adele leaving, he wasn't quite over being *left*.

He swallowed hard against the lump of bitter anger that lodged at the back of his throat when he thought about those red taillights driving away.

"Did you have a good day at school?" Will looked away from the icy road for a second to glance at his daughter.

They'd moved here from South Carolina six months ago and he'd forgotten just how brutal life could be in the snowbelt.

She lifted a mittened hand and pulled down the bit of scarf over her mouth. "It was good. Ms. Potter taught us about perspective yesterday and it was free draw today so I drew a picture of a flower from the bottom like I was a worm looking up at it and then she yelled at Tony for being late. Again."

He waited with bated breath for her to tell him about the pictures she'd drawn for Ms. Potter. But she just put her scarf back over her lips and stared out the dark window at the Christmas lights still hanging around the eaves of the Presbyterian Church.

"How about school school? You know math class and recess?"

"We had music class today. It was fun."

He smiled ruefully. Penny was her mother's daughter, that's for sure. Adele had been a free spirit, interested in art of any kind. She was a wonderful musician, but couldn't balance her checkbook. He'd taken care of all the practical things. She'd claimed that's what had made their relationship work.

Not that it had stopped her from running off with the actor.

"You know your mom really liked music."

"I remember."

"Yeah?" *Be cool. Let her talk.* He resisted his every inclination *not* to talk about Adele. He reached over and turned down the radio.

"I remember her playing the piano and, sometimes when she taught those singing lessons, she'd let me sit in the same room."

He smiled at her. "I didn't know that."

Penny shrugged, and he got the terrible impression that, in Penny's opinion, there was lots he didn't know.

"Do you miss your mom?" he asked, and Penny finally turned to him, her blue eyes unreadable in the dark car.

"Sure," she told him like he should know that. "Do you?"

His mind went slow and still. "I don't know, Penny. I miss having a mom for you. I miss being a family like that…"

"We're a family."

He smiled and nodded, though he wanted to pull over and wrap his arms around his sweet and solemn girl. "You're right. You're totally right."

"Do you want a new wife?"

Will could only gape at Penny. "What makes you think that?"

She shrugged, her winter coat rustling against the seat belt. "Mom's been gone a long time. Seems like you should get a girlfriend or something."

He tipped his head back and howled. "Have you been talking to Aunt Elaine?"

"No."

"Cousin Alyssa?"

Penny's mouth tipped up, but she tried to smother her smile. His niece Alyssa was obsessed with boyfriends. She was at that preteen age, when all energies were focused on boys and lip gloss and eye-rolling.

"I don't want a girlfriend," he told his daughter.

"But—"

"I do not want a girlfriend." he repeated. "Tell your cousin that."

He felt empty inside. Adele and her betrayal had cleared

him of any inclination toward romance. He'd seen behind the curtain and knew that all of those things that made Valentine's Day so special to so many people—the hearts and flowers, the moonlight and candles—were tricks. Shams.

Dressings for empty windows.

It wasn't real. Not for him. Not anymore.

"When I talked to Mom on Wednesday, she said you can go out to California this summer once school is out." The words felt ripped from his throat. He'd rather eat mud than let his daughter go out there.

"Ms. Potter has an art camp in the summer. I want to do that."

He heaved a sigh, relieved in a dark, selfish place that Penny hadn't leaped at the opportunity. "Okay. But maybe you can do both. Art camp and see your mom."

"Is she going to come here?" she asked and he nearly laughed at the image of the beautiful and sophisticated Adele in Fenelon Falls. She'd always turned up her nose at the town he'd come from.

"I don't think so, honey. She'd want you to go to California for the visit."

Penny looked at him with those big blue eyes that everyone said were just like his. "I want to stay with you," she said, and Will's heart just split right open.

Adele certainly hadn't pushed the idea of a visit. She'd given up all rights in the divorce. He'd been the one pressuring her to have some sort of role in her daughter's life, and she'd begrudgingly offered the summer trip. But if Adele wasn't interested and Penny didn't want to go to California—he wasn't going to push it.

"Okay." He nodded. "Summer in Fenelon Falls."

"Are we going to Grandma and Grandpa's right now?" she asked, changing the subject.

Thank you, God.

"It's Friday night," he said with a grin. "That's where we go. Are you excited?"

"I'm excited about seeing Alyssa and Bethany and Heather," she said, listing her girl cousins.

"But not Joe?" he asked with a smile.

She shook her head. "He's a boy." She put the scarf back over her mouth and that seemed to be the end of the discussion.

"Does he have cooties?" he asked.

"Cootie's aren't real, Dad." She told him that as if she'd read it in the *New England Journal of Medicine.* "But he licks his finger and tries to put it in my ear and he chews with his mouth open and—" she pursed her lips "—he's gross."

Will smiled and focused on the road. "Got it. I won't let him close to my ears."

Since moving back to Fenelon Falls from South Carolina, Friday nights had changed from a quiet night of pizza and the rewatching of some Disney movie his daughter never tired of to a night of chaos. He had three siblings still in town. All of them had kids and all of them would be at his parents' place.

Will smiled just thinking about it.

His family and their loud and boisterous style of love was why, after it became very clear that Adele wasn't coming home, he had packed Penny up and moved her. Well, that and the fact the house he, Penny and Adele had lived in was growing haunted by the ghosts of a family he didn't recognize anymore.

He'd come up here to forget the past. And to help his daughter. He shook his head thinking of those pictures. Ms. Potter and her art class were a blessing. If she could help him and Penny he would spend the rest of his life thanking her.

Ms. Potter.

There'd been an odd moment in her classroom tonight. Just at the end. He'd been so spellbound by the empathy in her brown eyes he'd almost hugged her. It had been the strangest thing. While staring into her eyes, he could almost feel her arms around him. His hands at her back. It had been so long since he'd felt the soft press of a woman and for that moment he could almost taste it, salty and thick in his throat.

He coughed and shrugged off his jacket, suddenly warm in the car.

He'd been alone too long, that much was clear.

Adele had left two years ago. Almost to the day.

Two lonely years ago. And until tonight he'd been able to ignore just how lonely he was.

If he searched, he wouldn't be able to find someone as different from Adele as Rebecca Potter. Sure, they had the art stuff in common, but Rebecca was reserved. She actually reminded him of his daughter—still waters and all that.

He admitted after the intense fire of Adele, that the quiet but stimulating company of Rebecca Potter felt like a salve.

But was that really what he wanted? Was that right for him and Penny?

Out of the corner of his eye he watched his daughter breathe on the passenger window and then draw a heart with her finger in the steam.

CHAPTER THREE

January 26—Friday

WHEN HER WHOLE LIFE was said and done and Rebecca was sent to hell, for her impure thoughts and the lies she'd told her parents, instead of burning for all eternity tied to some rock, she'd be back at her folks' house, suffering through another Friday night dinner.

Elle had warned her that her mother was going to be on the rampage after the big fight she and Elle had had last weekend. Rebecca had the sick feeling she was a bone between two dogs. She should stand up for herself—tell her mother to back off—but she didn't. She let Aunt Elle fight her battles for her.

At the dinner table, Rebecca braced herself for Jane Potter's worst.

Coward.

"We could use you tomorrow," her father said from his throne at the end of the table, his bald head gleaming in the candlelight. When she'd been young she'd thought every bald man was a little like Mr. Clean—slightly dangerous, with that twinkle in his eye. It had been a disappointment when her dad lost his hair to discover he didn't have *any* Mr. Clean in him. He was just a bald, middle-aged accountant who loved his job. Nothing dangerous or twinkly in that.

"I don't think it's too much to ask for a few Saturdays a year as we go into tax season." He watched her over his glasses before taking a bite of lamb and chewing.

"Dad," she said, pushing her peas into her mashed potatoes and refusing to meet his censorious gaze. "You know I work at the café on Saturdays."

"Well, it's certainly not like Elle needs you. There's hardly anyone in there." Her mother leaned left, so she could see Rebecca around the lilies and candles in the middle of the table.

They sat in the formal dining room, surrounded by all the polished silver and china that the Potter Accounting Firm had allowed her parents to buy. If her mother could have worn it, she would have.

The sister who had done good. Married well. Had a quiet, perfectly behaved daughter who was following in Jane's boring footsteps.

Everything Aunt Elle wasn't.

"I certainly hope that you aren't going to be a part of that dateathon."

"You mean, am I signing up for it?"

Dad actually laughed. "Heaven forbid, sweetheart. If you wanted to start dating, I've told you a million times I've got the perfect guy. Jake Cedeka from the club. I really don't understand your reluctance to meet him."

"What if it worked out, Dad?" She grimaced. "I'd be Rebecca Cedeka. It rhymes. I can't take that risk."

Dad smiled at her lame joke and the ball of tension that

sat in her stomach during family meals unwound slightly, allowing her to take a deep breath.

"So you're going to be Rebecca Potter for the rest of your life?" Jane asked.

Rebecca nodded, though the idea crushed her. "Maybe." She took another bite of potatoes, which subsequently stuck to the roof of her mouth. "It's worked for me so far."

"You are twenty-seven." The crystal goblet in Jane's hands hit the table with the weight of a brick. "You won't commit to working full-time at the firm. You insist on going down with the sinking ship your aunt calls a business…"

"Mom, she's your sister. I don't think it would kill you to stop by the Cup for a coffee to show your sister some support."

"My sister has been supported all her life. My father supported every flighty decision she ever made. I am not about to validate that…business by stepping foot in it."

The fight between Jane and Elle must have been a doozy. Her mother could be unfeeling at times, even stubborn, but she wasn't usually so mean.

Rebecca turned to her father, searching for a compassionate voice of reason. Dad just sat there, cutting green beans into bite-size pieces.

I must have been switched at birth, Rebecca thought for perhaps the millionth time.

"But—" Jane wrenched the conversation back to where she wanted it "—we were talking about you."

"I'm not signing up for the dateathon, Mom. Don't worry."

"All right then." Jane tilted her head. "Then how about those cards?"

Rebecca swallowed. Of course. The cards.

"What about them?"

"You are an accountant with the Potter Firm. There's a standard of behavior expected of you. You are acting just like your aunt, and she's never been a good influence…"

"I don't sign them, Mom. No one knows I make them."

"*I* know."

Jane yammered on and Rebecca's blood grew hot and thick. She knew it was wrong to let her mother's opinions matter so much. As Elle had said over and over again—her mother only had the power to wound Rebecca because she let her.

But twenty-seven years of habit was hard to break.

"I sold out last year, Mom," she said, foolishly trying to defend those small scraps of herself she sent out in the world. "People ask for more all the time. They ask for Christmas cards and birthday cards. I'd hardly call that stupid."

"If it's not stupid, why don't you make it official?" her father piped up, asking what was in fact the million-dollar question. "If everyone loves them and you are so proud of them why don't you sign them? Why doesn't everyone in town know that you make them?"

Because of Will. Because it's no one's business. It's private. Because…what if people laughed?

"Some people know…" She sounded like a petulant child. She stabbed a pea that shot off her plate and hit her untouched wine goblet. She put it back on her plate and set down her fork.

"You're clearly embarrassed by them, Rebecca. And if you'd just listen to your father and me instead of your aunt, you'd see we're only trying to help you get your life on track. Aren't you proud of who you are? Of the Potter name?"

She sighed, heavily. "Of course I am."

"Then work for us full-time." Phil shook his head. "I really don't understand why you have to make everything so dramatic, Rebecca."

Rebecca sucked in a deep breath and let it out nice and slow—something Aunt Elle told her might keep her from actually sticking her salad fork in her eye during these dinners. She repeated it, just to be on the safe side.

"I've decided the Fenelon Falls Young Artist Program is going to have a summer camp. I think I'll do a whole week on sidewalk chalk."

"Babysitting is not a job."

Her mother's opinion of the program struck deep, drew blood, but Becca pressed on, desperate to leave this dinner having said what she should.

"I've contacted the elementary school and they said I could use their blacktop. Won't that be cool?" She looked at her mother, imploring her to understand how important this was. How much she loved the idea of a group of kids filling a playground with sidewalk chalk murals.

Jane's eyes were cold. She didn't get it. She didn't care.

"How much money do you make teaching this program, anyway?" Phil asked, again getting to what he thought was the root of the matter. "Honey, we're just trying to help."

Rebecca, as she usually did on Friday nights, just gave up. She stopped the fight and took the silent and cowardly path of least resistance.

Phil and Jane continued to discuss her as if she wasn't there. And that was fine. Rebecca, as she'd done for years, concentrated on the shadows, the play of candlelight over lilies and crystal, the beautiful art that existed around her family, although she was the only one who saw it.

Later that night

"I'D BE MARRIED to a man who plays golf with my father…ugh." Rebecca cried, sloshing green tea over the edge of her favorite pig-shaped mug. "Can you imagine?"

"That's pretty bad." Lucky Morgan smiled into her own mug before taking a sip.

"Understatement of the year." Rebecca flopped back into Elle's comfy overstuffed chair in the far back corner of the Cup. On Friday nights, as soon as Elle turned over the Closed sign this little nook was theirs.

"Becca, they just want you to be happy," Elle said, rocking slowly and methodically in the old wicker rocking chair, next to the potbelly stove.

"So they say, but come on…" She looked at Elle and Lucky incredulously. They didn't need to pretend with her. "It's pretty clear they don't want to be embarrassed by me and my hobby and my glorified babysitting service anymore." The thought was so depressing that she reached for another shortbread cookie from the plate set on the ottoman within easy reach of all three of them.

It was their weekly shortbread night, conveniently scheduled just after her family dinner. Sometimes they had tea, half a cookie each and called it a night, but more often they had half a mug of tea before one of them would crack open a bottle of wine. And then the laughing would start and a second box of shortbread would be pulled from the cupboard.

Those were the best nights.

Rebecca drained her tea and hopped up to get the wineglasses from behind the counter, just so everyone was clear what kind of night they'd be having.

"They are easily embarrassed." Aunt Elle's eyes twinkled and Rebecca paused. Elle had eaten a thousand of Jane's poison apples over the years and she put up a good front. But Rebecca could see the tension in her aunt and wondered if maybe the poison was beginning to give her a little indigestion.

Not that Elle wasn't pressing on with fierce independence. *If only I had that kind of confidence,* Rebecca thought watching her aunt. *And those legs. I need to do more yoga or something. Whatever it is that's keeping Aunt Elle in such good shape.*

Then Rebecca made her weekly promise to stop eating shortbread… Tomorrow.

"And I think your mother feels threatened by the relationship you and I have," Elle said. "Maybe that's my fault. Maybe it's a good idea for you to work for your parents on Saturdays…"

"Don't be ridiculous, Aunt Elle."

Lucky traded her tea mug for the wineglass Rebecca offered her. "I think they'd get off your back, if you would treat the after-school program like a business…"

Rebecca rolled her eyes. Lucky could make a business out of waking up in the morning.

"No, come on." Lucky grabbed her hand before she could walk away. "Listen to me. Let's say you advertise instead of just rely on word-of-mouth. You offer to teach some free classes at the elementary school to stir up some interest." Lucky cast an excited gaze to Elle who nodded in agreement.

"She's right, you could really make a go of the program."

"See." Lucky tugged on her hand. "I get it, we both get

it—" she gestured to Elle "—your parents suck, but that's no reason why you shouldn't commit to doing what you want to do."

"I've committed," she protested weakly, "I've got summer camp…"

"Great!" Lucky beamed, her eyes bright in a way they hadn't been since New Year's. "That's the right idea. Now just do some advertising."

"Okay." Rebecca nodded reluctantly. "I hear you. I will advertise. I will make an effort." She squeezed Lucky's hand and let go, uncomfortable with all the attention. "I appreciate the pep talk and your belief in me. Thanks."

"It's what we're here for." Elle smiled and Rebecca handed her a wineglass and took her mug.

"Yeah, to kick your butt every once in a while," Lucky shouted as Rebecca went into the small kitchen.

She dropped off the mugs at the sink and grabbed one of the bottles of wine that sat above the fridge.

"Consider my butt kicked," she said coming back into the room. She handed the bottle and opener to Lucky, who always managed to open the bottle without breaking the cork or spilling it all over herself.

The cork popped out of the bottle of red wine and Rebecca and Elle leaned in so Lucky could fill their glasses.

"Where are you on the dateathon at the Cup?" Rebecca asked Elle, forcefully changing the subject.

Elle growled and her rocking took up a slightly more agitated pace. "Well, Max set up the Web site. We're live, whatever that means."

Lucky shot Rebecca a wicked grin and Rebecca buried her face in her wineglass to keep from sputtering. Arnold

Maxwell, the science teacher out at the high school and a man, who in Lucky's astute opinion had been pining for Aunt Elle since she moved back to town.

"But I think the good folks of Fenelon Falls need a kick start. So, ladies. Dear friends and conspirators." Aunt Elle sipped her wine and eyed them with a glint that could only be called predatory. "It's time for you both to put your friendship where your mouth is. I need guinea pigs for the dateathon."

Rebecca and Lucky both groaned.

"Hey," Rebecca said, switching focus. "Speaking of someone needing a kick in the butt, how about you play Cupid for yourself for a change and sign yourself up for that dateathon…"

"Now, there's an idea," Lucky agreed. "The town Cupid gets a little of her own medicine."

"I'm ready. More than ready." Unless it was the heat from the fire, Rebecca could have sworn that Elle was blushing. "But it's not like there's a whole lot of eligible bachelors hanging around Fenelon Falls…"

"Amen!" Rebecca raised her glass.

"Besides, keeping this business from going under is taking all the energy I have right now."

"So let me pay you more rent—" She'd much rather do that, than sign up for the dateathon. She believed in her aunt, but a dateathon? Yikes.

Elle put her hand up, stopping the old argument before it started. "I think that this dateathon is perfect. Exactly what the Cup and this town needs. I just need some help." She watched them pointedly. "From my friends." She leaned forward. "From my dear niece and devoted friend…"

"I can't," Lucky said, her voice sad and solemn. "It's too soon." She shrugged and pulled at the frayed ends of the afghan over her lap. "I did just propose to a man." The reminder was needless. Rebecca and Elle had been there at Christmas to help Lucky get over her surprise and grief when the answer had been no.

"Josh doesn't know what he's lost," Elle said, reaching over to squeeze Lucky's hand.

"You think?" Lucky asked, trying to smile but it came out all wrong. "Josh is my best friend...he knows me better than anyone. He knows me and he still didn't want me."

"What was he doing at your shop the other night?" Rebecca asked.

"Annoying me," Lucky said and then sighed. "He's just trying to make things normal between us. But then he kissed me and now nothing is normal."

"A kiss kiss?" Elle and Rebecca asked at the same time.

Lucky nodded. "Guys, I'm tired of even thinking about it. Can we not talk about Josh?"

"Of course," Elle agreed.

"But he *kissed* you?" Rebecca persisted. "What does that mean?"

"Becca, please let's just drop it. My head hurts, my heart hurts."

Rebecca nodded, reluctantly. One of them was getting kissed. It seemed like something that should be discussed. But Lucky took a sip of wine and kept her eyes downcast and Rebecca could see the glimmer of tears.

Only one thing to do, if wine and shortbread night was going to be saved from becoming a pity party.

"I have a crush," Rebecca blurted, and as expected

Lucky's eyes lit up. Elle groaned and rolled her head across the back of the rocker.

"You?" Lucky squealed. "A crush?"

"Yes," Rebecca said, though it was on the tip of her tongue to say that this one was different. This one was *more*. "I just can't seem to help myself."

"Who?" Lucky asked. She leaned forward and grabbed a cookie.

"Will Blakely."

Lucky's cookie paused on the way to her mouth, and Elle choked on a mouthful of wine.

Rebecca knew what they were thinking, that she was pinning her star on someone way out of her league.

"He's dreamy," Lucky agreed. "I mean seriously hot."

"And isn't Penny in your after-school program?" Elle asked.

Rebecca nodded. "Totally doomed, I know."

"Why?" Lucky and Elle asked at the same time.

"Why?" Rebecca laughed. "Because he's seriously hot. And seriously out of my league."

Lucky groaned. "There are no such things as leagues, Becca. There are just people who are compatible, and I bet you and Will are totally compatible."

"If you sign up for the dateathon, I could get him to sign up and then you'd know for sure." Elle had a one-track mind.

"Don't be ridiculous."

"You're the ridiculous one," Elle said. "He's lucky to have caught your eye. Someone as talented and fun and beautiful as you."

Rebecca rolled her eyes, but her esteem, which had

been smacked down by her mother's callousness, was able to recover. She smiled at her friends, glad as she was every Friday night that Lucky and Elle were in her life.

"To the three most eligible bachelorettes in Fenelon Falls," Rebecca said, holding her glass high. "Look out, Cupid, we're coming for you!"

Elle and Lucky touched their glasses to Rebecca's. Elle launched into her new Cupid assassination plan and soon Rebecca and Lucky were howling and red wine had sloshed over onto upholstery.

She thought of Will's sad, handsome face and felt those warm fires build low in her stomach. She thought of his hair, of the curl of his lip, the bright blue of his eyes.

Maybe they're right, she thought as the fruity red wine slid down her throat. *Maybe there are no leagues. Maybe it's just Will and me and Penny finding each other when we need to most.*

CHAPTER FOUR

January 27—Saturday

THE CUP WAS PRETTY FULL for a Saturday. Will managed to get a small table close to the far window and Penny insisted on going to the counter to place their usual order. He liked to go with her—just so he could hear her try to say "macchiato"—but she was going through a very independent streak and insisted on doing everything alone. Like dressing herself this morning.

His dear daughter approached the counter wearing last year's pink and silver dance recital costume over her jeans and boots— Rugged Barbie brought to life.

He unwound his scarf and chafed his hands together. Though the café was perfectly toasty, this winter was chilling him to the bone.

He usually met Josh here on Saturdays, but something was going on with his friend these days, and Will had a sinking feeling it had something to do with the flagging attendance at the church.

Will was worried Josh might have his eye on greener pastures.

"Hi, there." Will turned to find Police Chief Brass and his wife, Mirabel standing behind him, shrugging into their coats.

They were a study in opposites. Chief was a small, spare man, like a greyhound with a bad attitude and Mrs. Brass was one of those beautiful huskies, all blue eyes and fur.

"Chief Brass." Will and the chief exchanged firm handshakes.

"Either your daughter is dressing herself or you need some help," Edward said. Will laughed as they all watched Penny balancing on her toes at the counter talking to Ms. Potter.

"That's all her," Will laughed.

"They're so fun at that age," Mirabel said, pulling her fur-lined hood up and over her white hair.

"Mirabel, good to see you."

"You, too, Will. We don't see you enough," she said, her smile wide. They were good people and Chief Brass made Will's job as a county parole officer easier by working hand in hand with the county on efforts to stop juvenile crime in the area.

"I'm not sure your husband would agree with you," Will said. "Chief and I spend a lot of time together."

"And he enjoys every minute of it, don't let him fool you." Mirabel gave her husband a sideways look. "He just said the other day that you were the best thing to happen to the county since we built the new elementary school."

Will felt himself begin to blush.

"Now, Mirabel, I didn't say that. I said—"

"Oh, stop and let the man have a compliment." She tugged on her gloves. "We need to get going. Have a good day, Will."

Before following his wife, the chief leaned in a little closer. "We picked up Tony DeLona on Friday night."

Will hung his head. He'd known it was just a matter

of time, but he couldn't help being disappointed. "What did he do?"

"Vandalism and public mischief. You'll be seeing his family on Monday."

"Thanks for the heads-up." He patted Brass on the back and watched him walk out the door.

Penny came back from the counter with two plates in her hand. Muffins for each of them. Ms. Potter followed with two steaming mugs.

"They didn't have blueberry," Penny said, setting the plates down with a clatter. "So I got you chocolate chip, like me."

"Now, that's the breakfast of champions," he said with a grin. He leaned back and Ms. Potter slid his machiatto in front of him and he found himself engulfed by her scent—paint, perfume and sugary cinnamon. He had to bite back a sudden, surprising moan.

Penny's talk about girlfriends had kept him up late fantasizing about all the things he could do with a girlfriend. And that moment with Ms. Potter in the studios hadn't helped. Not at all. Too many of those fantasies involved her.

He'd woken up like a teenager with a dirty secret.

"Thank you," he whispered, blinking hard to get his equilibrium back. He was screwed up. The demons of loneliness and lust had him and he couldn't shake them loose.

"No problem." She smiled at him and the bright winter sunlight flooding through the windows made her skin glow. And her hair… He'd always thought it was just brown. But it wasn't. There was red in there and blond.

It was…

"Pretty." he said aloud and wanted to smack himself upside the head.

"I'm sorry?" Ms. Potter said.

"Um…that's pretty nice of you to bring the drinks. Thank you, Ms. Potter," he managed to say without cringing. Even Penny was looking at him strangely.

"My pleasure," she murmured, her voice low and smoky. "You can call me Rebecca. Or Becca. Everyone does."

"That's her real name," Penny supplied. She leaned in and took a sip from her mug without lifting it. When she sat back she had a perfect chocolate mustache.

"Great, Rebecca." Her name was sweet on his tongue. He found himself staring at her eyes. They were like whiskey or scotch, gold and amber and fluid in a way.

"Oh!" Penny cried, her attention captured by something over his shoulder. "Elle's put up more Valentine's Day cards!" She scooted off her chair and was gone.

"She really loves this holiday," Rebecca said as they watched Penny bob and weave through the small crowd.

"I can't seem to cure her of it," Will said and mentally winced. He sounded like the Grinch or something…the anti-Cupid.

"Well, enjoy your drinks," she said, turning away from him, and those demons that had a firm grip on his better sense had him reaching for her arm. Contact. Just above her elbow.

"Rebecca," he murmured and she turned, her hand covering the spot he'd just touched, like she'd been burned by his fingers. He wanted to do it again. "I want to thank you again for your help with Penny. You have a real way with kids."

"She's special," she said with a smile.

"Yes, she is, but I think you are, too." He swallowed and looked away from the pink climbing her fair cheeks. "You should think about expanding your program, maybe doing something for kids from broken homes."

"Really?" Her brows creased over her eyes as if she'd never considered the value of what she was doing for the kids in town.

"Absolutely. I know Tony DeLona's folks are probably wishing someone would help him talk about how he's feeling…"

"Tony's in my class twice a week."

"See if you can get him to draw a picture like you did with Penny. I'm telling you, art therapy has been gaining respect. Young kids don't have a lot of the tools at hand to deal with their feelings and things like divorce…" Rebecca's head was tilted and her careful study made him flustered. "Well, think about it." He shrugged and broke the edge of his chocolate chip muffin.

"I will," she murmured but didn't move. She nodded and then like sunrise a slow smile spread over her face. Dimples appeared in her cheeks and Will took a sip of coffee too hot, because it prevented him from muttering any more foolishness. "Thank you, Will."

He nodded back, his mouth full.

She returned to the counter and the meager line of customers. He forced himself not to stare after her.

Rebecca Potter is beautiful, he thought and took another sip of his coffee. *And I am an idiot.*

He had half-baked notions of asking her on a date. Of reaching across a table and touching the pale skin of her wrists. Of watching her smile at him in candlelight.

To cure himself he remembered those taillights driving away two Valentine's Days ago.

PENNY WATCHED HER DAD and Becca through the shelves that held all the Valentine's Day cards and books. As Alyssa would say, something was up. Dad shoved half his muffin in his mouth and the dents were back in Becca's cheeks.

So far, so good. Now, onto the next step.

She turned and faced the small stacks of Valentine's Day cards. She liked the one with the big tongue that had a knot in it. "You make me tongue-tied," Penny read.

She didn't get it, but maybe it was an adult thing. It looked funny and funny was good. Funny was what she was after.

This was the perfect card for Dad. For her whole plan. Penny wanted to get it for Dad and write Becca's name in it. The thought made her want to giggle and dance. Perfect. It was all going to be perfect. Except for one thing. She didn't have any money. She couldn't ask Dad for some because then he'd *know* and the surprise would be ruined.

She bit her lip.

God, I'm really, really sorry. And I promise to save up my allowance and give it to Elle as soon as I have enough. And I won't complain about going to church, and I'll even be nice to Joe when he's being gross. I'll do the dishes and won't walk into the bathroom when the door is shut.

She looked over her shoulder to make sure Dad wasn't watching, then lifted the hem of her pink skirt and slid the card into the waistband of her jeans.

"Excuse me?" a voice behind her asked, and Penny spun around to find Elle.

Oh, no. Oh-no-oh-no-oh-no.

She was caught. And she was caught by Elle. Tears burned her eyes and her stomach cramped.

"What are you doing, Penny?" Elle touched her shoulder and Penny just wanted to die.

"Stealing," she whispered and the tears slid down her cheeks.

"I see that, but why?"

"I wanted to give this to my dad." She handed the card to Elle.

"That's a strange valentine to give your dad." Elle's eyes were so nice and understanding, Penny cried harder and the truth flew out of her mouth before she could think of something better to say.

"I was going to sign Becca…Ms. Potter's name."

Elle's mouth dropped open.

"Don't take me to jail," Penny whispered. "I won't ever do it again."

"Oh, you sweet little genius, I won't take you to jail." Elle crouched down and wrapped Penny in a big hug. Penny wiped her eyes on Elle's shoulder. She smelled like roses and something spicy that made Penny's nose tingle. "I'm going to help you."

"Help me steal the card?" Penny asked.

"No, I'm going to help you play Cupid." Elle smiled and hugged her close.

Adults are so weird, Penny thought.

REBECCA SHUT THE DOOR to the storeroom behind her and, with only the foam cups and bowls as witness, did an ecstatic, out-of-control happy dance. She shook her butt and screamed into the stack of aprons Elle kept in the milk crates.

She didn't even care when Lucky walked in during the middle of her wild woman routine.

"What is going on? I came in to talk to you about the church and saw you duck in here like you were on fire."

Rebecca wrapped her arms around Lucky's neck and forced her to do some happy dancing with her.

"I think I am going to do an art program for at-risk kids." Rebecca gave the lesser news first, because the big news, the heat in Will's eyes, his stammer and long look, his touch on her arm, those things were too precious. She couldn't just say, *I think maybe he might like me, too.*

"That's a fantastic idea!" Lucky said.

"I know." Rebecca shivered again and Lucky laughed hard in her ear. "I know. It's all so perfect."

"What else has gotten into you?" Lucky managed to get Rebecca's arms from around her neck and hold her out at arm's length.

Rebecca put her hand over her mouth, keeping the wonderful news to herself for just one minute longer. But finally she burst. "Will called me pretty. He just said it. He tried to pretend he was talking about something else, but…" She closed her eyes. "He kept blushing and he like…" she shook her head, "looked at me and stopped talking for a second and then sort of twitched and shoved half his muffin in his mouth."

"Really?" Lucky asked. "So…"

"I think I'm going to ask him out. I mean for a drink or something. Right? That's what I should do? Or should he do it? Who does that?" She swung right back into doubt. "Oh, I should forget it. Right? He's probably just sleepless or something… He has heartburn. Or…"

"Stop it." Lucky shook her. "Stop it, just stop it. If you got a vibe from him then of course you ask him out."

"But what if the vibe was wrong—"

Lucky started to laugh, and Rebecca realized how she sounded. "Okay, you're right. I'm an adult. I'm…" She shrugged and laughed, feeling like a kid before her first bike ride sans training wheels. "I'm going to ask him out."

"Yes!" Lucky hissed. "Good for you."

"You know the last time I asked a guy out—"

"I know, I know. Eric Northfield in the fifth grade." Lucky brushed back Rebecca's hair and started to straighten the red T-shirt she wore. "And he told you he liked your best friend. Heartbreaking, but seriously, get over that."

"Right." Rebecca took one last bit of strength from the adoration in her friend's eyes. "Off I go."

Lucky pulled open the door to the storeroom and there in the alcove in front of her precious Valentine's Day cards stood Will.

Due to sudden paralysis Lucky had to give her a shove, and she stumbled out next to him. He looked up from the two cards he held.

Your Kiss Heals Me and *Baby, You Move Me* with the picture of a man carrying a woman on the palm of his hands.

He's getting me a valentine. He doesn't realize they're all for him. That he's the Love God, that his kiss…

"I don't understand how people can believe in this," he said.

"What?" she whispered.

"This Valentine's Day stuff." The sadness was back in his eyes, but her own sudden pain made her immune to his.

"You don't?" she asked, her mouth sticky. *This wasn't how this was supposed to go.*

He put down the cards. "Romance is for people still foolish enough to believe in true love. Love is work." He shook his head. "And most of the time it doesn't work at all." He touched the corner of *You Are My Best Day*.

She was unable to move or laugh or say anything.

"Think about what I said." He turned to her. "About the class for kids from broken homes."

"I will," she whispered with a weak smile and then took two steps backward and ducked into the storeroom.

Stupid. She collapsed onto the stacked milk crates and thunked her head sideways against the wall. *So stupid.*

CHAPTER FIVE

January 31—Wednesday

"YOU'RE JOKING about these, right?" Lucky asked, looking up from the cards Rebecca had given her. It was Wednesday and Elle and Lucky had called an emergency shortbread night on account of "everyone's crappy mood."

They'd skipped the tea and gone straight to wine.

"Who's joking?" Rebecca asked around a mouthful of shortbread.

"Well…" Elle set her stack down on her knee. "Clearly we're having some Valentine's Day issues."

"No issues." Rebecca poured herself some more wine and set the bottle back on the windowsill behind her. Snow gathered in quiet heaps against the glass. The winter storm all the weathermen were talking about was on its way. "I just want to reach out to a new audience."

Lucky howled and red wine sloshed on to her black sweater and all over the cards.

"Hey," Rebecca protested. "Just because you don't like them…"

"Becca!" Lucky held up one of the cards, now with a big burgundy stain on the pink paper and read it. "'Sorry to hear about your broken heart. Get well soon.'" She set that down on her lap and read the second one. "'My cats and I wish you a flealess Valentine's Day and a quick, painless death.' That just screams happily ever after."

"The older—"

"I like this one," Elle chimed in, holding up the card with a trail of broken hearts across the front. "'Careful, it's spreading.' Very clever."

"We can't sell these," Lucky said.

"I can't even read them, they're so depressing."

Rebecca drank some more wine and studied the red tassels of her favorite blanket. She didn't know what to say. They were right. Of course they were. Those cards were awful, but it was all she had inside of her. Every time she sat down with that red card stock in front of her the only thing she could see were the hollow depths of Will's eyes. He'd never feel for her what she felt for him, and it had taken those moments, those stupid moments when he had proved it, to highlight the fact that her feelings weren't just a crush.

"We must be the saddest trio in Fenelon Falls tonight," Rebecca sighed. She hadn't been locked up in her own grief so much not to see what was happening to her friends. Elle was fighting with Jane and her daughter was on the other side of the country and something was going on with Max, but she didn't seem too happy about it. And Lucky was losing Josh to a bigger church in the city. Rachel Conner, the little girl with cancer, was back in the hospital for testing, and Lucky was right in the middle of all of it. As usual.

It seemed this Valentine's Day was bound to be the worst on record. "Let's go back to those Cupid assassination plans we were talking about."

"Hear, hear," Elle agreed, raising her glass in a mock toast. "I've been thinking of hiring a merc…"

"I for one am tired of this." Lucky sat up. "From now on…no more whining. Not about men. Not about our families. No more bitch sessions."

"But I don't have anything else to talk about," Rebecca groused. And that depressed her further. She finished her wine and set the glass by the chair. More booze was a bad idea. She sighed and looked up at the ceiling, as if answers were there.

Cheer up.

Get over Will.

Tell your mother you don't want to be an accountant.

It's not like the answers were secret. She knew them. She knew them by heart. She just lacked the courage to implement them.

She and Will had more in common than she thought.

"Of course you do!" Lucky plunked her fist down on the arm of the rocking chair.

"No, I don't. My mother gave me four more clients and I didn't fight her. Today I prayed for snow so I could cancel class tomorrow—just so I wouldn't have to see him again." She looked at her two friends. "See, I'm totally pathetic."

"Well." Lucky shook her head. "Pathetic or not, it's two weeks to Valentine's Day. I need cards for my shop. Elle needs cards for her shop. So in the immortal words of Cher—snap out of it!"

Rebecca smiled—her first real smile all night. "I guess I'm lucky you're not slapping me."

"Trust me," Lucky's eyes twinkled. "It's been tempting.

Count yourself fortunate that I am a woman of restraint, and I love you."

Rebecca reached out to grab her friend's hand. "I love you, too. And your violent tendencies. Let's talk about something cheerful."

"What about you, Elle?"

"Well." Elle smiled and lifted her eyebrows. "The Cup is doing better than ever. The dateathon is going gang-busters."

"You mean your Web site is going gang-busters." Lucky winked at Rebecca. "I've heard how well *you're* doing in the dateathon."

Elle blushed but waved her hand. "So far, it's been nothing but weirdos and kids. I think I'm sending out some kind of cosmic signal that's keeping the good guys away."

"Good guys like Max?"

Lucky, dark eyes dazzling, grilled Elle mercilessly about the finer points of her love life and Elle turned the table on Lucky. Soon, despite their previous bad moods, all three of them were laughing again.

The room was filled with the kind of love Rebecca could take for granted. These women buoyed her in all her worst moments. They kept her laughing. They kept her sane.

Suddenly, from the corners of Rebecca's mind—the place where lately only images of hairy legs and long empty nights had been found—a new kind of valentine emerged. Something affirming. Something different.

Rebecca threw off the blanket. "Toss those cards. I'll get you some new ones in a few days."

She said hasty goodbyes to her startled friends and headed, not to her apartment, but upstairs to her studio. She was tired of being a victim of Valentine's Day. Tired of being a victim to feelings she couldn't control, a mother who didn't listen, pining after a man who either didn't like her, or was too scared to take a chance.

Victim no more.

It was time for Cupid to grow up.

February 1—Thursday

REBECCA STOOD AT HER DESK and waved goodbye to Penny, who kept turning around in the doorway and looking at her with a perplexed expression. Maybe the little girl saw through her big fake smile and overcheery voice. Thank God her aunt Elaine had picked her up. If it had been Will standing there with his tousled hair and cold heart, she might have just exploded under the pressure of all her fake cheer.

"See you tomorrow!" she called, and Penny nodded and finally was gone.

Rebecca blew out a breath and collapsed back in her chair. Penny had been eyeing her all afternoon. Maybe it was Rebecca's overactive imagination, but the girl seemed like some kind of emotional Sherlock Holmes.

Her brainstorm last night for her new line of Valentines had manifested itself into about ten cards. She wanted to finish twenty more, so that Lucky and Elle each got plenty.

Hopefully her friends would like the results.

She'd even signed them, which made her feel a little like she was taking long, slow steps toward the edge of a cliff. She couldn't go back after this. She couldn't be the silent Cupid.

She stood and circled the room to straighten the endless mess the kids had left.

As she passed the bank of windows, she glanced down

at the sidewalk. A group of kids loitered outside of the café. Which might have been the least cool place in town to loiter, but maybe Elle was giving them the day-old cookies. Rebecca knew the Chess club had been hanging around a lot more often, but these boys didn't look like the chess types. One of the boys, without a hat or gloves or scarf, turned, and she recognized Tony, who hadn't shown up to her class for the past week.

She'd been so stupidly depressed about Will that she'd forgotten the idea for a program for kids from broken homes. Before she could think twice, she flew down the stairs.

"Hey, Becca!" Elle cried from behind the counter where she was counting inventory. "What are you doing in such a rush?"

"I'm not sure, Elle. I'm really not sure." If she paused or slowed, her courage would be gone and the moment wasted.

She opened the door and blinked into the snowy twilight.

"Tony!" she called and the three kids turned to her. "I need to speak to you."

One of the boys mocked her and punched Tony in the arm, but she kept her gaze locked on Tony's guilty brown ones and refused to acknowledge the other boys. "Can you come in for a minute?"

Tony looked at his friends and Rebecca couldn't help but feel the next minute was all important. "Tony?" She arched an eyebrow and channeled a little Clint Eastwood.

"Yeah." He ducked his head and walked away from his friends. She stood to the side and Tony entered the café. She turned back to the boys. "You guys can come in, too, if you want. It's warm."

They took off before she'd even finished the sentence.

"Let's go up to the studio," she said and Tony nodded, casting one last glance at the counter of baked goods. She grabbed a chocolate chocolate chip cookie from the jar and Elle winked at her as she walked by.

She took the stairs two at a time.

So what if she was going to be a spinster with twenty cats and tissues stuffed up the sleeves of her sweater, she'd make a difference in this town, in some kids.

"Sorry, Ms. Potter," Tony said, slinging his book bag on one of the tables. "I skipped art class this week."

She'd make a difference for Tony.

"Yeah, I noticed." She smiled at him and handed him the cookie. "Why don't you grab some scratch paper and whatever you want to draw with. Then we can talk about a few things."

Tony nodded, a tentative smile on his lips. He shoved the cookie in his mouth and grabbed a box of colored pencils and some of the paper she had stacked around the room.

She wasn't sure how to begin, or where to begin for that matter. But for once she was going to trust herself. She was going to trust her instincts and her art and this kid's good heart and see what happened.

She took another step toward the edge of that cliff.

"MOM, I'M SORRY, I just can't make it tomorrow," Rebecca said into the receiver and then held the phone about five inches from her ear. It made her mother sound like Charlie Brown's teacher.

"That's two weeks in a row!"

"Mom—"

"You haven't been at the office."

"I did the work at home. Mom—"

"I can't ever seem to get a hold of you. I'm tired of—"

Rebecca couldn't get a word in edgewise and finally her top, usually secured with superglue, blew right off. "Mom, I can't come to dinner because I'm behind on the cards. I have an appointment at Tilton School about my at-risk kid's program and because I've had all I can take of the guilt you serve with your roast lamb." She felt dizzy, light-headed. "Which is always too dry, by the way." She added that comment for spite, but it still felt good.

The silence from her mother was eerie. "I see," she finally said.

Rebecca rolled her eyes. "I'm an adult, Mom."

"You don't act like one."

She almost proved it by hanging up, but instead she lowered her forehead to the edge of her desk and looked down at her tennis shoes. "Can we just call a truce? Please? I can come over Sunday evening."

"Are you on drugs?" Jane asked, and Rebecca jerked upright.

"What?"

"I read an article in the church bulletin about how drugs can alter a person's personality. And frankly, sweetheart, you've been acting so strange lately. You've been argumentative and difficult at work. You've been sullen on Friday nights. I'm just…" Jane sighed and it sounded like she might be fighting tears and Rebecca was so surprised, so absolutely shocked, that she could only blink and gape like a fish on dry land.

"I'm just worried that you're changing. You are not the little girl I thought you were."

Rebecca had a recurring dream in which every conversation she had with her mother was being taped, so that she could just roll back all the completely crazy things her mother said. Like this.

"Mom, not only am I not on drugs. But—" she shook her head, saddened a little for her mother that she was so out of touch with her "—I'm not a little girl. What you think is strange behavior, is just me trying to figure myself out."

"You're a Potter, sweetie. What is there to figure out?"

"Lots, Mom. Lots."

"This is your aunt's fault! You've spent too much time with her and all of her worst traits are rubbing off on you!"

"What are you talking about—"

"Flighty, unable to commit, unreliable…"

"Mom!" Rebecca yelled. "I won't listen to you talk that way about the one person in this family who supports me. I don't care how you feel about it. This is my life."

When her mother didn't reply, Rebecca swallowed hard. The edge of that cliff loomed ever closer.

"Well, I guess we won't be seeing you for supper."

"I guess not."

Jane hung up on her and Rebecca could only stare at the receiver and blink. Was this a good thing? Was this independence?

All she knew was it was a relief not to have to see her parents tomorrow night, and while part of her did feel bad about the tone of her mother's voice, she shrugged off the guilt as a bad habit.

Her meeting with the principal of Tilton School was in regard to using the school for her after-school programs. Her classes were getting too big for the studio over the café and the tension between Jane, Elle and Rebecca was getting worse, and Rebecca worried that the studio space might be adding fuel to the fire.

Rebecca decided to run down and give Elle a heads-up. Jane was on a warpath.

CHAPTER SIX

February 2—Friday

HIS EIGHT-YEAR-OLD daughter was getting the best of him. Sure, she was clever and smart, but Will was an adult, an officer of the law no less, and he couldn't get her to crack. Not an inch.

He parked his Jeep and tucked the Valentine's Day card into his pocket. The third card he'd found in his briefcase since Monday. The third card signed Secret Admirer.

There was no other person who had as much access to his briefcase as his daughter, except for Chief Brass, and Will seriously doubted Brass was the secret admirer.

Will stepped out into the cold, but that Valentine burned a hole in his pocket.

He didn't know what to do. He'd confronted Penny. He'd thanked her. He'd told her how sweet the cards were. He'd told her she shouldn't spend her allowance on such things— she'd looked a little pale at that—but she hadn't cracked.

"Dad," she'd said each time, as if he was the slow kid in class. "I'm not your secret admirer. I'm your daughter."

He was beginning to think he was losing his mind. Or at least the part that helped him control his child. He'd called his sister Elaine today and asked if she was behind this nonsense. She'd laughed and told him she didn't have time to get her husband a Valentine's Day card, much less drive across town to sneak three into his briefcase.

He stepped into the Cup, the heat and sugary sweet air filling his nose with wonderful smells. Sometimes he just wanted to live at the Cup, among the caffeine and baked goods. He'd even become immune to the increasing Valentine's Day decorations. They no longer pricked his pride, reminding him of what he'd lost. They were just crepe paper and bows.

"Hiya, Will," Elle said, her head popping up over the baked goods case. "You want to be my guinea pig?"

"Elle, I'm not signing up for the dateathon," he repeated for the hundredth time. She was like a bulldog.

"I know." She held up a flour-dusted hand. "Your loss, though. The town is going dateathon crazy! I can't believe who *has* signed up."

Has Rebecca? he almost asked. But that would have been ludicrous. He had no business asking after his daughter's teacher. She should be signed up. In fact, he found it rather unbelievable that such a beautiful woman wasn't already involved.

The mysterious card seemed heavy in his pocket.

I Found You When I Needed You, it said. The picture was of a woman holding an old magnifying glass over her eye, making it huge. It was cute, clever. A step above or away from the usual sappy holiday greetings. All the mystery cards had been like that.

"I've noticed the place is much more crowded these days. Is that all from the dateathon?"

"Hallelujah!" Elle laughed. "Love is in the air, Will. Now,

come here and try my new Valentine's Day cake. I'm going to serve it as part of the Valentine's Day party we're planning."

She lifted a beautiful dark chocolate cake dusted in red and pink sugars. He nearly groaned just looking at it. He'd been burying his lonely and lustful demons in the Cup's cakes and cookies. Maybe if he got fat and diabetic he'd stop thinking about Rebecca.

"Looks good, Elle." He took the cake. The first bite was gooey, fudgy. He couldn't even talk for a second.

"Good?" she asked with a laugh.

He groaned.

"That's what I like to hear."

"I'm going to go get Penny," he said around the mouthful of heaven.

"I'll heat up some soup for you to take home," Elle said and darted back into the small kitchen.

Will turned and found himself face-to-face with the card and journal display. The cards were just like the ones he'd been given, but he'd never noticed. When he'd seen them on Saturday he'd just been so depressed he'd barely seen how fun the cards were.

"Hey, Elle?"

"Yeah?"

He touched the edge of a card with a picture of a woman on a curb holding a pair of broken wings. *It Doesn't Work Without You,* the card read. "Who makes these cards?"

"My niece."

He turned so fast he knocked a stack of journals to the floor. He crouched, his pulse racing as he picked up the books. "Rebecca did these?"

"Yep." Elle pointed to the cards. "You like them?"

I love them, he thought, but only nodded. "She's something else," he murmured.

"Yes, she is," Elle said, serious and deep affection in her voice.

A million words rushed to his lips. Questions about Rebecca. About her past. About her life. Things he didn't have the nerve to ask her himself. Things that, should he ask, would open doors in his life. Doors he'd shut two years ago.

I'm confused, almost came to his lips. *I'm so confused.*

"You should go on up," Elle said quietly and for a moment he thought she was saying he should go up and ask Rebecca his questions.

"Right," he said. "Penny's waiting."

He started to climb the steps and thought he heard Elle mutter, "idiot" under her breath. But that wouldn't have made any sense.

PENNY PUSHED her feet into her boots. They pinched at the toes, because they were on the wrong feet but she ignored that. She pulled her hat down over her hair and shrugged into her jacket, all while keeping one eye on her father while he wrote Rebecca a check for more classes.

Becca was not smiling. At all.

And Dad couldn't even look at her.

Things were not going well.

"Dad, I'm going to go say hi to Elle!" She took off down the stairs before he could stop her.

"Elle!" she whispered as loud as she could. "Elle? Where are you?"

"Back here, Penny!" Elle came out of the bright kitchen wiping her hands on a towel. "What's wrong?"

"Everything!" she wailed and threw herself against Elle's legs. "The cards aren't working! Dad's acting weird and so is Ms. Potter and no one is laughing. Those cards are supposed to be funny!"

Elle bent down and kissed the top of her head, which was really nice. It was nice to be hugged by a lady who smelled like sugar.

"I know." Elle took her hand and walked her over to one of the tables. "Have a seat," she said and Penny climbed into one of the chairs, and Elle fixed her boots so they were on the right feet. "The problem is," she said, "your father and my niece are two of the most stubborn people I've ever met."

"What's stubborn?"

"Stubborn is when you only do things your way."

"That's Dad all right." She nodded remembering their fight last night over her eating salad. He wouldn't let her down from the table until she'd eaten the whole thing. She'd tried to sit there and not eat it, but finally she'd given up and eaten *all* the spinach. Just because Dad was stubborn.

"So what are we going to do?"

"We're going to have to step it up," Elle said.

Penny liked that Elle took this as seriously as she did. "Yeah," Penny repeated, not sure what she was saying. "Step it up."

"Here's the new plan…"

"SO THAT SHOULD COVER IT." Will slid the check across the desk rather than hand it to Rebecca. He couldn't risk an accidental touch. His body would explode at contact.

"Great, thanks, Will. I'll add her to the Tuesday class." She smiled, but it was without dimples, and the warmth was gone from her eyes. He had the sneaking suspicion that she was mad at him. But that didn't make any sense. What had he...?

Then he remembered.

He groaned and shut his eyes. "I just found out you make those cards downstairs."

"With my own two hands." She wiggled her fingers at him, her brown eyes dark against the pale silk of her skin.

"I'm sorry for what I said about..." He heaved a sigh. "About your cards. They are beautiful and just because I have a heart of coal doesn't make them any less special."

Her mouth dropped open for a split second and then she smiled. The good smile. With dimples and pink on her cheeks.

"It's okay. Valentine's Day isn't for everyone."

He laughed through his nose. "An understatement."

"Is it personal? This anti-Valentine's Day theme in your life or do you feel such disdain for all the lesser holidays?"

He blushed, charmed by her teasing. "My feelings for Arbor Day are murderous." They smiled at each other and then he realized he didn't want to joke about this. He wanted to tell her, to share some of what weighed him down.

"My wife left me on Valentine's Day two years ago."

She sucked in a quick breath and her forehead furrowed with sympathy. He braced himself for the outpouring of pity. The disingenuous empathy everyone pretended when they heard such a clichéd story of heartbreak.

"That will ruin a holiday," she said with a sensitive smile.

Her humor was so appreciated—so unexpected—he practically barked with laughter. The studio, with all its glass and bare tables and chairs, seemed at the moment like an unlikely cocoon. And he could easily understand why his daughter so loved this class. Why she so trusted this woman.

It wasn't the understated beauty of her eyes, or skin or hair. It was her heart—as visible and lovely as all those other things.

"You know what's funny? I used to love it." He sighed and leaned back against the table. "I went all out when Adele and I were dating. Huge surprises and trips, scavenger hunts, the whole nine yards. I kept doing it when we were married, but when things started falling apart I realized just how empty these gestures I was making really were. I was trying to be romantic, trying to put in the effort, hoping she would, too."

"But she didn't?"

"She did leave on Valentine's Day. That was a pretty big gesture." He was joking about this. Miraculous!

"I've been thinking about what you said on Saturday— about romance being work…" She toyed with the end of one of her pens and watched him through her lashes.

He nodded, surprised by how painless this conversation was. He'd just opened his mouth and talked. It was that easy, but he'd never done it before. Not with his sister, his parents, no one.

"And I've realized that you're right. It is work, but when the work is honest, it pays off in honest ways. Right? Why should romance or love be any different than anything else? You get out what you put in."

"I put in a lot," he murmured. "And I got left."

"I'm sorry, Will. You and Penny deserve so much more."

He nodded again and then shook off the glum feelings like a dog coming out of water. "What about you? Has Elle got you lined up for the dateathon?"

"No." Rebecca laughed, wrapping the oversize red

sweater that obscured her lovely shape, around her waist. "Though avoiding it's been tough."

"You've been too busy for Cupid to get a good bead on you?" he asked. Her lips twitched and she seemed suddenly very interested in making sure her pot of black ink lined up perfectly at the end of her paper.

"I know it can seem ridiculous to keep believing in things like romance," she murmured, giving the pot a half-rotation. "I'm starting a class for kids from broken homes, for crying out loud. My parents' marriage seems like a business negotiation and my two best friends, the two most vivacious and exciting women I've ever met are somehow alone." She quit toying with the pot and shrugged. "But I can't seem to stop myself. I believe in romance and love and roses and candlelight. I guess I have hope for Cupid, yet."

She looked up at him, and he felt skewered. As if that rascal Cupid had lanced him, right through the chest.

"Seems foolish, huh?" She'd turned her laughter on herself and he wanted to touch her. To take away that need for self-protection.

"I wish I felt that way," he said honestly and the cocoon grew smaller.

"But you don't," she murmured and her smile, so bright moments ago, turned sad at the edges. The cocoon broke open. They weren't alone in the world anymore. The demons and the past were crowding around them.

"I guess not," he said because it was safer to say that than it was to say *I want to* or *help me feel that way.*

"I better go make sure Penny isn't eating cake for dinner."

Rebecca nodded and he walked away into the dark doorway and the stairwell beyond.

"STUPID…jerk…coming here…" Rebecca fumed. "I tried and I got left," she mocked him totally out of self-preservation and because he was long gone and no one was in her studio to see her being an ass.

She threw paper into stacks that slid right off the edge of desks. She broke a pot and tried to mop up the spill of black ink with her best card stock. Finally, she just fisted her hair in her hands and screamed.

She had been making efforts. Real serious inroads on her crush. She'd been clipping and trimming him out of her head and he'd shown up tonight like some dejected Prince Charming with his broken heart on his sleeve.

She slapped her open palm against her forehead. "Stop it. Stop it. Stop it. Cupid grows up. Cupid doesn't have crushes."

She repeated it until she'd convinced herself that she believed it.

CHAPTER SEVEN

February 3—Saturday

SATURDAY EVENING rolled around and instead of getting through the piles of paperwork he'd stacked up on his dining room table, Will found himself driving through a winter storm to the Cup. Penny had forgotten her book bag at Rebecca's on Friday and according to the frantic phone call he'd just received from Penny—at her cousin's house for a sleepover—she needed the book bag *now*.

Truth be told, he was glad for the distraction.

He'd been staring blindly at the paperwork for close to an hour. The house seemed too quiet. The dark too thick. His loneliness too…relentless.

He pulled into the Cup. The low lights were visible through the steamy windows but the parking lot was empty. Made sense. Who would go out for cappuccino in one of the worst storms of the year?

Who would go out retrieving their daughter's book bag in the worst snowstorm of the year?

He couldn't lie. He knew the answer. Rebecca often worked Saturday evenings and those demons chugging around inside him hoped he might see her here. In this empty café. With the lights low.

He pushed open the door to the welcome chime of the small bell and stomped his feet before looking up to see if Rebecca was there.

"Hi, Will." Her voice carried through the café and his heart, mired in the past for two long years, started to break free.

She's here, those demons chanted. *She's right here.*

In fact, she was behind the counter, surrounded by paper and pens and the beautiful glow of candlelight, which he assumed she'd lit in case the power went out.

For a moment, the combined potency of her beauty, the empty café, the way he'd been thinking about her made him speechless.

"You lost in the snow?" She tilted her head and smiled.

"I followed the cookie crumbs," he managed to say and then wondered if that made any sense at all. But she laughed and he was able to breathe and walk. He stepped up to the counter.

"My daughter left her book bag here last night. She needs it right now." He mimicked Penny, and Rebecca laughed. Her hair fell over her shoulder, a shimmering curtain of red and gold and glitter.

Touch it, the demons howled. *Just reach out and touch it!*

"We can go up and see—" She began to stand, but he put his hand on her shoulder to stop her. The thrill that ran up his arm and into his chest surprised and delighted him at the same time.

He was playing with fire. He knew that. He'd made it clear to her that he had nothing to offer a woman, but he still insisted on flirting, on standing in this dark room with possibility burning around them.

"There's no rush," he said, despite the fact that he'd rushed out into a storm to get the dumb bag. The idea of leaving her and this place seemed ludicrous.

She shrugged. "Okay, then can I get you something to drink?"

"Absolutely." He nodded and pulled up a stool and sat.

"The Potter Special?" Her eyes twinkled and he nodded.

"As long as it's not good for me, yes. The Potter Special should do the trick."

"I actually specialize in the not-good-for-you stuff." She turned away to the old espresso machine on the counter behind her. She began turning knobs and making noise and he didn't stop himself from studying her.

She was tall. He liked that. She stood straight. Her back an unbending line under the burgundy shirt she wore. Her hips were round, her legs long.

She was lovely to him in every possible way.

"Here we go," she said, a mug mounded with whipped cream in her hand. "Roughly all your daily calories in one mug."

Like a guilty fifteen-year-old, he accepted the mug and took a big sip. The tastes of caramel, cocoa, hot coffee and whipped cream exploded in his mouth.

"Good God," he said, looking down at the concoction. "That's fantastic."

"Told you. I'm thinking of getting it patented."

"Let me know if you need testimonials—" He smiled but she seemed serious.

"Actually, I could use a testimonial." She cleared her throat. "I'm trying to write a press release to send to area papers about my class for at-risk kids—"

"I'm glad to hear you're finally doing it."

"Thanks." Her smile was a flash of lightning in the darkened room. "Thanks for the encouragement. But I thought a quote from the county juvenile parole officer in my press release might make me sound official."

"It would be my pleasure. I had a meeting with Tony DeLona's folks today and urged them to seek your help with Tony."

"I had a talk with him after school the other day and his mom called this afternoon. Tony will be my first student."

"And Penny. You've made such progress with her."

"You know, it's so funny how simple it seems right now. You just listen to kids. You just let them talk or draw and you listen to what they need to say. It's astounding how few people really do that."

"It's not just kids." He smiled. "Sometimes it feels like no one listens to anyone anymore. We're all just waiting for our turn to talk."

"Not me," Rebecca laughed. "I'd much rather listen to you talk than bore you with whatever I might have to say."

"Don't sell yourself short, Rebecca. I bet you've got lots to say."

Their conversation ended in silence, and her gaze clung to his, and he, cowardly and dumb, looked away in order to break the intimacy.

"You…ah…working on more valentines?" He gestured at the red and pink card stock on the counter.

"Sort of." She chewed on her lip. "They're valentines for the other people in your life. You know? The people you forget to tell how you feel."

"Show me. I need something for Chief Brass."

She laughed and the heat of attraction between them dissipated, only to come back as her laugh ended in more silence.

Jeez, it's hot in here.

He set the mug down and took the cards she handed him.

"The first one is inspired by Penny," she said, without any of the shyness he sort of expected from her.

Will was speechless. She'd captured the spirit of his daughter in the sketch of a girl wearing a dance recital costume over blue jeans.

"You are my wonder, kid," he whispered the tag line, then swallowed the hard lump of emotion in his throat. His emotional reaction to the card, to the drawing and the sentiment caught him off guard.

"That's the best valentine I've ever seen," he told her. "Can I buy it?"

She shook her head. "I had intended to give it to you so you could give it to Penny. I sort of thought it was perfect for the two of you."

"It is," he breathed. Before he could get any more emotional he flipped to the second card.

The sketch was of a woman, who looked slightly like Rebecca. Like a quieter, rounded version of her and he wondered if that was how she saw herself, without the beauty of her smile, the sturdy grace of her shoulders. Without the sparkle he saw.

He wanted to change that. Badly.

In the drawing she was getting a kick in the butt.

"Dear valentine, you make me a better person," he read and smiled. "I'm quite familiar with the kick in the butt method of friendship."

"Most people are, that's why I thought it would work."

"Hey." He pointed at her tiny signature. "You signed it." She nodded. "I thought it was time."

"I agree. These cards are amazing. Really, Rebecca. You're amazing…"

For a second his words hung in the air, and he realized he couldn't cover them up. He couldn't pretend to have meant something else. He was forced to be honest, by his own loose tongue.

"You really are," he finished in a low voice.

"Thank you," she whispered. Her gaze met his and held. He couldn't pretend this moment wasn't happening. He wanted it to happen.

"You're giving me a vibe, right?" she asked. "I'm not making this up?"

He smiled at her blunt honesty. It was so refreshing. "No," he murmured. "This is real."

He wanted Rebecca to walk around the counter, and she did. He didn't flinch when her warm hand touched his face, his cheek, his ear.

"I'm stepping off a cliff," she whispered.

In the end he didn't know who kissed whom. They both leaned through the sweet smelling air and came to rest against each other.

Her lips were strong and sweet, like the rest of her and he turned his head, angling for more. Her fingers brushed his hair, his neck and the curve of his ear and he groaned.

Will stood, sliding his hands up her rib cage to her breasts and she leaned against him, soft and warm in all the best places.

While he'd certainly never forgotten how good it felt to

make out with a woman, he'd never dreamed how wonderful it would be to make out with Rebecca.

She tugged a little on his hair and pressed her hips harder against his. He wanted to lock the doors and spend the next several days kissing her.

"Will," she sighed.

He kissed his way down the pure white column of her neck.

"Will," she moaned.

His thumb grazed her breast and—

"Will." She pushed him away. Her eyes golden reflections of everything he felt. She laughed, nervously. "Someone could walk in…"

"Right." He swallowed, tried hard to catch his breath, but it was impossible with her so close and so suddenly irresistible. He reached for her and she for him, and they were kissing again, desperate this time for the touch of skin.

"Will!"

"I know…" He kissed her eyes. Her cheeks. "I know. We need to stop."

"Yes." She slid her hands across his ribs.

"We're going to stop."

"One more…"

"Yes…"

He hadn't felt this way since he was a teenager. He wanted to laugh and then suddenly he was. He practically giggled, madly into her hair. And so did she.

"This is crazy."

"You make me feel crazy." He pushed her away slightly. Removed his hand from under her shirt, from the soft, sweet skin he'd claimed as his own.

"Crazy good?" she asked, shy in the candlelight.

He blinked at her, unable to understand how she could turn him inside out.

"Crazy confused," he told her, sanity returning. What had he been thinking? Well, he hadn't, but still. This was his daughter's teacher, a woman he liked and respected. He had no business pulling her into his quicksand.

He blinked the passion from his eyes and saw the giddy warmth drain from hers. Her face went still and the distance, the mere inches between them, grew cavernous.

"Rebecca…"

"The next words out of your mouth had better not be I'm sorry." Her voice, while soft, was edged with steel.

She'd read his mind so he remained silent.

The rustle of her clothes as she stepped away from him seemed ominous.

"What's amazing here," she said, "is that I'm surprised." She walked back around the counter, as if the kissing hadn't happened, like she was erasing it. "I should have known."

"I'm just not ready…"

She shot him an acidic look that shut him right up.

"Be a grown-up, Will. Be honest with yourself. If you are ready to put your hand up my shirt, you're further along in the healing process than you want to admit."

Her words were a slap, and he could only step back and blink. He opened his mouth, unsure of what was going to come out, unsure of what lie or truth would reveal more of himself, but she held up her hand, stopping him.

"For weeks I've been calling what I felt for you a crush." She smiled tightly and his whole chest shrunk an inch. "I thought that by giving my feelings a cute little label, I could minimize them. Make them something sweet, almost laughable." She shook her head. "But I think I knew the moment you came in that first day with the crayons for Penny that you would outgrow any label I might make for you. And—" she took a deep breath "—I think I knew that no matter what, I was going to get hurt."

"I don't want to hurt you." He nearly leaped over the counter.

"I know." Her laugh was rusty. "It's why I like you. But I can't be your rebound. I can't be your first step back into the world, if you're going to try to minimize what you feel for me."

"I'm not—" He started to deny it, but her eyebrows shot up, and he shut up. He'd been about to apologize for the kiss, when his mouth was still damp from hers. If that wasn't minimizing what had occurred he didn't know what was.

"I'm not saying I love you. I don't know you well enough for that, but I do want to know you better. And that can't happen if you're too scared to try love again. If every kiss is going to be a mistake. Something to apologize for."

She'd reduced him to a puddle, a spineless glop of human fear and insecurity. Worse, one with nothing to say.

"Let me go see if Penny's bag is upstairs," she whispered. "You better get home before the storm gets any worse."

She walked away and left Will wondering how things could get any worse.

REBECCA STEPPED into her dark classroom, shut the door behind her and pressed the back of her head to the wood. She pressed harder. A solid reality at her back in what seemed like a world turned upside down.

Will was everything she thought she wanted and she'd turned him away.

"I'm a lunatic," she whispered into her silent studio. "Totally nuts." She laughed just to prove it.

But he doesn't deserve me.

She repeated the words to herself just to make sure they sunk in.

He doesn't deserve me. Not like that. Bumbling and sorry.

It never would have occurred to her a few weeks ago. She would have let him apologize after kissing her and the next time she'd seen him she would have died a thousand deaths wondering what he thought of her. And maybe in a few weeks when they'd be alone again she'd let him kiss her in some quiet moment when Penny wasn't watching and it would happen all over again.

But she was a grown-up. And so was he.

And she deserved better.

"Growing up sucks!" she muttered and grabbed the pink Barbie book bag in Penny's cubby.

CHAPTER EIGHT

February 7—Wednesday

"I'M INTRIGUED," Lucky said, pushing open the door to the studio. Elle was behind her, drying her hands on a rag slung over her shoulder. Rebecca was so glad to see them, glad and nervous. "The unveiling of your new cards. I can only hope they're better than the last ones."

"They'd better be—people are getting antsy for some cards. You're going to miss your opportunity to make money if you wait any longer to restock us," Elle said, clearly a little piqued by the situation. "Valentine's Day is a week away."

"Well, the wait is over." Rebecca handed them each twenty cards she'd slaved over the past five days. She had another ten waiting in case they really liked what they saw.

"These are…different." Lucky looked up from the cards.

"Okay, so far I've got different and…" She waited for Elle, who was still paging through the pile Rebecca had given her.

She paged past *Daughter, you make my heart sing,* with the picture of the Opera Heart. And *Son, you're the best thing that's happened to me,* with the picture of the man in a diamond mine.

"They're good," Elle finally said.

"Good, how? Good okay? Good like the best thing ever?" Rebecca chewed her lip. These women were supposed to be her friends. Where were the backflips, the hugs, the…

"They're different brilliant," Elle said, her smile huge. "They are different amazing."

"Are you lying?" Rebecca asked, skeptical of her aunt who, while a classy woman, was known to fudge the truth to suit the occasion. "Is she lying?" Rebecca asked Lucky.

"Nope." Lucky tucked the cards into her bag. "They are valentines for the other loves in your life. They'll be huge. You better start working on some more, I'm going to sell out of these in about four minutes."

Rebecca flung her arms out and laughed. "Wonderful. Great." She took a deep breath and finally, once and for all, finished the metamorphosis she'd started a week ago. In seven short days she'd shed all of the old Rebecca Potter. And now she was going to prove it.

It was painful, especially when the memories of Will's kisses came over her like a wave. Late at night she relived every touch, every sigh and heartbeat and wondered if someone else would ever make her feel so alive. So cherished and wanted.

She didn't know, but she owed it to herself to find out.

"Elle—" she braced herself "—sign me up for the dateathon."

February 8—Thursday

AFTER ART CLASS, while Dad was paying for their soups and sandwiches to take home, Elle pulled Penny into the storage room.

"I'm just borrowing your daughter for a second," Elle told Dad with a wave.

"Don't break her," he said, which would have been funny if Penny wasn't totally mad at him right now.

The storeroom door shut behind them.

"It didn't work!" they both said at the same time.

"What happened?" Elle asked.

"I don't know," Penny muttered. "He came here on Saturday night and got my bag but now…"

"Now things are worse!" Elle crossed her arms over her chest and sat down on a green crate. "Becca signed up for the dateathon."

Penny gasped. Becca was going to date someone else?

"Do you think they got in a fight?" Penny asked, remembering the fights Mom and Dad used to have. When things would break and Mom would leave for a day. She couldn't imagine Becca acting like that, but maybe she was wrong. Maybe she was wrong about the whole thing.

"No." Elle shook her head. "Becca's not much of a fighter. But I think something must have happened between them. It's like the arctic every time they're in the same room."

"So what should we do?"

Elle tapped her finger against her lips for a long minute. Penny got bored waiting and counted all the bottles of chocolate syrup on the shelf behind Elle's head. Ten bottles. That was a lot of chocolate syrup.

"I think it's time for us to step back," Elle said. "Let them figure things out for themselves."

"But Valentine's Day is only a week away!" Penny cried. "Dad hates Valentine's Day. He gets so sad. I want him to be happy this year."

Elle pulled her close for a hug. "How can he not be happy? He's got the sweetest daughter ever."

She rolled her eyes like Alyssa. "But I wanted him to have a girlfriend this year. I wanted him to be in love with Ms. Potter."

"Well, they're just going to have to do it themselves." Elle opened the door, ending their little talk, but Penny knew better. Leaving things up to Dad was a bad idea.

Penny waited until they were in the car heading home before she said anything. She'd learned something watching Mom and Dad fight for so long. You had to be careful not just of what you said, but *when* you said it. So she waited until Dad was humming along with the radio and his fingers were tapping against the steering wheel.

"Ms. Potter signed up for the dateathon," she said, pretending to play with the vent, but really she watched her dad from the corner of her eye.

"What?" Dad asked. They swerved a little, like he was trying not to hit something in the road.

"Elle told me Ms. Potter signed up for the dateathon and she's already really popular. Her Web site has gotten tons of hits."

"Tons?"

"Cool, huh?" Penny said, finally looking at her dad. "She should have a boyfriend."

He nodded. "Sure," he said and fiddled with the radio.

Penny turned her head to the window so he wouldn't see her smile.

February 9—Friday

"THANK YOU, WILL," Rebecca said, reading the quote he'd given her for her press release. He held his breath like some kind of lovelorn suitor. Which was ridiculous considering he'd smashed that option to pieces on Saturday. But when his daughter had told him about Becca joining the dateathon… Well, he hadn't slept at all last night. He'd written a quote for her, something he could have called her with, but no. He'd dropped his daughter off at his folks' house and now, here he was sweating through his shirt just to drop off a piece of paper.

"That's an incredibly generous quote." She swallowed, and he watched the smooth motion. *Why have I turned her away? Why am I such a coward?*

He'd spent the better part of last night trying to imagine asking her out on a date. And that was fine. Imaginary dates always went well. It was what would happen after six months of dating, when she'd get tired of his late hours. When he'd be the only one making the effort to keep them together. What would happen when he realized again that he had no idea how to keep a woman happy?

"I'll send that on to—"

"I heard you joined the dateathon," Will interrupted and Rebecca's eyes went wide.

She nodded. "I did."

He didn't know what to say. "Is it working out?" he finally managed to ask.

"So far so good."

Don't kiss anyone, he wanted to say. *Don't let those men touch your skin, or hold you close. They don't deserve it.*

"Is there anything else?" she asked.

"No." He shook his head. "We'll see you on Thursday."

He walked out to the Jeep, but couldn't get into it. He couldn't drive to his parents' house and pretend that everything was okay. Hot despite the gently falling snow gathering on the ground, he unzipped his jacket. He felt feverish. Restless.

He needed to walk.

After Adele had left he'd walked and walked until one day the decision to leave South Carolina and the home they'd made seemed easy. Seemed right.

He imagined Rebecca on a date at the Valentine's Day party that Elle had planned, waiting, eyes sparkling as she waited for her dream man to walk through the door.

A dream man who wasn't him.

He knew love existed. His parents, his brothers and sister were all proof of that—proof that love was possible between two people who worked at it.

Rebecca was the opposite of Adele. She was dependable, considerate and empathetic, probably to a fault. Sort of like him.

He stopped in his tracks.

She worked at relationships. Like him. Enjoyed the window-dressings of romance—the way he used to. Maybe the trick to a successful relationship was choosing a person who wouldn't require him to do all the work.

Rebecca Potter would meet him in the middle. He knew it.

He picked up his pace, zipped up his coat and walked.

He walked until his decision, scary and troublesome, was easy. Right.

He would be Rebecca's dream man.

February 10—Saturday

THE CUP was filled to the brim and Rebecca was working her tail off. The high school chess club seemed to have become regular devotees of the café and Rebecca cheerfully steamed up plenty of Potter Specials for the boys and served up the last of the Chocolate Valentine's Day cakes.

They whispered and huddled in the corner over a laptop and when Rebecca brought the last of their order she finally gave in to temptation.

"Hey, can you show me how to check my site?" she asked the boy sitting in front of the keyboard. He seemed to be their leader. "Max explained it to me, but I blanked out."

"Sure," the boy said. "You just need to remember your passwords."

That wasn't hard. Rebecca had the same passwords to everything in her life. She typed them in when the kid told her to and her page, with the drawing she'd made of herself, appeared on the screen.

"Thirteen hits!" one of the kids yelled. "Damn, Ms. Potter, you're hot!"

She smiled, torn between pleasure and the stifling regret of knowing none of those hits were from the man she really wanted. "Yes, I am, boys. I am hot." She smiled at them and headed back to the counter.

"Don't you want to check them out?" the boy at the keyboard asked.

"Maybe later," she said, without much heart.

Her life had taken a strange turn the past few days. Principal May at Tilton had been eager for her to teach her class at his school and she could move her program anytime. But she hated having to tell Elle that she was leaving. She hated leaving. But her mother was becoming nasty about the informal agreement Rebecca and Elle had regarding the rental of the space.

And if she needed added incentive, she'd been interviewed by the paper, and the story had come out this morning. It was supposed to be a story about the class for kids from broken homes, but it had turned into a sort of tell-all, about her cards and her after-school program.

It was an article about her.

Front page, full color.

She'd cringed and laughed off everyone's compliments over the photo but in reality had been secretly pleased by the way the photographer had made it appear as if she didn't have a double chin.

Secretly she'd been pleased about all of it.

"I need two hot cocoas," she told Lorna, who was helping out today. Rebecca turned her back to the bar to dump some dirty dishes in the buckets and the bell over the door rang.

Her whole body went cold. Then hot. Every muscle tight.

It was Saturday and Will and Penny usually came on Saturday. She would turn around and see him and it wouldn't be a big deal, because she was getting over her feelings for him.

She was.

Except she couldn't turn around.

"Coffee to go," she heard Chief Brass say, and she sighed in relief.

Getting over Will wasn't going to happen overnight. It would just take time.

February 13—Tuesday

WILL STARED blankly at the sign on the door of Rebecca's studio.

"Dad," Penny tugged on his hand. "I told you classes are canceled this week."

"I know, but why?" he asked. The cold, clear message on his answering machine today hadn't given him any good indication.

Sorry, guys. Classes canceled this week. We will start again next week same time, but in the Tilton School cafeteria, she'd said.

"And where is she now?" he asked his daughter who shrugged. He'd just spent the weekend figuring out his feelings for Rebecca and now he couldn't find her to tell her.

"Why'd they move classes?" he asked, before his daughter could answer his first question.

"I told you I didn't know in the car. What is wrong with you, Dad?"

Elle breezed past them looking like a woman with a bone to pick. He'd never seen her look quite so angry and wondered if maybe now wasn't the time, but Penny stepped in when he needed her.

"Hey, Elle? Where's Ms. Potter?" Penny asked and Elle turned to face them.

"I think she might stupidly be trying to talk some sense into her mother."

"Is everything okay?" Will asked. He put his hand on Elle's shoulder, which was up around her ear.

"It's fine." She managed a smile. "My sister is getting the best of me, as usual. But that's nothing for you guys to worry about. Are you here for dinner? I have some leftover wraps."

"Sure," Will said. "Is Rebecca coming back tonight?"

"I don't know. She might be back to pack her things." She went on to explain that Rebecca would no longer be renting the studio.

Suddenly the Cup O' Love didn't have as much appeal as it had when he knew Rebecca was upstairs working on her valentines.

"Dad?" Penny pulled on his hand. "What's wrong? You look funny."

"I do?" He smiled and then started laughing. He'd thought his Cupid had been killed two years ago. Run down by a red convertible, but as he thought about Rebecca's Valentines he was struck by an arrow.

"Dad, you're being weird."

"Hey, Elle, we're just going to head home. You still having that Valentine's Day party tomorrow night?"

"That's the plan."

"We'll see you there."

A slow smile creased her face. "You finally coming to your senses, Will Blakely?"

A blush burned his cheeks. Elle didn't miss much and he wasn't as good at hiding his feelings as he'd thought.

"Looks like it." He grinned.

"Will someone please tell me what's going on," Penny howled.

He looked down at his daughter. "I need your help tonight, kiddo. We've got lots of work to do."

"With what?"

"We're going to make a valentine for Rebecca."

IT WAS MIDNIGHT, and Becca packed the last of the finger-paints into the milk crate Elle had loaned her.

This is good, she reminded herself. *This is change and growth. The program can only get bigger.*

But it didn't make her feel any better about leaving her safe haven above the Cup. She loved this room with the huge windows and creaky floors. She even loved the draft that swept up the stairs anytime anyone opened the front door to the Cup.

She loved what kids had made here. What *she'd* made here.

"Onward and upward." She grabbed the milk crate and spun toward the door to come face-to-face with her mother.

"Jeez, Mom." She set the crate back down and put a hand over her leaping heart. "You scared me."

"Sorry."

Jane continued to stand in the doorway, her handbag in front of her like a shield.

"Did you need something?" Rebecca asked, unable to help her haughty tone.

Jane swallowed, opened her mouth and then shut it, and Becca sighed with weary frustration.

Don't apologize, she reminded herself. *You haven't done anything wrong. You're just living your life.*

"I saw the article in the paper today."

Rebecca braced herself for her mother's censure.

"It was good," she said and coughed awkwardly. "Enlightening."

"Thank you." Rebecca wondered if maybe she'd slipped down a rabbit hole.

"Mom—"

"I need to buy a Valentine's Day card," Jane finally said. "A few actually."

Rebecca took a moment to let the world settle back on its axis.

"You want one of my Valentine's Day cards?" She had to ask, just to be sure.

"I hear they're the best."

Rebecca smiled. That would matter to Mom. But still she recognized an olive branch when she saw one. "You can judge for yourself."

She grabbed the stack of "almost perfects" from the top of the milk carton. She'd rejected these cards because of little errors or ink splatter, but she hadn't had the heart to throw them away. Now she was reluctant to show them to her mother. She wished, desperately, she was handing over her very best work.

Her mother slid her purse onto her wrist and took the cards, and Rebecca, as much as she wished she could be indifferent, got very nervous.

She was eight years old again bringing home an art project for her mother's opinion.

She's going to hate them.

"They're lovely," Jane said. She looked up at Rebecca with a smile. A real smile. One that lit her eyes and put dimples in her cheeks. "Very special." She cleared her throat. "Like you. I don't tell you that enough."

Tears flooded Rebecca's eyes. It had been years since she'd felt the balm of her mother's good opinion, and she'd thought she'd outgrown the need—but here she was twenty-seven years old and nearly crying over her mother's compliment.

Her mom heaved a big breath. "Your aunt came in today and made me realize what I was trying to do to you, and while I am saddened that you don't want to work full-time at the firm, I understand and…respect what you're doing for kids and for yourself. I should have told you that long ago."

Thank you, Aunt Elle.

"Thank you, Mom." Rebecca finally said, her voice a scratch and whisper in the quiet studio.

"So," Jane said, opening the clutch on her purse. "How much do I owe you for these cards."

"They're not really for sale. They're my mistakes."

"They're perfect," her mother said. "How much do I owe you?"

Rebecca thought of Elle, of the way she did battle for Rebecca at every turn. It was time to return the favor.

"You can't buy them from me," Rebecca said. "You have to buy them downstairs at the Cup."

Jane blinked. "It's closed."

Rebecca nodded and smiled sympathetically at her mother, knowing what apologizing cost the proud woman. "You'll have to come in tomorrow and buy them from Aunt Elle."

Jane looked at her a long time and Rebecca looked right back. She felt so sure of herself, the ground beneath her feet these days was firm and steady and not even her mother could change that.

Finally Jane nodded. "I can do that," she said.

"I know you can, Mom." Rebecca picked up the box again. "Help me with the door, would you?"

Valentine's Day

REBECCA OPENLY STARED at Elle and Max all but making out at one of the café tables and couldn't stop smiling.

Her aunt had finally succumbed to Cupid and it was perfect! Between Mom showing up today and the very public display of affection going on over there, Elle's Valentine's Day was turning up roses.

"Well." Rebecca tapped at the dangling pink string of one of the red balloons that covered the ceiling. "I'm glad one of us is getting what we deserve," Rebecca murmured.

The whole dateathon idea was a success. All the tables were filled with people making small talk and trying not to stare at each other too long.

And the whole café was abuzz with Lucky's brave and bold move. The fact that Rebecca couldn't reach her on her cell phone or at the store was all the proof she needed that Lucky and Cupid had come to an understanding, too.

It was adorable.

And threatened to have Rebecca bawling her eyes out.

She'd looked at all thirteen of her hits the other day and not one of the men had seemed worth the time it would take for her to shave her legs and put on real clothes and pretend to forget Will Blakely for the span of an evening.

I'm gonna kill Cupid, the little bastard, if I see him, Rebecca thought, nursing her battered heart with wine made from some sour grapes.

"Hey, Ms. Potter?" Rebecca leaned over the counter to see Penny Blakely dressed in head to toe red, including a crown made out of plastic rubies.

"Wow, that's some crown," Rebecca said.

"Thank you, I was the Queen of Hearts for Halloween last year," Penny said.

"I'll bet you were a fantastic Queen of Hearts." Rebecca smiled at the charming little girl. Part of losing Will to his own cowardice was the pain of losing a little of Penny, too. Rebecca had spent some time fantasizing about what a happy family they'd make. She could have taken Penny into the Art Institute and—

"This is for you," Penny said, holding out a piece of folded red construction paper.

"Thanks, sweetie, but you've already given me your valentine, remember?"

"It's not from me," Penny said with a huge smile.

The construction paper was rough in her fingers, heavy in her hand. She looked at the folded card like it was a loaded gun.

"Are you going to open it?" Penny asked, bouncing on her tiptoes. Her crown slipped over one eye, and she impatiently shoved it back.

"Sure," she said, but didn't. She wasn't an idiot, something was happening here. This was a moment.

Finally she opened the card. Guessed she had it upside down and turned it over, but that didn't help the drawing much.

"You had it right the first time," Penny said. "Dad is a very bad drawer."

Joy and disbelief bubbled in her throat.

The drawing was of a stick man—covered in arrows, so many she thought initially it was a porcupine.

You got me, the caption read.

"Penny," she asked, unable to take her eyes from the crude black crayon drawing. "Where's your dad?"

Penny giggled and did a full pirouette—and Rebecca laughed, knowing exactly how she felt.

"He's upstairs in your old studio." She came close and whispered, "He's waiting for you!"

"Then I better go get him," she whispered back and leaned down to kiss the girl's cheek. "Thank you, Penny."

"Go already!" Elle cried and Rebecca looked up to realize that the whole café was watching her. Instead of panicking, instead of shrinking and freaking out, she made a bow, untied her apron and ran up the stairs.

A pink piece of construction paper was taped to the outside of her door.

Beware, it read, *Cupid On The Loose.*

There were pictures of Cupids in the corners of the paper. Penny had drawn them; Rebecca knew because she could tell what they were.

She took a deep breath and pushed open the door.

And gasped.

It was a cloudy twilight, dark and gloomy so the lit candles set on the floors, stood out in beautiful relief. So did the roses that had been stuffed in an oversize olive jar.

Tears blurred her eyes and it took her a second to find the man responsible, but he stood by the windows, his hands in his pockets.

His hair was smoothed back.

He looked nervous.

"Hi," he said with a silly little waist-high wave. He immediately put his hand back in his pocket and cleared his throat.

He was nervous.

Her heart started to beat erratically. Oh, what a man.

"You, uh… You're standing on your next valentine." He pointed to her feet, and she realized that scattered across the floor were a few more folded pieces of pink and red construction paper.

One was mashed under her tennis shoe.

She lifted her foot and grabbed the card.

I had no idea how cold I was without you, it said. But she couldn't tell what…

"That's me in an iceberg." Will told her. "I'm not much for drawing. But Penny did that one…" He pointed to a pink piece of paper and Rebecca bent to pick it up, and the tears she didn't fully realize she'd shed fell in big round blobs on the paper.

This is us now, the card read. *This is us with you.*

The picture was of the three of them, Penny, Will and Rebecca, all wrapped up in winter coats but there were no tears. There were big smiles and sparkles in the air. A dog with a spot over his eye with a big long tongue sat on Penny's foot. Will and Rebecca were holding hands.

"Will…" She covered her mouth with a trembling hand. "Will, what are you doing?"

"It's not me," he murmured, the tips of his ears red and his eyes filled with a raw mix of emotions. She knew what it had cost him to put himself out there like this. But his blue eyes gleamed with happiness.

"Cupid made me do it," he said with a shrug.

She swallowed…opened her mouth to say something

funny or clever. Something that would take away his nerves. But no words would be as effective as what she really wanted.

So she closed the distance between them, picking up the rest of the cards, until hands and heart were full, she stood right in front of him.

"You want to go out to dinner sometime?" he asked and she tipped her head back and laughed.

"Why not?"

"Want to meet my family?" he asked.

"Want to meet mine?" She grimaced and he touched the side of her face, an electric brush.

"I want everything. Your family, your success. Your funny heart. Your beautiful skin…"

It was too much. It was everything she'd ever wanted from Valentine's Day and a hundred times more. She almost couldn't take any more so she reached up on her tiptoes and kissed him, stemming his lovely words.

He breathed into her mouth, a soft huff of relief and his arms came around her, holding her tight.

They would go slow, she knew. He still carried some scars from his first marriage, but she had every intention of staying well within reach of Will Blakely.

"Happy Valentine's Day, Cupid," he whispered across her skin.

"Happy Valentine's Day, Love God."

PENNY SHOWED OFF her crown to Elle and Max. Max was a nice guy. She liked the way he looked at Elle, the way he kept touching her arm and her shoulder. It was nice. She hoped her dad was doing the same thing with Ms. Potter.

"Hey," she said, "do I get to call Ms. Potter Becca, now?" she asked.

Elle nodded. "I imagine you can." Elle crossed her legs and leaned in close. "What did you do, Penny?"

"With what?"

"With your dad. After I said that we should just give up and let them figure it out for themselves. You must have done something."

Penny thought about it. But in the end she took what was left of Max's chocolate cake and grinned at Elle.

"Nothing. It was Cupid, Elle. It was Cupid all along."

A heartfelt thanks to Laura Shin,
who never gave up on me.

LUCKY IN LOVE
Susan Floyd

Dear Reader,

Usually, writing is an isolating endeavor. Not with this anthology! Writing with Deb and Molly was an energetic, creatively exhilarating experience, from the conception of the stories to the final read through. As team leader, Deb kept us all on track and Molly (with Mick, in utero and out) provided the time line that got us to Valentine's Day. Finally, the creative generosity of Melinda Curtis set the tone for this lively immersion into Fenelon Falls.

Now that Elle and Becca have found their Valentine's sweethearts, time is running out for Lucky to make the good pastor Josh Watts see the light. Will Josh come around to realize that Lucky is the best thing in his life or will she have to take out that contract on Cupid?

I love to hear from readers and can be reached at P.O. Box 2883, Los Banos, CA 93635.

Enjoy!

Susan Floyd

PROLOGUE

New Year's Eve

LUCKY SHIVERED in the crisp night air as she waited for Josh in front of Fenelon Falls Community Church, a small steepled building on a hill just walking distance from the slowly reviving downtown. From the front steps, she gazed at the Christmas lights that seemed to make Main Street glow. The town's huge Christmas tree was lit from thick trunk to the very top, where a giant handmade star remained balanced, though winter winds whipped through the small town. Fenelon Falls had never looked so lovely, and Lucky felt her heart expand with love for the place she lived in. In a few days, those lights would be taken down and the Christmas tree cut up for firewood. But for now, everything was perfect.

She fumbled in her pocket, her gloved hands feeling for the ring box. She and Josh had been best friends for nearly twenty years. And for months now, Lucky had mulled this step over, looking at the situation from every aspect. Finally she had made the decision to hand her heart to him.

At Christmas, she'd given Josh a real kiss under the mistletoe. Not just the peck of a best friend, but a real, heartfelt kiss that had ended up embarrassing both of them because of the passion that had flared between them. Lucky had decided that was a good sign, even though Josh had looked shaken. Tonight, she was taking their relationship to the next, logical level. He'd always been there for her and she wanted a piece of paper that would tell him she would always be there for him. Always—for better or worse, for richer or poor. Becca, one of her best girlfriends, had some concerns. Elle on the other hand, had been nothing but encouraging. If it felt right, she said, Lucky should do it.

"Gorgeous night, isn't it?" Josh said in her ear, startling her so much she dropped the box.

As Lucky reached for it, he did, too. He was faster, retrieving the blue velvet box out of the snow. "What's this?" he asked, his eyes teasing her. "Something for me?"

Lucky wanted to deny it, but instead she looked away, as her body underwent a very premature hot flash.

"Oooh," Josh said, with a knowing glint in his eyes. "It *is* for me. You know how much I love presents."

"Josh, give it back." Lucky had changed her mind. She didn't want to do this now.

Josh pretended to open it.

"Josh, please. Give that to me."

"What is it, Luck? Another pair of cuff links?"

"I only got you that one pair." She defended herself. "How was I supposed to know that you needed a special kind of dress shirt to wear them with?"

"If it *is* for me, let me open it." He'd turned serious.

Lucky bit her lip. It was now or never. She nodded because her voice wouldn't work.

Josh opened the box and then stared at the ring. "What's this?" His voice was gruff.

"It's a ring." Lucky could barely get the words out.

"I can tell it's a ring," Josh replied. "What's it for?"

Lucky couldn't look at him. Why was this so embarrassing? It was Josh. They shared everything, even toothbrushes on occasion. So with her gaze firmly on her boots, she blurted, "Do you want to marry me?"

Josh didn't reply for such a long time that Lucky raised her head to see he was staring out at the town.

"You don't have to answer right away," she added. "You can take your time to think about it."

Josh closed his eyes, and Lucky felt her stomach cramp with dread. The Christmas kiss had been a fluke. But then he moved closer to her and under the clear night sky, with a million stars glittering above them, he kissed her, deeply and thoroughly. Lucky's heart felt big and full. He loved her. He loved her.

The kiss ended, and Josh pushed himself away from her. "I can't." The words seemed wrenched from him.

He was joking, right? Her mouth still tingled with the touch of his lips, the urgency in his kiss. She tried to close the distance, but he stepped back.

"Surely this isn't a surprise?" Lucky asked.

He shook his head. "I'm sorry."

"Sorry? What's there to be sorry about?"

"I can't, Lucky."

"What do you mean you can't?" she asked teasingly, trying to put her arms around him. "That word isn't part of your vocabulary."

She watched the red creep up Josh's strong neck. How well she knew that neck. She'd held on to it during her first slow dance at the Freshman Twilight Prom. And after her parents had been killed in a head-on collision with a big rig ten years ago. And it was his neck that she'd flung her arms around after she'd cut the ribbon to her shop, Lucky Duck Collectibles.

She just wanted to do that again, to tell him that, of course, he could marry her and, of course, they would have dozens of children and, of course, he loved her with all his heart.

But Josh stared at the Christmas-card-perfect downtown and said, "I was going to tell you later."

"Tell me what?"

"I'm closing the church."

CHAPTER ONE

Wednesday, January 10

LUCKY MORGAN felt the cold cement of the curb against her face as she strained to reach the necklace that was tenuously clinging to a twig lodged in the sewer. She'd been looking for it all day and by chance happened to see a glint of gold as she passed the gutter. She could barely see it in the dim light of the street lamp and the freezing slush had seeped through her clothes. Against her better judgment, she'd discarded her jacket and turned it into a makeshift cushion as she jammed her whole shoulder into the grate and gingerly felt around for the necklace, hoping that her fumblings weren't going to knock it off the twig. A stray cat watched from a safe distance, her wary eyes following Lucky's every motion.

"Too bad you don't have opposable thumbs," Lucky told her and watched the tabby disappear when an all-too-familiar vehicle rolled up to the curb. Lucky groaned and pushed herself up. She looked around hoping that there were other people present, but the rest of the stores had closed for the evening. She sat on her knees and stared at the sewer grate wondering if it was big enough for her to crawl into, then braced herself as the crunch of shoes told her someone was approaching.

"Here, let me," a masculine voice said right behind her.

Reluctantly Lucky met the too-familiar eyes, dark in the night, but brilliant blue in sunlight. She swallowed hard, a hundred different feelings swirling through her, threatening to overwhelm her.

"Come on, Lucky. Move." She felt a firm grip on her shoulder and reluctantly pushed herself to her feet. She surveyed her ex-best friend, seeing he wore a dress shirt sans tie under his open leather overcoat.

"You'll get dirty," she said, staring down. Those highly polished shoes and neatly pressed slacks were so not Josh. "Where are you going?" she asked as if she cared what he did on a Wednesday night. She didn't, of course.

But Josh, already kneeling, and using a pocket flashlight to peer into the grate, corrected her, "Coming from."

"Is that what you were trying to get?" he asked, as he directed the beam of light at the gold chain.

"Yeah. So, uh, where are you coming from?" Curiosity was a curse. She knew that if she didn't ask she wouldn't get hurt. But that didn't seem to help. What if he had a date?

Josh didn't answer her, but braced himself on the curb, so he wouldn't have to kneel on the wet pavement.

"You'll ruin your clothes," Lucky protested, but he was already coming up with the bit of chain.

She held out her hands, but Josh held on to it, studying it.

"Looks familiar," Josh said.

Lucky's mouth turned dry. She wasn't going to tell him he had been the one to give her that necklace nearly twenty years before—how old had they been? No more than twelve or thirteen.

"Doesn't look like it's worth much," he commented and

shot her a sidelong look. "At least not worth getting soaked to the bone."

"Just give me the necklace." Lucky tried to snatch it from him, but he held it out of her reach. His eyes twinkling like the ultimate annoying big brother. "Must have sentimental value."

"Yes, it does." Lucky nodded and grabbed her parka off the sidewalk. She put it on even though it was damp and pretended not to be frozen. She turned to him. "So give me the necklace." She didn't care that she was being rude, but then added, "Please."

After a moment of contemplation, Josh handed her the necklace. Lucky took it, careful not to come into contact with his large hand. She stuffed the necklace into her coat pocket.

"You're welcome," he said.

"Thank you," she muttered, as she hurried toward the safety of the Lucky Duck.

"You hate me so much you won't invite me in to warm up?" Josh called out to her. She turned back to look at him, a dark figure illuminated by the headlamps of his truck. His tone was jovial, but his body posture wasn't. Lucky stopped. It had been hard to know how to act around Josh lately. Even the simplest conversations had been complicated for them. Before it had seemed like she could read his mind and he could read hers, and they were forever finishing each other's sentences. But the man in front of her wasn't her Josh at all. Her Josh was compassionate and caring. This Josh was all about the bottom line. And while she could forgive him for not wanting to marry her, forgiving him for closing the church was another matter entirely.

Josh shrugged. "Okay. I'll see you later, then." He headed back to his truck, fishing the keys out of his pocket.

"Wait!" Lucky blurted, and then wanted to take it back. But she gestured for him to follow her.

"How'd you lose it?" Josh asked as he held open the door to the shop for her, always the gentleman.

"Must have slipped off my neck," Lucky replied, jerking when Josh placed his hand on her back to usher her in.

"Kind of edgy, aren't you?" Josh commented as he closed the door securely behind him. "Your shop display looks good."

"Thanks." She answered offhandedly but she felt a small glimmer of accomplishment. She'd worked hard to make the Valentine's Day display attractive and eye-catching. Her efforts were proving successful, too. She was getting twice the foot traffic that she'd had last year. Probably the result of more people moving into town and discovering her little store. Not knowing what else to say, she wiped off the three specks of dust that had accumulated on the closest display and looked at everything but him.

"Uh-huh." Josh seemed to see right through her. "Didn't see you on Sunday."

"Well, you know, it's that time of the year," Lucky said as she hung her damp coat on a hook by the entrance.

"What time of the year? The time of the year to skip church? You know, Mrs. Simmons really missed you. I'm not nearly as good at filling her in about the latest gossip and you know that my handwriting sucks. When you're ninety, every visit is a blessing." Josh's tone was ever so slightly reproving. He paused and added, "I missed you, too."

Lucky didn't say anything. What *could* she say? For years,

every Sunday after service, she and Josh had been a team, visiting the homebound, church members or not. Once Elle had established the Cup O' Love, they'd drop in, order coffee if it was cold, frappuccinos if it was hot, then sit in Elle's comfy chairs and talk about everything and anything. But after New Year's Eve she couldn't bear to watch Josh do what he did best—inspire and encourage, with humor and humility. It was pointless. No one would attend if they knew he was closing the church and moving on.

"I didn't tell anyone," Josh said, his voice gentle.

"About?" Lucky stared at him.

Josh cleared his throat. "About us."

But Lucky didn't feel reassured at all.

He continued, his words tumbling out, as if he were afraid that she wasn't going to listen. "It's not like I announced why you weren't there. But your absence was felt."

Of course she would be missed. Each year for the past fifteen, ever since Josh's father had died of an unexpected heart attack and his mother of grief not long after, more people left the church. Josh had been young when he took over, just out of seminary school. Lucky knew he'd turned down several opportunities to carry on what his father and grandfather had started. And he'd done a fabulous job.

However the downturn in the economy had hit Fenelon Falls hard. The closing of the main industrial plants had made Fenelon Falls a virtual ghost town, only now being revived by commuters who'd been priced out of the housing market in Chicago. But they were too exhausted to think about sacrificing Sunday mornings for church.

And that left only a dozen or so active members attending Sunday services. Intellectually Lucky understood why

Josh wanted to close the church. It was disheartening to see the congregation dwindle away. But with ebb there was also flow. More people *would* start coming back to the community church. She couldn't believe that after all this time, after all that Josh's family had invested in the community and the church that he would walk away.

"Luck, you have every right to be angry with me," Josh's voice was pained. "But I need you to talk to me."

Lucky put the Closed sign in the window, then walked to the storeroom where she had some extra clothes. She wanted to respond to Josh. She wanted to tell him that she understood and everything was going to be okay. But she couldn't because her heart was breaking, and everything that had been good and right between them was all but gone.

JOSH WATCHED THE DOOR to the back room shut and wondered if that was Lucky's not so subtle way of telling him she was no longer going to be his friend. He hadn't had a decent conversation with her since New Year's Eve. Not that he blamed her. If he could have taken back that evening, he would have. Lucky didn't deserve to be rejected that way. She deserved to be cherished and loved by a man who was going to give her his heart and soul. She didn't need someone like him, at least, not in the way she thought she did. He started toward the door to let himself out.

But then he stopped. It would be awkward, but Lucky would get over it. She always did. She was the most resilient person he knew. Even when things got really bad, she'd always been right there, radiating joy and hope with laughter that was unmistakable. It originated from her belly and gathered volume as it worked its way up her throat, and it was always infectious. When Lucky was laughing, everyone around her was laughing, too.

Josh swallowed and stared at the elaborate display of rubber ducks behind the cash register. The yellow and orange of the ducks were in sharp contrast to the pinks and reds that dominated Lucky Duck Collectibles right now. Just like Lucky, they stood out. He missed her. What he needed was time alone with her. Once he got that, he'd be able to talk to her again. And as soon as Lucky got over being embarrassed, their new relationship would be that much better.

But as he waited, he began to have doubts. Lucky wasn't ready, he knew that. But his time in Fenelon Falls was quickly slipping away.

A soft rap on the front door startled him. It was Becca Potter. He quickly opened the door.

"Josh." Becca sounded surprised and she seemed to be having trouble looking him in the eye. No doubt Becca knew everything. She and Elle were Lucky's best girl-friends. "Is Lucky here?"

Josh gestured toward the closed door in the back. "She's changing."

"Did she find her necklace?"

"Yes. It was in the gutter." Josh was glad to at least be privy to even that small piece of information about Lucky. Ten days without Lucky had felt like a lifetime.

"Oh." Becca nodded and a silence fell between them.

Josh shifted uneasily for the twenty seconds or so, then finally asked, "So what have you got there?"

"A poster." Becca seemed to shrink in on herself. "Uh, for Valentine's Day. To advertise the cards I, uh, make."

"Yes. Lucky told me," Josh remembered, happy to latch onto any conversation. "Your cards. So you're going to sell them again. That's great. Fenelon Falls is going to have a good Valentine's Day. I hear Elle's running some kind of dateathon."

"Hey, Bec," Lucky called from the back. "I'm here. I just needed to change—" She walked toward them as she tugged down her—actually his—sweatshirt. "Is that the flier for your cards?" Lucky asked, her face delighted.

Josh felt a small flare of envy. Since he'd told her that he was closing the church, Lucky had stopped looking at him that way, and now she was Miss Sunshine, bundled in one of his sweatshirts, the necklace he'd rescued dangling in the V of the collar. He saw it was a heart and felt another burst of jealousy. Who could have given her that? He knew she wouldn't tell him if he asked.

"No," Becca was saying. "But I brought a poster."

Lucky tsked. "If you made up the fliers with an order form, I could get you a whole slew of new customers."

"Hey, you found your necklace," Becca gently deflected Lucky's attention.

Lucky covered the heart with her hand. "Thank goodness. I wouldn't have felt right without it." She studied the poster that Becca held, then nodded. "This does look great! It will do for a start. How are the art classes going?"

Becca smiled. "I love them. My students are so nice."

"Penny Blakely is enrolled, right?" Josh asked, wanting to be part of the conversation. "Will said something about it. He really appreciates how you're handling Penny."

Becca flushed deep red from her neck to her forehead. Lucky gave a short shake of her head.

"What?" Josh mouthed to her when Becca stared at the floor.

Lucky just raised her eyebrows. "Bec, if your cards are going to turn out anything like this, you'll do a brisk business."

"I'm beginning to think like Aunt Elle. Valentine's Day is much too overrated," Becca finally said. "She's right. Cupid should be taken out." Josh was surprised by the vehemence in her voice.

"It's a nice time to think about the ones we love." Josh was trying to be helpful, but that only netted himself another exasperated look from Lucky and more embarrassment from Becca.

"Don't mind her," Lucky said with a laugh. "She's suffering from a serious case of Cupidious neglecticus."

"I'm going now." Becca headed for the door before either of them could reply. But Josh didn't miss the meaningful glance Becca shot to Lucky. Lucky just smiled as she escorted Becca out. Once the other woman left, Lucky turned and stared at him. Her face had lost any mirth. "I don't want to keep you, Josh. I'm sure you've got a lot to do."

"I'll give you a ride home," he offered.

"I can walk." Lucky shook her head as she headed for the storeroom.

Josh caught her arm. "It's freezing outside. I'll run you home."

"I've got my jacket." She waved at it, then looked dismayed as she took in the soggy mess.

Josh resisted the urge to laugh. "You had a jacket," he said. "But you're going to have to put that in the washer." He started to take his off.

"No, you need it," Lucky protested. "And I didn't say I'd go with you."

Josh ignored her and held out his coat.

She shook her head a second time.

"What? You can't wear my coat?" he asked impatiently. "You're already wearing my sweatshirt."

Lucky gasped and looked down. When she raised her head, uncharacteristic meekness filled her face. "Okay," she said and allowed him to slip it over her shoulders. It swamped her.

"I've still got to set the alarm," she said.

Josh handed her the keys to his truck. "Does it still work the same?"

"Yes."

"Your password is—"

"—my birthday," Lucky finished. "Do you remember my birthday?"

Josh gave an impatient click of his tongue. Did she think that just because he'd refused her proposal that he'd forgotten every little thing about her? "Lucky, just go wait in the truck."

CHAPTER TWO

Still Wednesday, January 10

LUCKY WAITED in Josh's truck, feeling the warmth of his jacket around her. She nuzzled her face into the collar and inhaled deeply. She smelled leather and aftershave and Josh. She still couldn't believe he was actually going to close the church. Of course, she knew things had to change. Nothing stayed the same. But Josh had always been her constant. She'd never considered life without him, without his smile when she approached or his sane reasoning when her brain worked too fast.

"Stupid, stupid, stupid," she scolded herself. If there was a handy wall available, she'd knock her head against it. Instead, she sat in his truck, feeling like a stranger even though the passenger seat had molded over the years to fit her rump. She looked around and saw the CDs she'd given him for his birthday, the plastic Jesus she'd stuck to his dash and the furry dice she'd hung from his rearview mirror. Jesus was frowning. See, even he knew. She opened the door, ready to slide out.

But Josh was striding in her direction, and Lucky reluctantly swung her legs back into the cab and shut the door. The truck dipped with Josh's easy heave into the driver's seat.

"Now you're freezing," Lucky commented.

"I'll be fine." His words were clipped.

Lucky kept her mouth shut. She'd heard the impatience in his voice. He'd always carried the woes of the world on his shoulders, felt personally responsible for them, gave and gave to the small community congregation. Could that be why he was shutting down the church? Because he thought Fenelon Falls would suck the life right out of him, if he stayed? Or that he wouldn't have anything left to give to anyone if he kept the church open? If that *was* the case...

"Stupid," Lucky muttered.

"What?" Josh glanced at her as he shifted into gear.

"Nothing."

"You said something," he insisted as he pulled onto the main drag and headed toward her cottage.

"Just talking to myself." Lucky lapsed into silence. It would be better once she got home. She'd pop a frozen dinner into the microwave and spend a quiet Wednesday evening—doing what? Nothing. Even though the ride was less than five minutes, it seemed an hour had passed before he parked outside of her front door.

"That wasn't so bad," he commented, flashing her a quick look. He'd forced enthusiasm into his smile.

Lucky got her keys out of her pocket before opening the door. "Thanks for the ride," she said as she slid out and shut the heavy truck door firmly. As she hurried up the walkway, she heard Josh cut the engine and get out. He must want his jacket back. She fumbled to get the key in the lock, aware that Josh was now standing very close, close enough for her to feel his breath on the back of her neck. She pushed open the door and the chill of the house hit her face.

"Oh, we need heat in here." She flipped on the lights before shrugging out of his jacket and handing it back to him.

"I can start a fire," Josh offered as he draped his jacket over the back of her armchair. Lucky frowned. He didn't look like he was leaving anytime soon.

"The heater will do fine," she lied. The heater took a couple of hours to really get up and going. But she wasn't about to— Too late. Josh was already crouching down, crumpling sheets of newspaper, stacking the firewood in an optimum way, as he had done for her a hundred other times. Soon, Josh had the fire crackling, and he put his hands out to warm them.

Lucky's heart beat faster as he stood. He was like a handsome stranger she just couldn't stop staring at.

"I have two frozen dinners." The words came out before she could stop them.

"Is that an offer for dinner?" Josh brightened.

Lucky nodded, even though she knew it was a bad idea. "Yes."

Josh sat down on her couch, where he could see her in the kitchen. Lucky stuck her head in the freezer, looking for two different dinners. They always shared. Her fingers worked to open the dinners from their cardboard box, and she ended up ripping the boxes, then had to piece together the instructions. Microwave or oven? Microwave would be quicker, but they wouldn't be ready at the same time. She resigned herself to the fact that Josh was staying for a while, and set the oven to preheat, put the dinners on a cookie sheet, trying to calm down the entire time. When there was nothing else to do she walked back into the living room.

"What now?" Josh asked.

"We wait." She'd found a clean, long-sleeve T-shirt and tossed it to him. "You might as well get comfortable."

"Hey! This is where this went," he accused her. "I've been looking for it."

She shrugged. "Finders keepers," she murmured and then quickly turned away as Josh stripped off his soggy dress shirt.

"Okay, turn around. I'm decent, now," he said teasingly. "So what are your plans tonight?"

Lucky waved in the general direction of the computer in the corner of the room. "I've got a ton of paperwork. I've also got to check my eBay store. I've got several auctions closing tonight."

"Okay. Don't let me disturb you." Josh moved to sit on the couch closest to the computer. They'd spent many an evening in exactly those positions. "You're still doing good business?" His question was polite. He shifted to a more comfortable position, his head resting on the back of the sofa, his long legs stretched out in front of him, angled because the coffee table was in the way.

"Enough to stay open." What a silly question. It wasn't like Josh to ask silly questions. Horror passed through her. Surely this wasn't some awkward warmup for a deeper conversation. She walked across the room and sat down to turn the computer on. He couldn't want to talk about or, for goodness' sake, *process* what had happened on New Year's Eve. She was doing her best not to think about that night, about her life without Josh.

"Lucky, we need to talk." Josh shifted again, so he could see her better as she peered at her computer screen.

"About?" She tried to make her voice light. Now would be a good time for the earth underneath her feet to open up and swallow her whole before spitting her out some volcano in Hawaii. Or Japan. She wasn't picky.

"About the church and me and—and why…"

She could feel his eyes on her, but she wasn't going to turn and face him. If she looked into those eyes, she would have to forgive him for doing what it was he had to do. Just the thought of the church closing made her want to cry. She clutched the little heart around her neck and zipped it up and down the chain.

Desperate to avoid the conversation she didn't want, she asked, "So where were you coming from all dressed up like that?"

JOSH CLEARED his throat. Lucky wasn't going to like what he had to tell her. She'd avoided him for ten days after he'd told her about closing the church. After this, she'd never talk to him again. "Do you really want to know?"

"I'm not sure." She kept her eyes on the screen, her hand working the mouse. He wanted her to look at him, so he would know exactly how she was feeling.

"I need you to understand."

"About?" Her voice was cautious.

"Everything, everything that's happened since New Year's. I need you. I need my friend." Josh couldn't say it any plainer than that.

Lucky was silent and finally, she swiveled her chair around and looked at him. What he saw on her face was hurt and a deep sadness that he knew he had caused.

"I can't stand us not talking," Josh whispered.

Lucky's lips tightened, and she shook her head. "I can't talk to you about this when I don't understand it." Her voice broke. "I know I can't expect you to feel the same as me about us, but the church? How long have you been thinking about this? If you were so unhappy, why didn't you say something?"

Josh grabbed her hand, surprised to find it was ice cold. He rubbed it between his two hands to warm it up. "You deserve an explanation. And it ties into the reason I'm all dressed up."

Lucky looked at him warily, almost as if she knew it was going to be bad news.

"It's not you," he said hurriedly.

She didn't look convinced.

"I was coming back from a job interview when I saw you facedown in the gutter," Josh explained. "I thought you were dead."

She stared at him for a half a second and then nodded for him to continue.

"It's in Chicago."

She frowned, her eyebrows nearly touching. Funny he was just noticing that for the first time. He wouldn't have thought there was anything about Lucky he didn't know.

"I'd start next month."

Lucky still didn't say anything.

He tightened his grip on her hand. "Please talk to me."

"You know, those big city folks are different." She nodded, looking pleased with herself. "So different that they'll hate you and you won't get the job at all," Lucky said matter-of-factly, then added, "Of course, they'll hate you a lot. You're too openminded and not at all by the book. So we don't have to worry." She gave a sigh of relief and smiled hopefully at him.

"They offered me the position before I left."

She smacked her lips. "There you go. A real church wouldn't do that. Plus, it's a long commute to Chicago. I know folks make it every day, but why would you want to do that?"

Heart pounding in his ears, he gave her another piece of information. "I wouldn't commute."

"Not commute?"

"No, I'd move to Chicago."

She yanked her hand out of his and shook her head. "No. You're not telling me this." She put her hands over her ears as if that action could stop any more bad news hurtling her way. He knew he was hurting her. They'd been tied to each other for more years than he could count. This move would hurt them both. But he had to do it and he wanted her approval. He wanted her to be happy for him. His next words were out of his mouth before he could stop them.

"I took the job, Luck."

Lucky got up from the chair and walked into the kitchen.

LUCKY COULDN'T be hearing what she was hearing. She suppressed the urge to burst into tears. Closing the church was bad enough, but leaving? It was unthinkable. Josh couldn't leave, much less move to Chicago. She stared at the frozen dinners, still frozen and sitting on the cookie sheet.

"It helps if you put them in," Josh said from the doorway.

"I was preheating the oven," she retorted as she opened the oven door and pushed the dinners in. She set the timer and said over her shoulder, "If you're hungry, my feelings won't be hurt if you leave."

"Ah, Luck." Josh's voice was tinged with regret. He touched her arm and she flinched. But he pulled her into a deep hug anyway. For several moments they remained still. Lucky felt the hard plane of his chest against her cheek, smelled fabric softener in his shirt and wished time would stop. Then she gently pushed herself away from him.

"Was it the proposal?" She had to ask. She would never forgive herself if her proposal was the reason he suddenly wanted to live in Chicago. "Was it too weird? I mean I can change churches and we can pretend to be strangers—"

"No!"

His emphatic tone was reassuring, but not in the way she wanted.

"It's not you," Josh reassured her. "I told you that."

"Then what is it?" Fenelon Falls had everything anyone could want, unless of course he or she wanted cultural events, a major sports team or a big shopping mall. But other than that, the little town had people who would embrace a stranger and made sure that no one was ever hungry or cold. Josh hadn't shown any interest in opera or sports—except the local high school football team, which he supported wholeheartedly.

"You remember my seminary friends?" Josh began. He didn't look at her when he said this.

"Yeah, Joe and Paul." The rock in her chest thudded down to her stomach. She knew about Joe and Paul. They were missionaries, who had dedicated their lives to helping the needy. They traveled to other countries, building new schools, tending to the sick, digging wells for fresh water.

"You know where they are now?"

She knew exactly where they were. But she couldn't believe the conversation was going in this direction. "Wasn't Joe in Somalia?" she remarked.

He nodded. "And Paul?"

"The last you said he was in Mongolia." It was sounding worse and worse.

"And remember I told you about Amanda—"

"Your old girlfriend."

"She's in South America with her husband."

"And?"

He looked away, as if he didn't want to voice the words.

"And?" Surely he wasn't going to say what she knew he was going to say. She couldn't bear it. She stepped back putting some distance between them, crossed her arms over her chest and asked a third time, "And?"

"And I'm in Fenelon Falls."

CHAPTER THREE

LUCKY COULD ONLY STARE at Josh. Her mind was whirling, not accepting what he was saying. After a minute, she croaked, "What's wrong with Fenelon Falls?"

Josh shook his head. She could see that he was struggling with how to explain this to her. Finally he sighed and said, "Nothing. Nothing is wrong with Fenelon Falls. If anything it's an idyllic place. It's perfect."

"If it's perfect, why close the church? Why the new job?"

Josh looked at the floor for a long time. "It's too much."

Lucky didn't think she'd heard him correctly. "Too much?"

He nodded. "I'm going crazy here. I worry all the time. That church is going to fall down at any time, and I don't have the energy to build a new one."

"But we can help. All you needed to do was ask," Lucky said.

"There's no one to ask." Now Josh was the one crossing his arms over his chest. "Let's face it. In a few months, it'll be just you and me at the service. It's a joke. My ministry here is a joke."

Lucky shook her head. "You're not a joke. We need you. I need you." Lucky couldn't have said it any differently, but she felt her heart break when she saw the defensiveness of his stance. "It's not going to be like this all the time. More people move to town every year. Eventually, the church will be full again."

"I can't wait that long. It seems as if I've been paddling upstream for too many years. I'm starting to think I dread Sundays. And I have to tell you that it would be nice to get a paycheck and not have every cent that comes in go to repairing the church."

"But your grandfather and your father," Lucky whispered. "You're leaving that history. Throwing it away."

Josh closed his eyes and clenched his jaw.

"You're throwing *me* away." Lucky hadn't meant to say it like that. Worse, when the words came out, so did the tears she'd been trying to hold back for the past ten days. She curled into herself and sank to the floor. She'd never thought she'd feel this kind of pain again. When her parents had been killed, the pain had been so intense she'd thought she would go crazy from it. But at least she'd had Josh. She'd been able to cling to his warmth, listen to his beating heart and know that she would survive. Now, he was going to take that security away.

She felt Josh next to her, pulling her up off the floor, hugging her close to him. She wanted to push him away but instead, she buried her face into his chest, and after several long minutes, Lucky had cried herself out. She sniffled and then awkwardly stepped out of his arms. She couldn't face him.

"Well, now, I feel stupid." She looked around the kitchen and found a paper towel to blow her nose on.

"Don't." It was a gentle command.

She knew her attempt at a smile was pathetic. But when

she finally looked up, Josh was staring at her, his eyes intense with love. After a slight hesitation, he cupped his hand around her face and gently wiped her cheek with his thumb.

"Ah, Luck," he muttered before he kissed her. It was an experimental kind of kiss, soft yet firm at the same time.

Lucky closed her eyes, her brain not quite in sync with what her mouth was doing. Why exactly were her toes curling? A fine shiver traveled down her back as Josh shifted his hands to tilt her face toward his. Those beautiful blue eyes stared down at her as if he were seeing her for the first time.

Then he bent his head again for a different kind of kiss, a more possessive, insistent kiss. Lucky pressed her hands against his shoulders, reveling in the feel of hard muscle against her palm, and clung to him as she accepted the gentle probing of his lips. But before another second passed, he was pulling himself away, thrusting his fingers into his short hair and looking around the kitchen in dismay.

"I'm sorry," Josh said, his voice hoarse. "I didn't mean to do that."

Lucky tried to smile but she just couldn't make her lips turn up. What could she say? Nothing that would make him change his mind and stay in Fenelon Falls. He was looking at her with a kind of desperation that she'd never seen before. She knew that he wanted her to tell him it was okay, that everything was going to work out. And no doubt it would. Time really did heal most wounds. But now, she felt scraped raw and she couldn't say a word.

"I'm sorry, Luck. I shouldn't have done that." Josh backed out of the kitchen, already reaching for his coat. "I'm sorry. I just wanted to talk, to tell you about the job. I shouldn't have kissed you. I don't know what I was thinking."

Lucky could think of no reply and found even the warmth from the cozy fire couldn't penetrate the chill she was feeling. She was going to start to cry and she didn't want to cry in front of him again.

"Thanks for the rescue," she said, once more zipping the pendant along the chain. "I think you need to go now."

"Luck—" His voice was quiet, unsure.

"No, Josh. Don't do this to yourself or to me. We've got a lot of history together and most of it's good. Let's leave it at that."

"I can't, Lucky. I need you to under—"

"I will understand, Josh. But not right now." She turned away and blotted her eyes with her sleeve. "Please go."

"Okay. Lucky, I'm really sorry."

"I know you are." She tried to smile. "That's the part that hurts the most."

Josh put his coat on and he rested both of his hands on her shoulders and kissed the back of her head. "I never meant to hurt you."

She nodded, squeezing her eyes shut, but the tears still slipped through. "Well, better now than a nasty divorce and bitter custody battle over the kids, right?" She laughed even though it wasn't funny and she felt like her heart was breaking all over again.

He turned her around and just looking at the pain in his face made her want to cry. He brushed her tears away and pulled her into a deep hug. She sniffled against his shirt and then with every bit of willpower she had, she placed her palms against the flat planes of his chest and gently pushed him away. "Go. Now."

He dropped his arms. "See you on Sunday?"

"I'll think about it."

"Avoiding me isn't going to make it better."

She rolled her eyes. "It's the best I can do right now."

"Well, I'll be looking for you Sunday."

"Nobody else gets your jokes?" She gave him a weepy smile.

"No one laughs at them," he agreed. "Just you."

She nodded and watched him walk out the front door. He looked back once and got into the truck. A few seconds later she heard the engine rev and a beam of light flash across the door as he drove across the street to the small rectory behind the church.

Lucky exhaled and wiped her face again. She was exhausted and terribly sad. No matter how much she told herself that she didn't love Josh, deep down she knew she always would.

Sunday, January 14

As Josh started his sermon, he saw Lucky slip into the back pew. He immediately forgot what he was saying and had to look at his notes. The sparse congregation chuckled at his slip and he sent a grin in Lucky's direction. But she wasn't laughing. In fact, she looked as if she'd rather be anywhere else than where she was.

At the end of the service, she slipped out the door before he could catch her. In good weather, the reception after the service would be held in the front courtyard, but in winter, they pushed the folding chairs back against the wall so people could mingle and catch up with the week's events. He shook hands and listened intently to what his parishioners were telling him and accepted compliments about his sermon—all the while looking for Lucky to appear by the kitchen where the hospitality committee served coffee and sweet pastries. Lucky wasn't one to pass up pastry.

Josh knew she wouldn't want to be around him, especially after what had happened on Wednesday. That evening had confirmed what he'd already known, leaving Fenelon Falls meant he was leaving Lucky. She was integral to this community, and he couldn't imagine her transplanted to the city. So much of Lucky's identity was woven into the fabric of this town, from the Welcome sign she helped to create for the Chamber of Commerce to her trips with him to visit housebound people to her weekly teas with Elle and Becca at the Cup O' Love, where he suspected they drank harder stuff than tea.

Lucky was everywhere and anywhere in this town, including his heart. Even now he was scanning for a glimpse of her, straining to hear laughter burst out like the first crocus of spring. But there was only pleasant after-service chatter.

He could identify each person by name in the room. And he had history with almost every single one of them. He knew their fathers and mothers, sons and daughters. He was as much a part of the church landscape as the old train station was to the town. He'd grown up in this small parish, the son of the good Pastor Watts, a third generation clergyman.

But he just didn't have it in him to keep the church going. Through tragedy, death and moving, the stalwart members of the congregation had dwindled to just a dozen or so. Like Max Maxwell, who'd been a regular each Sunday when his wife was alive, but since her death rarely came anymore. It was too much and Josh didn't blame him. Fenelon Falls

Community Church was a sinking ship, with not enough new membership to offset those who were leaving.

In his father's tenure, the church had had lean times, but nothing like this. The congregation had been large, over three hundred strong, with many anonymous donors who gave generously to support the church. The truth was Josh had very little left over from his parents' healthy savings. That and the church property. The building with the elegant steeple that defined the landscape of Fenelon Falls was eroding into a splintered heap.

With the closing of the plants and the farmers simply hanging on from one season to the next, he couldn't in good conscience ask for donations. And he admitted it. He lived in a different era than his father had. During his father's and his grandfather's time, Sunday was the day that people set aside for worship, for communion. Now churches competed with video games and twenty-four-hour supermarkets. Most other churches were emphasizing *performance* to try to compete with cable television.

After the congregation went home and the Sunday helpers had put away the coffeepot for another week and realigned the chairs in rows for the next service, Josh realized Lucky wouldn't be joining him for their usual rounds. But at least she'd come to the service.

He swapped his robe for his parka, gathered up his sermon portfolio and made sure that the side doors to the church were locked. Then he made sure the hymnals were back in place on the folding seats along with the Bibles.

"Nice sermon, Pastor."

He suppressed a smile. Lucky always could read his mind. Just when he needed to talk to someone, she would appear, as if she were an angel sent just to keep him on the straight and narrow.

"Nice of you to show up," he replied, not looking up at her, just walking up and down, occasionally flipping a hymnal over or separating the Bibles so they were accessible from both ends of the rows.

"I can't disappoint Mrs. Simmons two weeks in a row, can I?"

"No, I don't think she'd ever forgive you if you did," Josh teased and was rewarded with one of Lucky's exasperated looks. "Besides, the middle of the month's bills are due this week."

"I noticed you didn't say anything about leaving." Lucky was staring at him intently. "Have you changed your mind?"

"No. I'm still going."

"So when are you going to tell everyone?" Lucky asked.

"Next week. There are some funds that will need to be dispersed to the people who need it." He sounded a lot calmer than he felt. "Like your pew fund."

Lucky nodded. "I guess we don't need those now, do we?" She looked forlorn.

Josh knew that had once been Lucky's dream. Real pews. But since the space served as both the sanctuary and fellowship hall, pews had been impractical, not to mention expensive. Folding chairs were a much more prudent option.

"So, hey. I want to show you something," Josh said and sat down, patting the seat beside him. After Lucky sat next to him, Josh opened the well-used portfolio, careful not to spill out all his notes. He sorted through the pile and handed her a brochure.

"That's the church in Chicago. The one I'm going to."

Lucky took it with surprise. "The church has a brochure?"

He nodded. "Just look at it."

"Spas have brochures, summer camps have brochures. Churches don't have brochures. At least not in full color."

"Churches with a lot of people have brochures." He pointed to a bulleted list. "Look at what they have. A soup kitchen and a homeless shelter. And a hundred-voice choir."

"And twenty-three ministers," Lucky noted dryly. She looked up at him, her eyes enormous. "What does a church need with twenty-three ministers? Are you sure this is a step up?"

"I'll have a chance to work with some of the best thinkers of our time."

"Doing what?"

"I'll start as an associate, then move up to full clergy."

"Associate? An assistant?" Lucky was skeptical.

"Not assistant, associate."

Lucky gave him back the brochure, as if she couldn't think about it anymore. "When do you start?"

"They want me by the middle of February."

"Uh-huh."

"But they'll give me time to wrap up things here."

Lucky didn't say anything. She just stared straight ahead.

"Lucky, look at me." It was a soft command and she unwillingly turned to him. Then, he saw what he didn't want. She was begging him to stay.

"I don't want to let you go," she whispered. She clasped his hands. "You're my best friend."

He cleared his throat and he squeezed her hands tight.

He didn't want to be without her, either. They had been through so much together. Was he crazy? He would never find someone who knew him the way Lucky did. He broke eye contact, then said, "I'm not going far, Luck."

"But what if I want to talk to you?" She sounded about twelve years old.

"There's the telephone, e-mail, visits. You have my cell number."

She exhaled a sigh. "That's not the same. You know, it's a completely different world out there."

Josh nodded. "You're right. And that's why I've got to go." Then he voiced a thought that had been swirling around in his head since the kiss in her kitchen that had left him shaken, a thought he hadn't dared to utter before. "But you can come, too."

CHAPTER FOUR

LUCKY STRAIGHTENED in her chair, her eye trained on Josh's face. Had she heard him right? There was no way he was asking her to go with him. But a rush of emotion—disbelief mixed with impulsive hope—made her voice catch in her throat.

"What?" she croaked.

Josh looked a little shell-shocked himself. He stood quickly and turned his back to her.

Lucky didn't say a word, but her mind was mulling this new thought over. She *could* go with Josh. It was an option she hadn't considered. Apparently, based on Josh's silence, one he hadn't considered, either. But what about the Lucky Duck? And Elle and Becca? And who would visit Mrs. Simmons to help her write out her checks? Images from her life flitted through her brain. She had a *great* life. Her bungalow was paid for, the Duck was starting to turn a profit, and she had good friends. Not to mention roots that were intertwined with the town of Fenelon Falls. Most people would work and save for years to have exactly what she had. She had everything…except Josh.

She sucked in a deep breath and said, "I don't know."

Josh finally turned around.

She couldn't tell if he was relieved or disappointed. And all he did was nod, as if he didn't know, either.

She glanced at her watch. "It's time to go visit Mrs. Simmons."

JOSH SIPPED on hot cocoa, made from a packaged mix. It was a poor substitute for the Cup's cocoa, but he would drink every drop. As he changed the batteries in the smoke detectors, he listened to Lucky chat with Mrs. Simmons, who'd attended services with Josh's grandfather. Mrs. Simmons had outlived her husband and her two children and was still independent within the confines of her small house. During the winter months, she didn't attend church services so he and Lucky dropped by every Sunday to check on her and to help her with any chores that she needed done. After missing last week, Lucky was making up for lost time. She'd shed her parka in Mrs. Simmons overheated living room, rolled up her sleeves and was sitting on the floor in front of a large pile of papers.

"You missed two puzzles here," Lucky was saying. "I don't want to toss something you want to finish."

"Let me see, dear," Mrs. Simmons replied, peering at what Lucky held out in front of her. "Oh, you can throw all those away."

Josh heard the rustle of papers and then Lucky said, "What about this mail?"

"That's junk mail." Mrs. Simmons waved the mail away. "I missed you last Sunday."

Josh held his breath, but Lucky didn't hesitate. "I was a little under the weather. So I trusted Josh to do the heavy lifting. Are you sure this is junk mail? There's the heat bill. Oh, and the telephone bill."

"I thought I paid the phone bill." Mrs. Simmons pondered. "Look in my checkbook, will you, dear? I thought something else had happened to you. Josh didn't say that you were sick. I figured the two of you had had some kind of disagreement."

"It doesn't look like it," Lucky said, referring to Mrs. Simmons's check register. "Did Josh pay some bills for you last week?"

"Josh, did you pay bills last time?" Mrs. Simmons asked.

He brought the stepstool to the living room to check the smoke alarm there. "No. I didn't."

Lucky just nodded and started writing out the check to the energy company. She carefully recorded the amount in Mrs. Simmons's checkbook, and then gave Mrs. Simmons the check to sign, explaining what she had just withdrawn. Mrs. Simmons's hand shook as she signed her name. By the time she was finished signing, Lucky had the check to the phone company written out.

"I'll take those to the post office tomorrow morning so they go in the eight o'clock mail," Lucky said.

They both watched Mrs. Simmons carefully put the check in the envelope and then lick the flap. She sealed it with a definitive rub of her fist. "I've got stamps in that drawer." She pointed to the telephone table.

Lucky fished through the drawer and found a half used sheet. "Christmas stamps?"

"Yes. Those are the ones." Mrs. Simmons nodded as she took it. "Got too many, so many of my friends are dead." Both he and Lucky watched as Mrs. Simmons's trembling hand carefully peeled off the stamp and stuck it to the envelope. After she repeated the action, she gave Lucky the envelopes.

"Thank you so much for coming to visit an old woman," Mrs. Simmons said. "Would you like more cocoa?"

"No, thank you." Lucky patted her hand.

"Is there anything else we can do for you?" Josh asked. The elderly woman shook her head.

"How about the toilet?" Lucky asked. "Are you still having problems with it?"

Mrs. Simmons brightened. "No, Seth Conner came and fixed it."

"Seth did?" Lucky sat down. "When did he do that?"

"Wednesday."

"How's he doing?" Josh asked. "I haven't seen him lately."

Mrs. Simmons frowned. "Not very well."

"Really?" Lucky asked. "What's up?"

"The baby, little Rachel. She's sick again."

Lucky sat up straight. "I thought she was in remission."

"She was." Mrs. Simmons sighed. "But she needs more tests and he's having trouble with the insurance people. He didn't say that, but I'm sure he is. I tried to give him money for fixing my toilet but he wouldn't take it."

"I'll talk to Herb Chambers. He'll know if Seth needs anything," Josh said as he handed Lucky her parka.

"He won't take money. Too much pride," Mrs. Simmons warned them.

Lucky planted a gentle kiss on her wrinkled cheek. "He won't even know."

Now it was Mrs. Simmons patting Lucky's hand. "You're a good girl. I'm so glad you two are back together again. Never let something like a little quarrel get in the way of a good friendship."

Lucky just waved as she walked out, heading quickly to his truck, getting in, without saying a word.

Josh started the truck and let it idle while it warmed up.

"How are you going to tell her that you're closing the church?" Lucky asked. Her mouth was tight, the way it always was when she disagreed with him.

"I can't wait for Mrs. Simmons to die before I leave," Josh replied, his tone more terse than he intended. "I never said that it would be easy."

"You could have better timing." Lucky was equally terse.

"Tell me, Lucky. When *is* a good time to leave?" Josh couldn't help the sarcasm that crept into his voice. "After the roof of the church collapses and kills the eleven remaining members of the congregation?"

"We can raise money for a new roof," Lucky countered. "For that matter, the Duck is doing okay. I have plenty in savings. I can give you all of it."

Josh exhaled. "It's not just the money. It's everything. It's the fact that I've been tied to the church since my dad died. I've been working my tail off and—"

"And we appreciate you for that." Lucky's tone changed. "Everyone knows how hard you work, how much you contribute. That's why this is unthinkable."

"It's not getting better, Luck. It's not." Josh shook his head. "We've got to let it go."

"I don't want to let it go. It's our history, Josh. Even much more yours than mine."

"Then you should believe me when I say it's done." Josh revved the engine as he put the truck in gear.

LADEN DOWN with several bags of groceries, Lucky staggered up the icy walk to the small bungalow, Josh following right behind her. Seth Conner opened the door for her and took Lucky's load, and his children crowded around them.

"What's this?" Seth asked.

"We're starving," Lucky said, leading the way to the small kitchen. It was neat and clean. No one would ever suspect that a family of eight lived here. She looked meaningfully at Josh who was doing a quick survey of the children. "And I was saying to the pastor here that I hadn't seen you folks since before Christmas."

"Lucky got the idea to have a picnic," Josh finished, rolling his eyes to Seth. "You know how Lucky is when she gets a crazy idea. If she wants a picnic it doesn't matter if there's snow."

Lucky made a face at him and turned her attention to the children. They were looking a little thin, and she made a mental note to drop by later in the week with another load of groceries. She summoned a cheerful smile.

"We could have a picnic in the living room," Lucky said in inspiration. She looked at the preteen who was standing shyly in the corner. "Missy, there's got to be a blanket that we can use."

The eldest of the children smiled. "I know what we can use, Miss Lucky. We have a large sheet." She darted out of the kitchen and two other children followed her.

"Where's Em?" Lucky asked. She fished through the paper bags and brought out a loaf of bread. As if choreographed, Josh started unpacking the rest of the groceries and recruited the middle boys to help him stock the refrigerator, which was painfully empty. Assembly-line fashion, he passed gallons of whole milk, cartons of eggs, packages of lunch meat and fresh vegetables to the boys. She felt as if she could cry. How could Josh think his work was done?

She took a deep breath and exhaled slowly, trying to call up the most cheerful smile she could. Then she focused her attention on Seth. "So Emily left you in charge, huh?"

"She's at her folks'," Seth answered, averting his eyes.

"She's with Rachel until the day after the day after tomorrow," piped up Christopher. His head barely reached the large table that was wedged in the kitchen nook. He climbed up on a wooden chair to get a better view.

"Really?" Lucky asked casually, though she felt for the little girl.

Seth stood in the doorway, his arm raised, his hand hanging onto the frame. "Rachel's got to have more tests."

"She's sick again," Christopher informed them. "And has to be at the hospital."

"I'm sorry," Josh said. He put his hands on the heads of the two boys. "Is there anything we can do?"

Seth shook his head. "Nothing."

"Is it bad?" Lucky asked as she handed Josh a jar of mustard, which he opened for her while she found a knife.

"Not too bad," Seth hedged.

As if they'd done it a thousand times, Josh tossed her a package of lunch meat, which she caught with one hand. "Not too bad means?"

"Her white blood cells are lower than they should be."

"I am so sorry." She opened the lunch meat and started layering generous portions on the bread. "Are you sure that there's nothing that we can do?"

After a long silence, Seth passed his hands over his eyes. His voice cracked just a little and he said, "Just pray for us. Josh, you must have the emergency line up to Big Man, right?"

Lucky couldn't help herself. She stopped what she was doing and went and gave Seth the biggest hug she could muster. "We'll all pray for you and Emily and Rachel." Seth's returning squeeze confirmed that a hug was exactly what he needed.

"And for me, too!" Christopher put in, clambering off his chair to squeeze Lucky's leg.

Lucky patted the little guy on the back. "I'll send a very special prayer up for Christopher Conner." She looked up at Seth. "If you need to be with Emily and Rachel, call me and I'll come and look after the kids."

Seth backed up with a tight smile. "We might have to take you up on that." He cleared his throat and then clapped his hands and said loudly, "So where's Missy-Meister with that picnic blanket?"

Missy burst into the kitchen with an old sheet, and Seth went to help her spread it out.

Missy came back in. "Can I help?"

"Sure." Lucky shot her a big smile. "You can open those bags of potato chips. Josh, where's the cheese?"

"American or Swiss?"

"American," she answered, winking at Missy who had grabbed the chips. Josh came up behind her, the package already open, giving a slice of cheese to each of the children who carefully removed each slice from its plastic wrapper. "Put it on here," Lucky instructed them and soon there was a whole pile of sandwiches.

"Carrots and celery, too." Josh came up with two bags of precut carrot and celery sticks and gave one to each of the boys, while Lucky carried the sandwiches to the living room. She sat down on the sheet and before long the sandwiches had disappeared and chips were scattered everywhere.

"Sorry about the mess," Lucky apologized. "I didn't mean to make more work for you."

Seth shook his head. "Nothing a vacuum won't take care of."

Missy, who was sitting next to her father, wriggled her way under his arm.

"Thanks, you guys," Seth said meaningfully. "You've helped a lot."

Lucky just shrugged and shot a look at the too-quiet Josh. "We're glad to. That's what neighbors are for."

After they'd cleaned up and heard the gossip from Missy, Lucky and Josh were ready to leave. All the Conner children gathered around the door to say goodbye. Seth and Josh exchanged handshakes and Lucky gave Seth another reassuring hug, which led to a series of hugs with each the children. "Remember if you or Emily need some time, just call. I'd be happy to come over," Lucky said as she gave Christopher one last squeeze.

"And let us know about Rachel's test results," Josh added.

Seth nodded. "Will do. You both be safe out there. We're lucky to have the two of you."

Lucky shot a glance at Josh to see if Seth's words had made any impact, but his face didn't reveal anything. Could she go with Josh, even if she didn't think he was doing the right thing?

"Where to next?" Lucky asked as they pulled away from the Conner house.

Josh didn't reply. And she could see he was a million

miles away. Lucky didn't interrupt his thoughts. She was starting to feel bad about what she'd said. She'd been speaking out of her own hurt, from her need to cling to what had always been between them. She was doing a disservice to Josh if she thought he'd made any of these decisions lightly. She knew he felt the Conners's pain as much as if Rachel were his own child.

"I'll take you home."

"You sure?" Lucky didn't want the drive to end. She didn't want Josh to be silent.

But he only nodded and returned his gaze to the snow covered landscape in front of him. As they drove up the hill to the church, Lucky said, "You want to come over for a movie or something?"

Josh shook his head. "No, thanks."

"Okay." Lucky opened the door and slid out. "I'll see you later, I guess."

"Luck?" Josh called before she could shut the door.

The way he said her name had her heart beating hard with hope. "Yes?"

"Thanks for coming today." His eyes remained enigmatic, but she could tell he was being sincere.

She could only manage to nod.

CHAPTER FIVE

Thursday, January 18

OVER THE PAST FEW DAYS, Lucky had tried to make an effort to be optimistic. But her mind was stuffed full of plans and contingencies. She had a page of all the reasons why she should stay in Fenelon Falls. On the other side, she'd written one word. *Josh.* Cupid wasn't helping her much here. If he was on the job, he'd somehow convince Josh to stay. Maybe she shouldn't have threatened to assassinate him.

Running into him—Josh, not Cupid—at the post office, the supermarket, in the street right outside her shop made her even more confused. When she'd gotten home the previous day, her driveway and the walkway up to her front door had been shoveled. She knew Josh had done it. She'd also seen a slew of repair trucks in front of the church and that puzzled her even more. She'd tried to coax out of Mr. Chambers the reason he was at the church, but the electrician was uncharacteristically closemouthed. Her heart did a little jig. Maybe Josh was reconsidering.

She wanted to talk to Elle and Becca, but she just couldn't. Now, she was pondering her life, as she rearranged her store window, putting in Valentine's Day notepads and stuffed animals and large Mylar hearts. The display was her favorite kind of work. She changed her store window every few days, giving centerstage to different products. It was an effective strategy that got more people to come in. She also put Becca's poster in the window, much to the artist's chagrin, but Lucky had already had many people put in their order for the special handmade cards, even though they didn't know Becca created them. The added benefit of working on the storefront was that she could see all sorts of comings and goings, including Herbert Chambers parking his truck right in front of her shop.

Lucky was surprised when he opened the door and walked inside. This had to be the first time he'd ever been in her shop. She'd known him and his wife, Cora, for her entire life. When she was younger, the Chambers had sat in the front every Sunday, but when Tommy, their only child, was killed, they'd become active members, the most stalwart of the group.

Without a hello or how are you, the electrician got right to the point. "Came to pick you up."

"What for?" Lucky smiled her greeting.

"We've got to go."

"But I can't just leave," she protested.

"Put the Gone Fishing sign on." Mr. Chambers obviously wasn't taking "no" for an answer.

"Can I at least get my coat?" Lucky asked, although she was already heading to the storeroom. When she returned, Mr. Chambers had already put the Will Be Back sign in the window. Mr. Chambers wasted no time, scooting her into his truck after she locked the door and started it up.

Before he could put the gear in Drive, she asked, "What's this all about?"

"The pastor wanted me to pick you up."

"Why?"

"He's calling a meeting."

"A meeting?" Lucky felt her heart drop to her stomach. Josh was going to make the announcement about the church, about his new job. And he'd known that if he asked her, she wouldn't attend. He was right. She would have found a reason not to go. She didn't want to watch him throw away Fenelon Falls.

When she and Mr. Chambers walked into the church, Josh looked up, and she saw the firm determination in his face. Lucky greeted everyone in the small group. Jane, Elle's sister and also the church treasurer, had taken time from her busy accounting practice to be there. So was Ginny, who organized the after-service reception, as well as Cora, Mr. Chambers's wife, who did double duty as secretary and Sunday school coordinator, when there were enough children to have Sunday School, which there hadn't been in well over a year.

As she took her seat, Lucky felt helpless. She knew in her heart that if Josh had just held out a few more years, the congregation would rebound and once again thrive as it had when his father was alive.

After clearing his throat to gain everyone's attention, Josh began to speak. "First, let me thank you all for coming out on such short notice," he said to everyone, though he gave Lucky a meaningful glance. "I know you're interrupting your workday to be here. Jane, especially, you."

Jane did look a little frazzled. Lucky knew because Becca and Elle were such close friends, Jane often felt ignored. Part of it was her personality, which was strong, even overbearing at times. But inside, Jane had a good heart. It just seemed that when it came to Becca, Jane never truly listened to what Becca wanted. And Elle did.

Josh coughed and then said, "This is probably the hardest thing that I've ever had to do." He rushed his words. "Many of you were here with my grandfather or my father. As you know, we've been having problems with our membership."

"Who's the problem?" Lucky asked and looked around teasingly. "I think we can take 'em."

Everyone chuckled, even Josh. Good. She got a smile out of him. But it wasn't enough.

"After a lot of hard thinking," Josh continued, "I've decided to take a new position at another church."

Before anyone could make more than a small gasp of dismay, he added, "In another town."

Josh cast a quick glance in Lucky's direction as if asking her to help him out, but she kept her expression as neutral as possible. If Josh was going to do this, he was on his own.

"So what happens to the church?" Jane finally asked.

"As you all know, the church property is owned by me and my family," Josh carefully replied. "I'm selling the church property and the rectory."

Lucky sucked in her breath in shock. That was news to her. Now, they wouldn't even have a location. Josh was really ridding himself of Fenelon Falls, as if the town was his albatross.

"I've talked to the other ministers in town," Josh offered them. "And they are more than happy to welcome those of you who want to join them. You know, they're all good churches, newer churches with more programs…" His voice trailed off as he looked at the faces of his parishioners trying to digest this new information.

"Do you have a buyer?" Mr. Chambers asked.

"Nothing's final. But I've been offered a good sum for the property. Things are different now. People have lives that are so jam-packed there's little time on Sunday for church. And with the layoffs—" He cut short the rest of the sentence.

"What do the buyers want to do with the church?" The question shot out of Lucky's mouth. Even to her ears, it sounded sharp and critical, and she saw Josh wince.

However, he hesitated for only a fraction of a moment before replying, "It's a warehouse store that will bring new jobs to Fenelon Falls."

"Minimum wage jobs," Lucky said before she could stop herself. Then she clamped her mouth shut tightly. She wasn't going to turn this into a sparring match.

"Any kind of growth is good for the city," Jane pointed out.

"Are you selling for the money?" Lucky asked Josh, unable to stop her questions from coming.

Josh ignored her and continued, "With the proceeds of the sale, I'd like to set up an endowment that perhaps Jane would be the executor of and that those who wished could be part of an executive board that would make financial decisions for the endowment."

"What kind of financial decisions?" Jane was clearly interested, but Lucky couldn't believe it. She looked around and found that rather than being outraged, disappointed, or just plain mad, the others were sitting there, considering the possibilities. Was she the only one who felt Josh was doing something incredibly stupid?

"Mrs. Simmons is going to need someone to check in on

her daily," Josh answered. "I'd like her to receive a modest amount regularly to supplement her social security."

Lucky was the only one who didn't nod in agreement.

"Also the Conners need help with some of Rachel's medical expenses."

"I know that it's not going to be a lot of money," Josh said, holding out his hands to them. "But it certainly would be enough to get folks through these tough times. I know this is a shock, but I wanted to give you as much notice as I could. I'm moving to Chicago the middle of next month."

"Don't we have a say in this?" Lucky asked. "Isn't there something in the bylaws that says you can't just arbitrarily shut us down?"

Ginny patted Lucky's knee. "It's hard for all of us, but I think that the pastor is making a good decision."

Lucky couldn't argue with her friend. Ginny's husband had been one of those laid off. Now he was traveling two hours one way for not much more than a minimum wage job. With a new business in town, he'd be able to work closer to home.

After the meeting adjourned, Lucky stayed seated even though the Chambers offered to run her back to the Lucky Duck. Soon only she and Josh were left.

"What are you doing?" she said. "Have you gone crazy?"

Josh shook his head and began returning the chairs to their orderly rows. "You know, Luck. I think this is the sanest I've ever been. Selling the property is a good compromise. It will benefit the community and it will benefit me."

"So we're going to have a Mega Mart as part of Fenelon Falls landscape?"

Josh was silent. Finally he said, "Things change all the time. You know that better than anyone."

Lucky could feel tears pressing behind her eyes. She was going to cry, yet again. "But if you sell the property and tear down the church you can't come back, even if you wanted to."

Josh looked away from her, his jaw working. He'd never been good at expressing his feelings, even to her. Yet she could often anticipate what he worried about, ease his problems before they became something big. How had she missed the fact he didn't want to live in Fenelon Falls?

"You actually think that this is the best solution?" she asked.

"I don't want to go through this anymore, Lucky." Impatience tinged his voice. "Believe me, it's for the best."

"The best for whom?" Lucky felt the tears spill over. She wiped them away.

"You know, Lucky." Josh sat down next to her, but his presence wasn't comforting. He handed her a handkerchief, but didn't touch her, didn't pull her into a hug, didn't put his arm around her. "For you, everything has to stay the same in order to be good. It's not that way for me." His tone was hard, clipped. "I would have thought you'd know that." He rose impatiently, but didn't go very far.

Lucky was surprised. Josh never spoke to her like that.

Pulling herself out of her pity party, she searched his face. His expression was unyielding but his eyes were vulnerable, and Lucky finally understood. Josh had always supported the community. He'd given and given and given.

She reached out and caught his wrist. He tried to shake

her off, but she held on, making him look at her. She'd been so stupid not to have recognized it months ago.

"So tell me, Josh," she asked with a whisper. "When was it that you lost your faith?"

CHAPTER SIX

TRUST LUCKY to be the one who would actually articulate what Josh had only begun to realize. He wanted to deny Lucky's words, but he couldn't do what amounted to a lie.

Lucky just sat there, as if she was seeing him for the first time, the pad of her thumb rubbing the inside of his wrist. He didn't find it comforting. "I get it, now. You think you're not doing enough. That's why you want a job at a church with twenty-three other ministers. It's too hard on you to do this on your own." Her voice was imbued with sympathy. "You think that if you are around these ministers, you'll get your faith back. You'll find your way back."

Josh couldn't talk. It was a terrible thing to be a minister and have nothing left to give. No matter how much he tried, he couldn't be his father. He cleared his throat. "You can still come with me," he said quietly. "The offer still stands."

Lucky shook her head. "You're not going to find what you're looking for in Chicago, Josh."

"What are you talking about?" Josh was ready to put an end to this conversation.

"You think you're going to find your faith in that big church, but all it's going to do is keep you busy. You'll be so busy you won't have to think about why you feel the way you feel." Lucky still hung on to him, her voice urgent.

Josh carefully extracted his wrist from her grasp. "I know exactly why I feel like I feel."

Lucky clearly didn't believe him.

He tried a different tactic, forcing himself to remain calm. "Just know that what works for you, Lucky, is the very thing that's killing me."

"Leaving isn't going to help, Josh."

"That's what you say, but I won't know until I get there," he replied. "So, Lucky, this is it. All right? I know you don't agree. But let's just leave it like that. You stay here and I'll go to Chicago. I can't be part of your fairy-tale life." The last part was said with such force and bitterness, that Josh was ashamed.

If he'd meant to hurt Lucky, he'd accomplished his goal. Without another word, Lucky started to leave. Once at the front doors, she turned around to look at him. He knew she wanted him to bend, to give her a ride back to the Duck, somehow retying those strings that were slowly unraveling. But all he could do was watch the best thing in his life walk out of the door.

Thursday, February 1

LUCKY KNEW exactly when the whole town knew that the Fenelon Falls Community Church was closing by the exponential increase to the foot traffic to her shop. Sales had never been better as folks intent on digging out more information about Josh and what his new job was going to be ended up looking around and purchasing some small Valentine's gift. She hadn't seen Josh since their visits with Mrs. Simmons and the Conners the previous Sunday.

Emily and Rachel had been home and with Josh talking with Seth and Lucky chatting with Em, they did a very good job of hiding their discord.

Over the week, Lucky had realized there was no way she'd be able to go with him. Josh could leave Fenelon Falls, but she couldn't. Too many people needed her. And while she knew Becca and Elle would do just fine without her, Lucky wasn't so sure she'd do fine without them. Chicago was a different world. She would have no friends, nothing, not even a job. But no matter how great her misgivings were about Josh's decisions, she tried to sound positive about his new move to the inquiring minds that pressed her for information.

"He's going to a gorgeous church," she said to one customer.

"They've got a huge choir and several ministers," she said to another.

"They have a brochure," she kept repeating. "It looks like Josh will have his work cut out for him."

"Too bad about Josh," Elle commented, fingering a soft puffy heart. "I know you really wanted things to work out between you two."

Lucky shrugged. She knew it wasn't the money or the fact that the church building was falling apart or even the lack of a congregation that had Josh leaving. It was Josh. He had lost his faith. The irony overwhelmed her with sadness. He was going through a crisis of faith and the only place he thought he could find it was in a big church in a city where faith battled daily with despair. But that didn't matter because she also knew that nothing could convince Josh he could find his faith right here in Fenelon Falls.

"I guess he needs to spread his wings. I'll survive." Lucky was tired of these conversations, but Elle was her friend.

"It's too bad that there isn't some kind of compromise," Elle said, her eyes filled with compassion.

Lucky just snorted. "According to Josh, selling the church *is* compromising." Lucky didn't stop counting her inventory, checking off what had sold well, what she wanted to reorder next year and what would go on the sale table on February 15.

"The endowment is certainly a generous gift to the community. Jane is already researching the best way to invest the money and how to protect Josh from any nasty surprises taxwise," Elle was saying.

"The best gift to the community is Josh's presence. If he stayed, he wouldn't have to deal with any nasty tax surprises." Nothing was going to change Lucky's mind, no matter how sensible Elle was being. She felt for her precious gold heart. She'd gotten Ed the jeweler to solder the clasp on so it wouldn't slip off again. She might be losing Josh, but she wasn't going to lose this necklace.

"Maybe he can't," Elle suggested. "Maybe he's at a place where he doesn't have enough perspective to see beyond leaving. But just because he leaves doesn't mean he can't come back."

Lucky knew what her friend was trying to tell her, but there were other issues. "Do you want a Mega Mart staring down at the Cup?"

Elle laughed. "As long as they don't sell coffee, I'm good with it. Now, if it were a Starbucks, that'd be a different story."

"So what did you think of those last cards of Bec's?"

Lucky changed the subject, hoping Elle was wise enough to follow her lead. "I can't believe how bad they were. I mean, she's the nicest person in the world, but to wish someone a flealess Valentine's Day is scraping rock bottom."

Elle winced. "You know how it is. She's distracted. Between Will and her mother."

"Things still tense with Jane? I thought she looked a little distracted."

Elle was silent. Finally the older woman confided with a grimace, "You know what Jane said to me the other day?"

Lucky shook her head. She'd spent so much time feeling sorry for herself that she hadn't really been thinking about anyone else. She stopped what she was doing so she could focus her attention on Elle.

Elle laughed but it didn't reach her eyes, making Lucky realize how serious the troubles between the sisters were.

"What did she say?"

"I don't even believe that she could say those words."

"What?"

"She said she hated me."

"That's terrible." Lucky hugged her friend. "I am so sorry. You know, Jane is just an unhappy person. And I think she feels like you're closer to Bec than she is. I'm sure she didn't mean it."

Elle shut her eyes tightly and took a deep breath. "I'm fine. And yes she did mean it."

The bell on the front door rang and three more customers came in. Elle allowed Lucky to greet them, and after a few short moments, Lucky joined her again. "Don't worry. Time takes care of such things. And anyway, things can't always stay the same. Eventually Jane will come around."

"Did those words come out of your mouth?" Elle asked with surprise. "That's growth."

"My growth?" Lucky asked, feeling a little defensive. How did the conversation get back to her and Josh? "What are you talking about?" She gave Elle an annoyed look.

Elle laughed. "We're quite a pair, aren't we? The battle's half won if you can admit that change happens and what you think you want isn't really what you want at all. The Fenelon Falls Community Church endowment is going to do a lot of good for a lot of people."

"But it means Josh is leaving." Lucky hated that she couldn't be happy for him.

"But he doesn't have to go alone. You said he asked you to go with him."

Lucky shook her head. "Just because he's making a bad decision, doesn't mean that I also have to. I don't want to leave Fenelon Falls. Everything and everyone I love is here. Who would I eat shortbread with?"

"I think you need to figure out what you want more. It might not be what you think it is." Seeing that Lucky wasn't going to say anything more, Elle straightened as she saw a horde of teenagers heading for the Cup O' Love. "Oh. Duty calls."

Lucky peered out and saw that Max was part of the group. "And someone else is calling, too."

Elle shook her head. "He's the one person not calling."

"Maybe you should call him," Lucky suggested.

"You said it, I didn't," Elle said as she went out the door. "Oh hi, Josh. Your ears burning?"

Lucky flushed red and shot Elle an evil look that was completely wasted on her.

"BYE, ELLE." Josh looked around the Duck, his hands in his pockets. It looked even more pink in the daytime. He'd never realized that so many items could be shaped like a heart. Sparkly, glittery and, yes, *pink* stuff launched themselves at him as he trod the love gauntlet to the counter Lucky was hiding behind. "And what is the purpose of this holiday?" Josh mused out loud.

"It's about love, all right?" Her voice came from under the counter.

Josh leaned way over and saw just a bit of Lucky's hair. "Are you hiding from me or something?"

Lucky popped up like a jack-in-the-box, startling him and scoffed, "No, I'm not hiding from you. Why would I be hiding from you?"

"I don't know. Elle just said that my ears should be burning. Were you talking about me?"

Lucky had a pair of scissors in her mouth. "No."

Josh always knew when Lucky was lying to him. Her eyes gave her away every single time.

"So what were you saying?"

She shook her head. "I wasn't saying anything."

"Okay, then what were you thinking?" Josh knew Lucky drew very definite lines between what she said and what she thought.

She frowned, her reading glasses making her look very schoolmarmish. "Nothing you haven't heard before."

"I just came in to say hi. Let you know I'm leaving in

two weeks. A week from next Wednesday." He threw the information out to her. She hadn't told him if she was going to come, too. Not that he really expected her to. She was too deeply rooted here.

"Okay" was all she said.

"I'm going through all the stuff in the rectory." He could see she didn't really want to talk to him, but he wasn't ready to leave. "I thought there might be a few things you'd want. I'm finding a lot of your stuff."

"All right." Lucky nodded. "That sounds fine."

Josh couldn't stand it. She was already distancing herself from him. Probably so she wouldn't be so hurt when he actually left. He'd always known he would lose Lucky, but he hadn't expected the pain and emotion he'd feel.

Lucky picked up her clipboard and left the protection of the counter, crossing to the part of the store that was farthest from him. Silently she started to count the stuffed bears. After a pause, he went over and joined her.

"So when do you want to come?" he asked.

"There are only five. I thought there were six," she muttered.

"Isn't your inventory on the computer?"

"Yes," she answered. "But I like to do an actual hands-on count." She burrowed into the stack of cuddly bears.

It was obvious she was acting this way so she wouldn't have to look at him. And that left Josh with no choice. He stepped in front of her to block further access to the shelves.

"Josh, move," she said, her voice was impatient. "I'm trying to work."

"Not before you and I talk."

"Talk?" Lucky stopped what she was doing and looked up at him. "What on earth do we have to talk about?"

"About my leaving, about whether you're going to come with me." There, he'd said it. This wasn't exactly the most romantic of settings, but still better than the backward proposal he'd given her two Sundays ago. Then, he hadn't thought everything through. But now, more than ever, he had to know her decision.

"No." She shook her head.

The abruptness of her answer startled him. "No?"

She rose and held the clipboard tightly to her chest. She repeated, "No. I'm not going to go with you. You might be able to leave, but I can't. I've got my business, the house is paid for, my friends are here, and there are people here who depend on me. My life is here, Josh." Lucky's expression was one of unhappy resolve, and Josh could feel the regret emanating from her. "I'm not going to abandon the people who love me the most."

"That's what you think I'm doing?"

Lucky swallowed, then nodded. "Yes, Josh. That's what I think. Now can you move, please?" Lucky squatted down again and started to count stuffed ducks.

Josh obliged but didn't leave. Her words still stung. She wasn't wrong to say what she felt. And of course she would feel abandoned, but it didn't make his chest hurt any less.

After a full tense minute, Lucky looked up. "Can I ask you something?"

"Sure." He welcomed Lucky's question. It meant he still had a chance to save their friendship.

"Do you love me? And if you lie to me, I'll know." She sounded like she was joking, but Josh knew differently.

"Don't do this, Lucky." Josh couldn't stop the thudding

in his ears and the tightness in his chest. He could only wish for a heart attack. "Let's not go there."

"But you just asked me to give up everything. Are you doing it because you want company or are you doing it because you love me?" She stood right in front of him, putting the clipboard aside.

He tried to answer her question another way. If avoidance was impossible, maybe a little misdirection might give him time to assimilate conflicting emotions that bombarded him the moment Lucky asked about love. "Of course I love you, Lucky. We couldn't have had the kind of friendship we have without a strong base of love."

But Lucky wasn't going to be put off. She wrapped her arms around his neck and buried her face into his chest. Her voice was muffled. "Is it just a strong base of friendship, Josh? If I asked you to marry me again, would you? Do you love me like that? For better or worse, for richer or poorer?"

She lifted her face and gently placed her lips on his. Josh groaned, as his arms wrapped around her body, which seemed to fit right into him. *For better or worse, for richer or poorer.* How many times had he recited those vows? How funny he hadn't fully understood what they meant before now. He depended on Lucky. He so wanted her approval, her support. Against his will, he deepened the kiss, knowing that he was doing exactly the wrong thing. He could feel her tremble and her mouth open as she moaned. And that sound was his undoing. He was suddenly overwhelmed by the passion that smoldered between them. Where had it come from?

Lucky pulled back, her hands resting on his forearms,

her eyes shining with love for him. "No one who loved me like a friend would kiss me like that. So, Josh, will you admit it? Do you love me?"

CHAPTER SEVEN

JOSH CLOSED HIS EYES. Trust Lucky to make his escape from Fenelon Falls hard. She was the one person who could force him to examine emotions he didn't feel like sharing with anyone. It would be better if no one knew how he felt. It would be so easy to lie, to make her believe that what had happened here and on New Year's Eve was something fleeting. That he'd never cared for her as more than a good friend.

"Josh?" In the way Lucky spoke his name, he could hear all her hopes and dreams for happiness. But he couldn't be the one to give her that, at least right now. Even if there were times he thought his own happiness was linked to hers. "Please say something."

"Yes, Lucky, I love you." He said the words, but he didn't like the confusion they brought with them. And because he didn't know how to tell her how he felt he added, his voice sharp to his ears, "Are you satisfied? Is that what you wanted me to say?"

"That isn't quite the *way* I wanted you to say it," Lucky replied with a quick, teasing smile she didn't feel. Infusing humor into a conversation gone bad had worked for them in the past, but this time, Josh didn't smile. She pressed her hands together and discovered she was shaking. What should have been elation, felt like guilt, because she'd coerced from Josh something he wasn't ready to give.

Josh *didn't* look like a man in love. He looked like a man pulled in two different directions, irritated because neither choice was right. She added wryly, "I guess I thought it'd be a lot, er, more."

"Sorry to disappoint," Josh said and glanced at his watch, and Lucky knew what was coming next. "I've got to go." Yes, that was it. The blunt rejection, much like a blind date gone really bad.

"Josh." Lucky took a couple of steps to block his exit and put her hand on the sleeve of his jacket. "Please, don't leave like this."

"Like what?" he asked. His eyes weren't on her face, but on the icy sidewalk outside the shop.

"Like you are now."

Josh sighed heavily. "You know, Lucky, you wanted me to tell you if I loved you. And I did. That's it. That's all there is. That's all I have in me." His eyes met hers, and she could see the confusion in them and knew the only reason he hadn't bolted out the door was that he was too well mannered.

But even manners weren't going to keep him here. He gently broke free of her grasp and walked out of the store. As she watched him go, Lucky couldn't help feeling that he was finally walking out of her life. He loved her but nothing had changed. His admission didn't mean he was staying or that he wanted to build a life with her. All she'd accomplished was to take something Josh didn't want to give her.

Saturday, February 3

JOSH SORTED THROUGH his belongings, wondering when he'd accumulated so much stuff. Some of these things were from his parents—may they rest in peace—but most of it was his own. He grimly acknowledged that he hadn't anticipated leaving the rectory, so he'd become a bit of a pack rat. Now was as good a time as any to get rid of things he didn't need. The meteorologists had predicted a huge winter storm would hit tonight, and Josh could hear the wind picking up.

Most of the boxes would have to go into storage. He'd already arranged to rent a room from one of the other ministers who had a young family. The only thing left to do was pack.

Other than make things right with Lucky. She didn't deserve his anger. He'd acted like a jerk, and more than anything he wanted to apologize and ask her to be his friend again. Of course, knowing Lucky, it would be easier for her to let him go if she *was* angry with him. Besides, he didn't believe she'd stay angry forever. And with a real salary at his new position, he'd be able to pay off the credit card bills he'd run up to pay for church repairs the Sunday offerings didn't cover. Once he had something to offer, he'd come back, see if Lucky was still available. If she was, then *he'd* propose, giving her the best diamond ring he could find on eBay.

A rapid knocking on the front door startled him. He looked at the clock. It was nearly eleven.

"I see the light!" Lucky yelled and the knocking persisted.

"I'm coming, I'm coming." Josh wove his way through his box maze and swung open the door. The meteorologists hadn't lied. He couldn't even see Lucky's house across the street. But he could see Lucky standing on his front steps, covered from head to toe, with just enough space between hat and scarf to reveal her eyes. "Come in, come in." He pulled her into the house.

Shivering, Lucky stamped the snow from her boots. And he realized how much he already missed her. And he knew that was only going to get worse. Determined to get through her visit quickly, he asked, "Are you crazy? You shouldn't be out in this weather. We could have lost you."

She unzipped her parka and shrugged out of it. "Power went out at my house," Lucky began as she took off her ski cap and started to unwind a very long, colorful scarf from around her head and ears.

"Really?" Josh asked, taking her coat, hat and scarf and hanging them on the old wooden coat tree.

"Yeah. It's pretty cold over there, so I thought I'd see how you were faring." Her voice trailed off when she noticed the boxes. She looked as if she'd just been punched in the stomach.

"I'm fine, as you can see. Doing a little packing," he admitted and steered her past the boxes to the sofa.

"Just a little." Lucky deliberately turned her back to the boxes, but he needed something to do, so he kept on wrapping the myriad crystal and resin angel figurines that people had given his family over the past four decades. When he was little, his mother had told him all the angels were symbols of his father's good deeds, promising him that when he grew up, he would have his own collection. But times had changed. People didn't give away angels anymore. "Uh, Luck." He coughed. "About the other day—"

Lucky waved her hand. "Don't worry about it."

"I just want to apologize—"

"It's forgotten." She cut him off. She picked up a finger painting and looked at it from different angles. "Is it my imagination or does this resemble a duck looking up?"

Josh peered at him. "You know, I've never realized that before."

"Missy Conner did this."

Josh nodded. "I think she was three or four."

Lucky put the picture down and then started to help him wrap figurines. "These are beautiful."

"It's been a long time since someone's given me an angel."

Lucky didn't reply, but continued packing. Josh was grateful for her company. Even though she didn't like his choice, she was helping him. After twenty minutes, he got up and stretched.

"You want some tea?" he asked.

"What?" Lucky looked up startled. Obviously she'd been a million miles away.

"Do you want some tea?"

"Yes, please." Then she popped up off the couch. "I can make it." She brushed past him into the small kitchen before he could stop her. Moments later he heard the kettle rattle and the faucet run. Then he heard what he thought was a muffled sob.

"Lucky?" He checked on her. "You okay?"

She had two mugs in her hands and was staring into the cupboard. She turned to him, accusingly. "You packed the tea *and* packed the dishes. I thought you weren't leaving until the middle of February."

"That's less than two weeks away," he said. "And I didn't pack the tea, I moved it. It's in the drawer now."

"Oh." Lucky looked down at the drawer he'd pulled out. "There it is."

She sniffed and watched the flame underneath the kettle. "I never thought you'd leave."

"People move in and out of our lives all the time."

"But not you and me."

The accusation he saw in her eyes pained him. "You and me, too. If I'm gone, you can focus on finding someone who can give you everything you want." He said it, but he would hate it if she did.

"But why would I want someone else, when I've got you?" She refocused her gaze on the kettle as if she could make it boil faster. "Or at least, I had you."

"Luck—"

A hard thumping on the front door made them both jump. Josh frowned and went to answer the door.

"Mr. Chambers, what's up?"

"Seth called me. Apparently Emily and Rachel have been in an accident. They're being transferred to a hospital in Chicago. He's got to go and he's looking for Lucky."

"I'll be right there," Lucky said. She'd followed him from the kitchen and was putting on her coat.

"I'll go with Seth. He's probably not in any shape to be driving in this storm," Josh said.

WHEN LUCKY and Josh got to the Conner house, all the lights were blazing, and Seth was pacing in front of the window. He swung the door open and Lucky gave him a big hug.

"Josh is going to drive you, and I'll look after the kids."

"They're all sleeping." Seth grabbed his coat. "I don't

know what I'm going to do if something bad has happened to Em—"

"We're not going to think like that. We're going to get to the hospital and then we'll take it from there," Josh said in his most comforting tone, and Lucky realized she'd never loved him more.

Sunday, February 4

LUCKY HAD HER HANDS full when all the Conner children woke up. Missy was a great help and with a minimum of fuss, all the children were dressed and fed and entertained with board games. Lucky had called Jane to cancel Sunday services. Josh had let her know that while the Conner car was totaled, Emily and Rachel only had some bumps and bruises; he would bring them home after the doctor released them.

Needing something to keep her busy, Lucky started cleaning the house, while the smaller children played in the living room. Missy helped her tidy the toys in the children's room before Lucky tackled the laundry.

As she matched tiny socks and listened to Missy mediate a quarrel she realized yet again how much she wanted this. A home and a family. And every mundane task that went with it. But what she really wanted was all that with Josh. And that wasn't going to happen.

After two hours of work, she rested and was immediately swarmed by young boys bringing her books to read. As she got to the end of her second reading of Dr. Seuss's *Go Dog Go,* the front door flew open and Emily walked in and hugged each of her children tightly, then gave Lucky a look of such gratitude that Lucky had to hold back the tears.

Seth came in behind Emily with Rachel asleep on his shoulder. He put his index finger to his lips, and the excited boys became silent, following Seth and Emily into Rachel's room to put her in the crib.

When Josh came in, Lucky just stared, so very glad to see him. Without any words, he crossed the room and pulled her close. His hug told her everything she needed to know. But she still heard him whisper. "I do love you, Luck."

And knew it wasn't enough.

CHAPTER EIGHT

Sunday, February 11

"SO I CAN'T BELIEVE you're going to let that man go," Mrs. Simmons said as Lucky wrote out the checks to cover her bills.

Lucky sipped her watery cocoa and tried as hard as she could to be polite. "What do you mean?" It was no coincidence that Lucky and Mrs. Simmons were alone. After the Conners's accident, Josh had kept his distance from her. It was as if spending time with that family had affected him in much the same way as it had her.

She'd helped him pack one more time, and she'd left the rectory after with a small box of knickknacks to remember him by. During their time together, they'd limited themselves to small talk and "remember when" memories, but they didn't talk about the fact that their love wasn't enough to overcome their differences.

Apparently Josh was leaving this week. He hadn't said whether or not the church property had actually been sold. And she didn't ask. She wouldn't be surprised if it hadn't. It was hard to assess land covered in three feet of snow. But come spring, the land around the church would be covered in daffodils, crocus and tulips, and she knew that it would sell in only a matter of days.

"I mean, why are you giving up on him?" Mrs. Simmons wasn't going to be put off.

"On who?" Lucky tried to pretend not to know who Mrs. Simmons was talking about. But when she looked up into the eyes that were staring at her with wisdom accumulated through ninety years of living, Lucky dropped the pretense. "Josh has to do what Josh has to do."

"He loves you, you know."

She did know that. He'd told her that in one of the saddest moments of her life. "That's why I'm letting him go. He obviously needs to find himself in Chicago."

"Bull pucky." The epithet flew from the sweet little old lady's mouth.

Lucky laughed despite her mood. "Was that a swear word?"

"It sure was." Mrs. Simmons leaned forward. "Lucille, the only way to help that man find himself is by sticking to him like glue. Trust me. Mr. Simmons and I were married for sixty-seven years, most of them happy."

"I don't think he wants me with him," Lucky said faintly. "And I can't leave my job."

"He might not think he does," Mrs. Simmons nodded wisely and grasped Lucky's writing hand. "And I know this isn't what a modern woman wants to hear, but your *job* is to keep reminding him why he was put on God's green earth. When he loses faith, you give it to him. When he finds it, you celebrate. And he does the same for you. That's all there's to it. And it doesn't happen on a cell phone or the ding-dang Internet."

Lucky was silent as she thought over what her friend had said. "I don't think I can change for him," she finally said.

Mrs. Simmons shook her gray head. "He doesn't want you to change, he simply wants you to be with him. Love doesn't just grow in Fenelon Falls. It grows wherever you are."

"But if I leave, who will come visit you?" Lucky asked.

"There have been more people visiting me than I can stand." Mrs. Simmons dismissed her with a wave of her frail hand. "Frankly, I need my alone time."

Lucky wiped the tears out of her eyes and hugged the older woman. "Thank you. Thank you."

Wednesday, February 14

VALENTINE'S DAY was as good a day to move as any, Josh thought. Most folks moved over the weekend and he figured there'd be less hassle on a Wednesday. Besides, Sunday had been his last service. Surprisingly nearly forty people had attended, all wishing him good luck on his new adventure, telling him not to forget Fenelon Falls. How could he? Lucky had come, too, but she'd sat in the back. Every time he'd looked at her, he'd found her eyes were trained on him. He wasn't sure why. Was she willing him to change his mind or trying to memorize the day? He hadn't had a chance to ask; she'd slipped away after. He'd seen her off and on since, but they hadn't spoken. He wondered if that meant what they'd had was gone forever.

A moving van pulled up, blocking his view of her little cottage. It took the four husky men no time at all to load the furniture. "Okay," the driver said. "We'll meet you at the storage unit in Chicago. I've got the address and you have my cell phone number in case there's a change in plans."

Josh nodded, but there wasn't going to be a change. He was going to get in his truck and drive away from Fenelon Falls. Elle was having her Valentine's Day Dateathon party tonight and he knew that Lucky had agreed to help out. Maybe later, he'd call and see how she was doing.

The moving van pulled away, leaving Josh looking at Lucky's house again. Impulsively he walked across the street. She wouldn't be home. She'd be at the Duck, selling last minute Valentine's gifts for the romantically challenged.

But he knocked anyway. And got no answer. He tried the door and found it was locked. Then he balanced the card he'd had Becca make for him on the doorknob. Lucky couldn't miss it and would know he was thinking about her. With resolve, Josh went back to the rectory, grabbed his duffel and walked through the back door of the church for the last time. The door closed behind him with a hollow and empty thud.

LUCKY SAT in Josh's truck, her overnight bag at her feet. She'd already given Elle and Becca her goodbye hugs, along with the expected tears—albeit excited tears. After the moving van had gone, she'd seen him walk across the street and knock on her door. Then she'd watched him put an envelope on the door. Even from this distance she recognized the shape of one of Becca's cards and felt around for the heart around her neck. She fiddled with it, knowing that she was doing the right thing, trusting that Mrs. Simmons and her ninety years of wisdom was guiding her in the right direction.

Then she saw him walk out of the church, pause to lock the double doors behind him and stare briefly at the snowy lines of the town that, from the vantage point of the church steps, resembled a Thomas Kinkade painting. Then he walked toward the truck.

Lucky held her breath. He hadn't seen her yet. Then the driver's side door opened and Josh started to swing his duffel bag into the back.

Josh stopped short when he realized she was there. "Lucky."

"Josh." She greeted him with a small smile.

"What are you doing here? Why aren't you at the shop?" Josh asked quickly.

"Mrs. Chambers said she would watch it for the next few days. Maybe longer if I need it."

"Few days?" Josh was wary. "What are you talking about?"

"I'm going with you." Lucky tried to sound as sure as she could but there was a tremor in her voice.

"What about the Duck, your house, your friends?" Josh's voice was strained. "You'd leave them?"

Lucky nodded.

"Why?"

"Because I love you, Josh. Where you go, I go."

"But your business?" Josh was still grappling with what Lucky was telling him. She could see that on his face.

"—is mostly on the Internet. I can do that anywhere. But to have a chance with you, I have to leave Fenelon Falls."

"Mr. Chambers told me that was exactly why I had to stay," Josh said quietly. "That I didn't need to stay for my grandfather or my father or the congregation. I needed to stay for you. But I can't. I've got to go, even if it means leaving you behind."

Lucky scooted across the bench seat and dangled her feet off the side of the truck. Then she tugged at his jacket until his hips were nestled against her thighs. Taking his face gently in her hands, she kissed him. His eyes closed and his lips clung to hers. After a moment of exploration, Lucky smiled. "That's the beauty of love, Josh. It's not about what either of us can do individually. It's about what we do when we're together. It's just about love. I *love* you, Josh. And if it means I sell knickknacks on the Internet and not in Fenelon Falls then that's what it means."

"But your store, your life."

"My store is taken care of and my life is with you, whether or not you want to marry me."

"I'm not going to let you do this." His voice cracked but his arms were wrapping around her. "I don't even know where I'm going."

She pressed her cheek to his chest and heard the muffled pound of his heart. "That's okay. If you get lost, you won't be on your own. Whatever you do, I'm there to support you." She pushed a box into his hands. "Happy Valentine's Day, Josh."

Josh looked at it guardedly.

Lucky laughed, feeling freer than she had in a long time. "It's not a ring and a proposal. But before you open it, do you remember this?" She pulled the heart off her neck and showed it to him.

He nodded. "Isn't that the necklace we got out of the gutter?"

Lucky smiled. "Don't you remember giving it to me?"

"*I* gave it to you?" Josh's forehead wrinkled.

Lucky nodded. "We were eleven or twelve. I'd lost the

necklace my mother told me not to wear because I'd lose it. I was sad for days, and you gave me this to replace it."

The look on his face told her Josh really didn't remember. But that didn't matter.

"You sort of tossed this at me and said it didn't mean you loved me or that we were going steady. You told me it was just to make me happy." Lucky felt her voice grow husky. "You knew what love was when you were twelve. Love is wanting another person to be happy." She tapped the box he held in his hand. "Open that now."

He almost dropped the box, but finally got it open, pulling out not a heart, but an angel.

"You're my angel, Josh." She traced her index finger over his lips. "Don't you get it? Even angels need angels sometimes."

And Josh did get it. But Lucky was mistaken. He wasn't the angel. She was.

First Week of October

LUCKY LAY ACROSS the first pew in the newest church in Fenelon Falls and stared at the glorious stained glass window behind Josh's head.

"Do you want to sleep there?" Josh teased his wife.

She turned over and grinned at him. "I do. I love them, I love them, I love them!" She slid back and forth on the smooth wood.

"Well, they're your dream." Josh said.

Lucky sat up and shook her head. "No, they're *our* dream."

So much had happened since February, more than Lucky could have even predicted. But it had started with her making Josh drive across the street so she could pick up the card he'd left on the door. Becca had outdone herself. A simple sketch of two rubber ducks bobbing together on the edge of a waterfall. Josh had been right. Change had to happen. They'd had to let the old church die in order for something new to rise. While Josh had worked at his new post in Chicago, Lucky had made the Internet her primary store. With Jane's financial advice, she'd sold her parents' cottage and ended up with enough money to start repairs on the old church, which had eventually led to tearing down the whole building, keeping only the front doors.

Josh hadn't really believed that fixing the building would be enough to bring back the congregation, but he believed in Lucky, so he'd told the people from Mega Mart the property was no longer for sale. Demonstrating uncharacteristic flexibility, Jane shelved the endowment project to spearhead the rebuilding effort. Ever resourceful, Jane had been the main force in getting things done. And then a wonderful thing happened and the people of Fenelon Falls had pitched in. The Chambers donated most of the lumber, Max, Elle and a group of brainy teenagers supplied much needed labor. The Conners, too, had helped. Even though Rachel had gone into full remission, they never forgot the support Josh and Lucky had given them. Even the support of the old congregation wouldn't have been enough, though, because there were some jobs they just couldn't do. But as often happened when Lucky became involved in a project, a miracle seemed to occur. At the second meeting of the rebuilding committee, a pair of brothers appeared. The brothers were contractors who'd moved to Fenelon Falls because they wanted their children to grow up in a town where neighbors cared enough to help neighbors. To set an example for their families, they offered their expertise to rebuild the church and became the first new members of the congregation.

Their first service had been that morning, and the trees of Fenelon Falls were burning red, orange and yellow. Mrs. Simmons had sat in the first pew, and with Mrs. Simmons came a whole slew of people.

The church was packed with old faces and many, many new ones.

"I counted eighty-three people," Lucky said.

Josh sat down next to her. "And I was looking just at you."

Lucky leaned into him, wriggling her way under his arm, and admired the new wedding band on her finger, the best ring Josh could find on eBay.

EPILOGUE

One Year Later

"SORRY! Sorry, I'm late," Lucky cried, bringing into the Cup a draft of cold February air. "I was over at the Conners' and I totally lost track of time."

"Don't worry," Elle said, kicking off her shoes and sliding down onto the couch with a sigh and a huge smile. "Jeez, I'm beat. Being a stepgrandma is wearing me out."

"I hear you," Rebecca groaned, kicking her feet up onto the ottoman and nearly upsetting the plate of shortbread. Between the growing demand for her cards, her after-school program and the wedding, she knew how Elle felt. Some days she was more beat than blissful, but usually she was able to keep a pretty good balance.

Lucky unwound her scarf and shrugged out of her coat, throwing both over the back of the plush purple chair that had been hers on shortbread night for three years now. From Cupid assassination plots to wedding plans, they'd come a long way.

"So, ladies?" Lucky asked with a merry twinkle. "What have I missed?"

Rebecca laughed. "I was just boring Elle with more wedding plans."

"I wasn't bored," Elle protested.

"Please, Aunt Elle, your eyes glazed over when I told you about the problems with the roses."

"They were sympathy tears."

Rebecca snorted.

"What do you say we skip the tea tonight?" Elle asked. "I've got a bottle of red that Max gave me for our 'Finally Got Our Heads Out of Our Butts' anniversary."

"I can't," Rebecca and Lucky said at the same time and slowly turned to look at each other. Lucky's hands rested on her flat belly.

"I know I'm not drinking so I can fit into my wedding dress. Why can't you?" asked Rebecca.

"We're having a baby," Lucky said, her face alight.

Elle and Rebecca leaped to their feet and pulled Lucky into their arms. They smiled at each other like three dorks until Elle started laughing.

"Well, thank God we never killed him," she said.

"Who?" Lucky asked.

"Cupid," Elle said. "The little twerp came through for us after all."

* * * * *

Happily ever after is just the beginning...

Turn the page for a sneak preview of
DANCING ON SUNDAY AFTERNOONS
by
Linda Cardillo

Harlequin Everlasting—Every great love
has a story to tell. ™
A brand-new line from Harlequin Books
launching this February!

Prologue

Giulia D'Orazio
1983

I had two husbands—Paolo and Salvatore.

Salvatore and I were married for thirty-two years. I still live in the house he bought for us; I still sleep in our bed. All around me are the signs of our life together. My bedroom window looks out over the garden he planted. In the middle of the city, he coaxed tomatoes, peppers, zucchini—even grapes for his wine—out of the ground. On weekends, he used to drive up to his cousin's farm in Waterbury and bring back manure. In the winter, he wrapped the peach tree and the fig tree with rags and black rubber hoses against the cold, his massive, coarse hands gentling those trees as if they were his fragile-skinned babies. My neighbor, Dominic Grazza, does that for me now. My boys have no time for the garden.

In the front of the house, Salvatore planted roses. The roses I take care of myself. They are giant, cream-colored, fragrant. In the afternoons, I like to sit out on the porch with my coffee, protected from the eyes of the neighborhood by that curtain of flowers.

Salvatore died in this house thirty-five years ago. In the last months, he lay on the sofa in the parlor so he could be in the middle of everything. Except for the two oldest boys, all the children were still at home and we ate together every evening. Salvatore could see the dining room table from the sofa, and he could hear everything that was said. "I'm not dead, yet," he told me. "I want to know what's going on."

When my first grandchild, Cara, was born, we brought her to him, and he held her on his chest, stroking her tiny head. Sometimes they fell asleep together.

Over on the radiator cover in the corner of the parlor is the portrait Salvatore and I had taken on our twenty-fifth anniversary. This brooch I'm wearing today, with the diamonds—I'm wearing it in the photograph also—Salvatore gave it to me that day. Upstairs on my dresser is a jewelry box filled with necklaces and bracelets and earrings. All from Salvatore.

I am surrounded by the things Salvatore gave me, or did for me. But, God forgive me, as I lie alone now in my bed, it is Paolo I remember.

Paolo left me nothing. Nothing, that is, that my family, especially my sisters, thought had any value. No house. No diamonds. Not even a photograph.

But after he was gone, and I could catch my breath from the pain, I knew that I still had something. In the middle of the night, I sat alone and held them in my hands, reading the words over and over until I heard his voice in my head. I had Paolo's letters.

* * * * *

This February...

Catch NASCAR Superstar **Carl Edwards** *in*

SPEED DATING!

Kendall assesses risk for a living—so she's the last person you'd expect to see on the arm of a race-car driver who thrives on the unpredictable. But when a bizarre turn of events—and NASCAR hotshot Dylan Hargreave—inspire her to trade in her ever-so-structured existence for "life in the fast lane" she starts to feel she might be on to something!

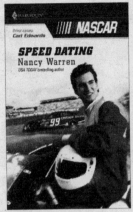

Silhouette®

Romantic
SUSPENSE

Excitement, danger and passion guaranteed!

Same great authors and riveting editorial
you've come to know and love.

Look for our new name next month
as Silhouette Intimate Moments® becomes
Silhouette® Romantic Suspense.

Bestselling author
Marie Ferrarella
is back with a hot
new miniseries—
The Doctors Pulaski:
Medicine just got
more interesting....

Check out her
first title,
HER LAWMAN
ON CALL,
next month.

Look for it wherever
you buy books!

Visit Silhouette Books at www.eHarlequin.com   SIMRS0107

REQUEST YOUR FREE BOOKS!
2 FREE NOVELS PLUS 2 FREE GIFTS!

HARLEQUIN®

Super Romance®

Exciting, emotional, unexpected!

YES! Please send me 2 FREE Harlequin Superromance® novels and my 2 FREE gifts. After receiving them, if I don't wish to receive any more books, I can return the shipping statement marked "cancel." If I don't cancel, I will receive 6 brand-new novels every month and be billed just $4.69 per book in the U.S., or $5.24 per book in Canada, plus 25¢ shipping and handling per book and applicable taxes, if any*. That's a savings of close to 15% off the cover price! I understand that accepting the 2 free books and gifts places me under no obligation to buy anything. I can always return a shipment and cancel at any time. Even if I never buy another book from Harlequin, the two free books and gifts are mine to keep forever.   135 HDN EEX7 336 HDN EEYK

Name	(PLEASE PRINT)
Address	Apt.
City	State/Prov.	Zip/Postal Code

Signature (if under 18, a parent or guardian must sign)

Mail to the **Harlequin Reader Service®:**
IN U.S.A.: P.O. Box 1867, Buffalo, NY 14240-1867
IN CANADA: P.O. Box 609, Fort Erie, Ontario L2A 5X3

Not valid to current Harlequin Superromance subscribers.

Want to try two free books from another line?
Call 1-800-873-8635 or visit www.morefreebooks.com.

* Terms and prices subject to change without notice. NY residents add applicable sales tax. Canadian residents will be charged applicable provincial taxes and GST. This offer is limited to one order per household. All orders subject to approval. Credit or debit balances in a customer's account(s) may be offset by any other outstanding balance owed by or to the customer. Please allow 4 to 6 weeks for delivery.

Your Privacy: Harlequin is committed to protecting your privacy. Our Privacy Policy is available online at www.eHarlequin.com or upon request from the Reader Service. From time to time we make our lists of customers available to reputable firms who may have a product or service of interest to you. If you would prefer we not share your name and address, please check here. ☐

HSR07

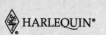

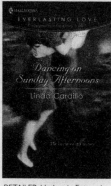

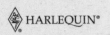

EVERLASTING LOVE™

Every great love has a story to tell™

Fall from Grace
Kristi Gold

Save $1.⁰⁰ off

the purchase of
any Harlequin
Everlasting Love novel

Coupon valid from January 1, 2007
until April 30, 2007.

Valid at retail outlets in Canada only.
Limit one coupon per customer.

52607370

HECDNCPN0407

HARLEQUIN®

Super Romance®

Is it really possible to find true love
when you're single...with kids?

Introducing an exciting new five-book miniseries,

SINGLES...WITH KIDS

When Margo almost loses her bistro...and custody of
her children...she realizes a real family is about more
than owning a pretty house and being a perfect mother.
And then there's the new man in her life, Robert...
Like the other single parents in her support group, she
has to make sure he wants the whole package.

Starting in February 2007 with

LOVE AND THE SINGLE MOM

by C.J. Carmichael

(Harlequin Superromance #1398)

ALSO WATCH FOR:

THE SISTER SWITCH Pamela Ford (#1404, on sale March 2007)
ALL-AMERICAN FATHER Anna DeStefano (#1410, on sale April 2007)
THE BEST-KEPT SECRET Melinda Curtis (#1416, on sale May 2007)
BLAME IT ON THE DOG Amy Frazier (#1422, on sale June 2007)

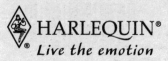

HARLEQUIN®
Live the emotion